MW01128878

Fighting For You
(The Connor Family, Book 5)

LAYLA HAGEN

Dear Reader,

If you want to receive news about my upcoming books and sales, you can sign up for my newsletter HERE: http://laylahagen.com/mailing-list-sign-up/

Chapter One
Jace

"Uncle Jace, can we do the step-over again?"

"Buddy, we don't have time. If we're late, your mom will kick my—" I'd been about to say ass but caught myself just in time.

"It's okay. I know you wanted to say ass. I'm a big boy now. I'm nine years old."

"Yeah, but Lori will kick more than my ass if she hears me cursing around you."

Milo grinned. "But you always tease Mom."

"I know, but here's a secret. I choose my battles. It's a very important lesson."

As a pro soccer player, and as Milo's uncle, I was very proud that he shared my love for the game. He'd watched my team practice, and after it was over, he insisted I show him a few moves in more detail. I was always up for training him, but today we didn't have much time. Management had called a meeting, and I couldn't be late, and Lori wanted to take Milo to dinner.

She was waiting for us in front of the locker rooms, smiling.

"What are you two so smug about?" she

inquired.

"Can't we have our secrets?" I countered, throwing Milo a furtive glance.

"Uh-uh. Secrets usually mean you're up to no good."

"Not this time," Milo chimed in.

She watched us suspiciously but didn't press. "Well, we have to get going. See you on Friday."

After they left, I headed to the shower, then upstairs with my teammates.

"Any clue what this is about? Graham mention anything at Friday dinner?" My fellow forward Levi asked.

I shook my head. "Nothing."

Levi eyed me skeptically. Ever since the owner of our soccer club, Graham Frazier, had married my sister Lori, my teammates had constantly asked for insider information. Graham and I never talked shop during the family's weekly Friday dinner. Those were for catching up with all my siblings and showing Milo new moves.

The headquarters of the LA Lords was in the building next to the stadium. Our gym was on the lower level. Management offices were on the upper floors.

After we all sat down at the oval table in the meeting room, Graham walked in with Tina, our VP of business operations, and a very pretty blonde I'd never seen before. She was wearing a simple black dress with a wide belt around her waist, and her blonde hair was tied up in a bun. She was also wearing black-rimmed, rectangular glasses. They framed her blue eyes beautifully.

I sat straighter in my chair, paying attention when Graham spoke.

"Good afternoon, team. Thank you for coming up. I'll keep this brief. As you know, Bree left last month, and we haven't been able to find someone new for our sponsorship business development position. I'm confident that Brooke is the perfect fit for us."

Brooke gave Graham a small nod, then took one step forward, surveying everyone at the table.

"I'm Brooke Derringer. The name might ring a bell." She pointed at the back of the room, where coach Stephen Derringer stood, smiling proudly. "Your coach is my father, but I promise you that's not why Tina here hired me."

I liked that she took the bull by the horns and addressed this directly, even though her boldness earned her several smirks and even a snicker from Henry, our goalkeeper. I cocked a brow at him, and he toned it down. I wasn't the team's captain, but I was the most valuable player, and my opinion carried weight.

"I have seven years of experience in managing and securing sponsorships and endorsement contracts. I believe I can bring a fresh perspective, as well as new opportunities from my contacts."

A few of my teammates were smirking again. I was going to have a word with them later. As far as I was concerned, Brooke seemed capable, and I trusted

Graham's judgment when it came to hiring. They didn't need the approval or opinion of the team. The team had two jobs. One: play the best game we could. Two: be on our best behavior so sponsors would flock to us.

Approving management hires was not on our task list. Frankly, it surprised me that Graham had even called this meeting. New hires usually went unnoticed by the team. I suspected that Brooke had asked for it so that she could clear the air on her kinship with the coach.

"I promised Graham I'll keep this short, so I'm just going to walk you through a few things I plan to bring to the table right away. I'm aware that there are already numerous contracts in place, but I have a list of additional sponsors I'd like to approach. I believe it will benefit the team. I would also like to set up one-on-one sessions with each of you, to find out more about you and find additional individual endorsement opportunities. I know that your agents usually deal with your individual contracts, so if you wish, they can participate too. My philosophy is that what helps you personally also helps the team as a whole."

I was impressed with her go-getter attitude, and I was looking forward to my one-on-one session with her. Thanks to GQ designating me sexiest soccer player of the year three times in a row, I already had many endorsement contracts. The title brought me unexpected fame, which came with some downsides as well, but I had nothing to complain about.

GQ's attention had been sheer luck, but then again, I'd been a lucky guy most of my life. That was not to say that I wasn't busting my ass and giving the team one hundred percent of my dedication, but I was aware that I would not be here today if the stars had not aligned in my favor.

It was the middle of July, just past midseason, and we'd had a string of victories. I'd scored the most goals, which had earned me the MVP tag. At twenty-eight, I still had a few good years ahead of me, but careers in pro sports were fickle. You were only as good as your last season, not to mention an injury could prematurely end a career. It was important to book as many marketing gigs as possible while I was riding the wave.

I was curious what Brooke would come up with. I was trying not to check her out, but I couldn't help myself. I was sitting at the far end of the oval table, so I had a direct view. The conservative librarian look was smoking hot on her. It made me want to take off those glasses and look closer. How did she look with her hair undone and rumpled? With those pink lips slightly swollen from kissing?

She turned to scribble the names of potential sponsors on the whiteboard behind her, giving me an excellent view of her ass. I made a concerted effort to focus on her writing.

As she cleared her throat, turning around, I went back to trying not to check her out. Or more accurately... I went back to trying not to be obvious about it.

***

Brooke

I looked around the room, inspecting the players' expressions. I knew I'd encounter some skepticism given that Dad was the head coach, but I was determined to win them over. I wasn't going to accomplish that in the fifteen minutes we had today, but eventually, I'd prove myself and build credibility.

Dad had wanted to tell the team himself, but I insisted on holding this meeting. I preferred to gauge everyone's reactions myself. I've always been too stubborn for my own good. My sister lovingly mocked me for that.

When this opportunity came up, I simply couldn't say no. I loved a new challenge, and unfortunately, I couldn't remain at my old workplace.

Dad caught my eye and winked. I knew how proud he was, how happy I'd made him when I accepted this position.

"A sports gear company in Washington is looking for a soccer team to showcase their new line. I will send you all an email as soon as we conclude this meeting. Inside, you will find all the details. Take your time and think about it, discuss it among yourselves. If you're interested, I will move forward with it. As far as logistics are concerned, you would all have to fly out of town for two days for a photo shoot, but I already checked the game calendar, and we could schedule it during the break after your away game in Texas."

A few players nodded, even as their eyes widened. They were clearly surprised that I was moving so quickly, but no one had time to waste. Also, I knew that coming up with an example during the first meeting went a long way in establishing my expertise, not only with the team but also Graham and my direct boss, Tina.

"Any questions?"

"Some of us already have contracts with other sports gear companies. Would that be a problem?" Jace Connor asked.

"I took the liberty of reviewing the contracts you have as a team and consulted your agents for your individual contracts, and while you have noncompete clauses, this opportunity wouldn't go against it since this is catalog only."

Jace smiled appreciatively. I smiled back, then pried my gaze off him, moving on to the rest of the players. I wasn't supposed to have favorites, but everyone had weaknesses, right?

With light brown hair and green eyes, Jace Connor was by far the sexiest of all. The team posed for a calendar each year in various states of undress. I *might* have kept the January page (Jace's month) up after the thirty-first, but I bet so did half of California. He'd been shirtless. I almost couldn't believe he was as attractive in person as on the calendar, or the screen. I easily understood why GQ had designated him sexiest soccer player.

He was also possibly a heartbreaker if Twitter was to be believed, which could go either way with sponsors. Some loved associating their brand with a bad boy, but most shied away from it. In my experience, they were right to do so. Bad boys usually attracted scandals. But Jace hadn't been involved in anything major during all his years with the Lords. In any case, I couldn't wait to work with him. I told them more about the opportunity in Washington.

"Any other questions?" I asked after I gave a lengthy answer about noncompete clauses. My gaze flew to Jace again almost of its own volition. He spoke up, flashing that killer smile.

"Sounds great to me. Where do I sign up?"

Chapter Two
Jace

Friday dinners had been a fixture in our family for years. My oldest sister Valentina had started the tradition after Will, the second-oldest of the family, turned eighteen and moved out. Once I arrived at her house, I went straight to the kitchen and kissed her cheek.

"Sister, this smells great. As usual."

My sister was the best cook I knew. I'd been of that opinion as a kid, and it hadn't changed as an adult, even after testing many restaurants.

"Where are your girls?" I asked.

"Raiding my closet."

"Of course."

"Hey! I have great fashion sense. Of course the girls want to take advantage of it."

Val's fiancé had two nieces they were raising together. Peyton was seven. April was fifteen and already sharing Val's shopaholic tendencies. After annoying Val by stealing a piece of cake, I skidded out to the backyard. Milo was already stretching. We practiced right until Lori came to inform us that everyone had arrived, and then we headed inside.

Our Friday dinners were loud and crazy, and I loved them. We were six siblings, so I'd grown up in a big household where a third of the inhabitants (usually Hailey and me) was up to no good most of the time. I was the youngest, and Hailey was just two years older than me. Lori was the middle sister, and Will had always considered himself part of the older group, which I supposed he was since Val and Landon were twins. After our parents passed away, the two of them raised the rest of us.

They'd both received scholarships to Harvard and dropped out to return to LA and take over Dad's pub as well as claim responsibility for all of us. I had only been nine at the time, so my memories were fuzzy, but even though I'd missed Mom and Dad greatly, I'd also started to consider Val and Landon as my parents. Even now, I felt more at home in Val's house than my own.

"You've bought a new table," I commented as we all sat down.

"Well, the old one was getting too small," Val said.

Our family had grown a lot over the past few years.

"I'll need a bigger living room once you two get hitched up," Val said jokingly, pointing between Hailey and me. We were the only single Connors left.

I caught Will's eye.

"Bet Hailey will get there first," Will said.

I shook my head. "Oh, come on, man. I was going to bet the same thing. I need you to bet against me."

"I'll do you a solid and bet you'll get there first," Hailey said. I grinned. Our betting habit had rubbed off on our sisters.

Hailey hadn't told us if she was dating anyone, though she shared more with our sisters, which was fine by me. I'd accidentally eavesdropped on their girl talk a few times, and… that was a little too much detail for me. Plus, I was well aware that I could be overprotective of my sisters, and they were all adults. They didn't need me hovering. I just couldn't help myself.

I could see Hailey springing on us that she was serious about someone.

As for me, I liked the way things were, or at least I told myself I did. After the first GQ title came out a few years ago, I became an internet sensation. Then, my fame carried out into the offline world, which was rare. Soccer wasn't one of the three popular sports in the US, but I wasn't fooling myself. I'd become known for my looks, not my game.

In the beginning, I'd rolled along with it. It was fun. I'd always been popular with the ladies, but that had taken popular to a whole new level. I'd relished the attention, taken advantage of it. Somewhere along the way, though, I'd realized that my newfound fame was attracting a lot of people who weren't interested in me, just in how they could benefit by hanging around with me. I was tired of that. Still, I couldn't see myself settling down anytime soon.

"Jace, I got the stills from the last photo shoot today but forgot to forward them to you. They're fantastic. I think half the girls in my office are a bit in love with you," Val said.

"Nah, they just like me shirtless."

"Thanks for agreeing to that, by the way."

"You know me. I take off my shirt for the calendar or my sister's campaigns."

Val ran a very successful cosmetics and fragrance company, and I was featured in a few of her ads. It was the first time Val had asked me for anything, and it hadn't even occurred to me to say no. I'd probably do whatever Val wanted me to do.

"And speaking of people who like you shirtless, Leta keeps talking about you."

Yeah, that was one thing I didn't want to do. Go out with Leta.

"Val, I thought you considered me too much of a heartbreaker to go out with any of your friends. I think I liked that way of thinking better."

Val pouted. Hailey laughed, and so did Lori, but I could tell she was one hundred percent behind the idea. Our middle sister was a wedding planner, and since neither Val and Carter or Will and his fiancé Paige had set a wedding date, it seemed she was waiting for Hailey or me to suddenly need her services. She was seven months pregnant, but I doubted she'd slow down even with a baby in tow.

"I admit I was wrong. You're on your way to becoming an honest man."

"Not going out with Leta."

I'd met her often enough to know we didn't have much in common.

"Be careful with the heartbreaker tag," Hailey advised. "It could turn and bite you in the ass."

I groaned, but Hailey was a PR pro, and I listened to her carefully whenever she gave me advice.

"Did you find someone to manage the sponsorship contracts?" she looked from me to Graham, who was sitting opposite her.

"Yes."

"You've had quite a few personnel changes this year."

There had been a changing of the guard at the Lords over the past year. In addition to Bree leaving, our former head of PR, Amber, had also gone on maternity leave. Graham's father had worked in PR at the club, but Graham had recently opened a restaurant, and his dad now oversaw marketing there.

"Yes. We hired Brooke Derringer," Graham went on.

"Any relation to the head coach?" Hailey asked.

"His daughter. She's a very talented business developer. It was perfect timing. Bree left, and we had a hard time replacing her. Then Coach Derringer came to me and said his daughter was looking for a change of scenery. She'll do great with us, I'm sure of it."

I was sure of it too. I couldn't get Brooke out of my mind. Those blue eyes were branded in my memory, and so was the curve of her waist and that of her neck. I'd fantasized more than once about tilting it just right so I could have all the access I wanted.

"She seems very competent," I offered. I kept the part where I thought she was smoking hot to myself. Graham wouldn't appreciate that comment.

During dinner, I talked to Will and Paige about my schedule this week. They ran an education center that offered various trainings to people from impoverished backgrounds, especially those who were homeless. I'd shown up a few times just to bring in a fun factor, but I was looking for ways to involve myself more.

"We'll find something," Paige said. I respected her a lot. She'd been the one who had the idea for the foundation and roped Will into it. My brother had been a detective with the LAPD before. I deeply believed that everyone should follow the career they wanted, but I couldn't lie: I was relieved that Will had switched to a safer job.

After dessert, Milo begged me to play soccer with him again. He was also preparing a surprise for Lori's birthday, and I was his partner in crime. He still needed help with a few details, and I was always full of ideas.

"You two look a little guilty," Hailey commented as Milo and I got up from the table.

"Course we do. I'm about to go be a bad influence," I supplied.

"I have to up my game in this department. You speak as if you were the only troublemaker."

I shrugged, exchanging a conspiratorial glance with Milo. "I think it's time for you to admit I'm the head troublemaker."

"I vote for Uncle Jace too," Milo said.

Hailey narrowed her eyes at Milo and me before we headed out.

We spoke about Lori's party more than we practiced, and after I ordered some supplies on my phone, I noticed an unread email from Brooke. She was informing us that she'd attend the photo session next Tuesday, and that she wanted to talk to each of us, get some information prior to our one-on-one meetings.

I sent back a short email.

Jace: Sounds good.

Brooke: If there's anything you'd like to discuss in particular, let me know and I can prepare some ideas.

I'd seen her at the club a few times, and it was clear that on the first day, she'd gone the extra mile to dress more conservatively, probably to make a good impression. The other glimpses I'd had of her, she'd been more casual: jeans and polo shirts, occasionally a skirt. She seemed to prefer keeping her hair in that tight bun, and her exposed neck turned out to be my kryptonite. Every time I glimpsed her, I wondered how it would feel to run my lips over that delicate skin. I emailed her back, trying to keep my mind out of the gutter.

Jace: I'm tied up with something this weekend, but we can just exchange ideas on Tuesday.

Brooke: Sure.

Her replies were fast. Why was she still working so late? Was she still at the club, or was she at home, perhaps sitting in a comfortable chair, with a glass of wine? Coach never spoke about his family, and I wanted to know more about Brooke.

I was looking forward to Tuesday, and even more to our one-on-one meeting.

Chapter Three
Brooke

Tuesday was only my fifth day on the job, but I was full of enthusiasm. Today, I was heading out to the pitch where the team was having their photos taken for one of our sponsors. It was almost dinnertime, and my presence was not required, but my purpose for heading there was twofold. One: I wanted to get to know the players better and schedule those one-on-one meetings. And two: I really, really wanted to indulge a little, watch all those Greek gods parade around. If anyone wanted to blame me for that, they could go ahead and do it. A girl had to indulge from time to time, and what better occasion than one where she could combine business with pleasure?

I loved my new workplace. I'd loved my old one too, but tensions had escalated to the point where I had to leave. Over the past few months, I'd been through quite a lot of changes. I didn't just have to leave my old job, but my ex-boyfriend proved that he wasn't the man I thought he was. Ever since, I couldn't help but sigh with melancholy whenever I saw a couple holding hands, or I held a cuddly newborn baby. Maybe love was simply not in the cards for me.

But hey, maybe everything did happen for a reason. If things had played out differently, I wouldn't be here today, and the LA Lords was an exciting place. Graham Frazier was one of the sharpest men I'd met. Soccer club owners were usually also involved in other businesses to support themselves, but the LA Lords was a very profitable endeavor. The club attracted numerous sponsors and sold a lot of merchandise. Graham had now opened a restaurant as well, but from what I'd heard, it was driven by his passion for cooking and not motivated by financial gain.

The players were already out on the field when I arrived. As the photographer called up the guys one by one, I approached the ones who were waiting their turn, keeping my iPad ready, making appointments. I'd just finished with Andrew, the captain, when I had the uncanny feeling that someone was watching me.

As discreetly as possible, I glanced to my right and caught Jace looking at me. *That look.* I didn't know if he was being charming on purpose, or if it came naturally for him, but my entire being reacted to it. I wasn't even sure he was charming in person. While that smile deserved its own category in the swoon-worthy department, he could very well be one of those people who exuded charisma until they opened their mouth. I'd barely exchanged a few words with him. He was still waiting his turn. I promptly turned my focus on my iPad, steeling myself before walking over to him.

"Hey, you!" he greeted jovially. "I was wondering when my turn would come."

"Sorry, but I knew the photographer scheduled you toward the end, and I wanted to get to the others before they left."

"Ah, I see. So I still have some waiting to do."

"I have a proposition for you. I'll talk really quick to Mark and Luke, then circle back to you before the photographer calls you up. I won't take much of your time. I just want to schedule that one-on-one meeting and find out if you're looking for something in particular so I can do some recon work for you."

"I have an even better proposition."

"Oh! Okay. Let's hear it."

"Wait until I'm done with the photo shoot, and then we can have that meeting tonight, over dinner."

"Dinner?"

"You have plans already?" He looked at me determinedly, as if he'd convince me to override those plans, whatever they were.

"No, but you want to spend dinner talking shop?"

"I don't mind. Insider tip: you can talk me into a lot of things if there's food involved. Just ask my family."

He came a little closer, holding me captive in place with those gorgeous green eyes.

"Be careful there. Who knows what you might end up signing."

"I'm just going to hope you won't take advantage. Too much."

Right. So he was even more charming in person than I'd thought. He took another step in my direction, until he was so close that I could see the hint of a five o'clock shadow on his jaw and cheeks. How would it feel against my skin?

Oh, no, no. I wouldn't go there. But those green eyes were relentlessly trained on me, further encouraging my thoughts to follow that path.

"What do you say?" he continued.

"I won't be able to do the recon work I mentioned."

"There's still time for that. Do we have a deal?" He shoved his hands in his pockets, moving his weight from his heels to the front, invading my private space a little.

"We have a deal." I nodded before heading over to Mark and Luke. My thoughts were on Jace the entire time I spoke to them. So far, he'd done justice to his media portrayal.

Charming? Check. Hot as all get out? Double check. Was he also the player they made him out to be?

As soon as the photographer announced the session was over, Jace walked to me.

"All yours," he announced, flashing me a crooked smile, looking even more breathtaking. Did this man ever not smile?

"I saw a Chinese restaurant just around the corner when I came here."

"Let's go there. Lead the way."

The restaurant was large, and we found an empty table all the way in the back. The place was decorated with Chinese motifs. Cute miniature dragons surrounded us, and the air was thick with various delicious smells.

As soon as we ordered, I told him, "So, Jace, as I said, this meeting is about finding out what you're looking for, if you have any specific wishes—types of endorsements you want to score or to avoid. I've looked at your existing workload, and you're booked solid, but you're also the Lords' most bankable player. I assume you want to take advantage."

"You're right about that. This career won't last forever, and this claim to fame will last even less. I'm not kidding myself that anyone is going to chase me in a few years' time."

I liked that he was down-to-earth and realistic. Judging by his easygoing nature, I'd figured he'd be easily swept up by his success. I was glad that I'd been wrong.

"Glad to hear we're on the same page. Anything you'd rather not book? I'm just going to take my iPad out and write everything down so I have a record of the conversation."

Jace pressed his lips together as if he was trying to suppress a smile. That was a first.

"What's that?" I inquired.

"What?"

"You look like you're trying not to laugh at me."

"You're very formal."

I blinked, confused. "This is work. Of course, I'm formal."

And there he went again—first trying to suppress a smile, then shaking his head. I crossed and uncrossed my legs under the table, opening up a new note on my iPad.

"Okay. So, any types of sponsorships you'd rather not do?"

"I'm open to pretty much everything, but I'd rather not take off my clothes."

I looked up in surprise. "But you did that for the calendar."

"That's a club deal, not an individual one."

"And you appear shirtless in most of the campaign pictures for Valentina's Laboratories."

"You looked those up?"

Apparently Jace was done trying to suppress a laugh. He quirked up the corners of his mouth in a smile I could only describe as... challenging. It threw me off. I blushed but kept eye contact.

"Of course I did. For research."

"You're very thorough." He tilted his head, studying me. "Which one do you like best?"

There was one where he looked particularly delectable, as if he'd just walked out of a shower, but hell would freeze over before I'd admit that.

Instead, I said in a casual tone, "I haven't looked at them that closely."

Jace wiggled his eyebrows. Shit. He knew I was bluffing. Before he had a chance to call me out on it, I asked, "But, circling back to our topic, why the sudden change of mind?"

"It's not that I've changed my mind. I've always had that rule, but I make exceptions. Valentina's Laboratories is owned by my sister— Valentina Connor."

"I didn't know that," I exclaimed. "It wasn't anywhere in the campaign details, and as you mentioned... I'm thorough in my research."

"Val and I thought it best not to publicize the family ties."

"Right. I can understand that. And it's an ongoing campaign, right?"

"Yes. Helps my sister, makes my fans happy. Why not?"

As I made a note of the ongoing nature of the campaign, I barely refrained from asking any personal questions. I wanted to know more about *Jace the man* than *Jace the MVP*.

"I think that takes out any underwear ads. Those almost always require you to take off clothes."

I could understand him not wanting to be objectified, but the thought of billboards of a shirtless Jace was making me very happy indeed. To be honest, he wasn't any less impressive even with clothes on. His cotton shirt did nothing to hide his muscles—it just showed off how extensively he trained.

"That's correct. I did turn down three offers."

"Noted. How do you feel about travel? If any sponsorship opportunities require you to fly to another location for a few days, would you be on board with that?"

"Sure, as long as it doesn't interfere with the games. I do however have a standing dinner with my family on Friday, so I'd prefer to be here on Fridays. I'm already missing dinners when I'm away for a game."

"Wow, every Friday, huh? Nice."

We were veering into personal territory, but I couldn't help myself. Before, I'd felt as if I knew him because I'd done my homework on all players. But now I felt as if I was discovering a whole new side of Jace, and I wanted to know more.

He nodded. "My sister Val started the tradition a few years back, insisting all six of us had to meet once a week to catch up. Now more than half are married. Some even have kids. It's an extremely loud affair but also a lot of fun. I'd rather not miss out, but I think I could always leave late at night on Fridays if anyone wants me over the weekend."

"I'll make sure to coordinate everything this way."

"Thanks."

I was dying to know more, but I bit back the impulse. Right, back to work. There wasn't any room for personal information here. I didn't want to be friends with any player. That was something Daddy always said. It was good to be friendly with them, but not friends, because that could make him less objective.

In my case, it was not about being objective. I'd work equally hard to get the best opportunities for every player, no matter if he was a decent person or a jackass. But for the first time in my career, I wanted to apply Dad's credo. He was very good at separating the personal and the professional.

I was just the opposite, which had cost me a lot. My previous job was at a fashion magazine. I'd become best friends with the founder, Cami. My boyfriend, Noah, had also worked with us.

When the opportunity to expand the business in London popped up, Cami suggested the three of us move away. I couldn't.

My family was going through a rough time: Dad had had a heart attack and required doting and attention (he tried to deny it, but I could be a pest). My sister Franci was going through a divorce. Mom had moved away after divorcing Dad years ago, and I could tell Franci and especially Dad needed me.

Cami and Noah grudgingly agreed that it made sense for me to remain in LA for a while, so I could run things here, but after the two of them moved away, it was as if they suddenly didn't want me to be part of the company anymore. They overturned every decision I made, dismissed every proposal I brought to the table. The friction between the three of us reached an all-time high when Noah broke up with me. It all came out of the blue. I was making plans for moving to London in about half a year, after my Dad and Franci were better, and Noah informed that he didn't see our relationship progressing anywhere. In fact, he wasn't seeing a future for us anymore.

My friendship with Cami had imploded at the same time, so I couldn't turn to my best friend for support.

Despite watching my parents' marriage disintegrate as I grew up, I'd dreamed about having a family of my own, but after the break-up, that changed.

Since leaving the magazine, I'd often wondered if things would have turned out differently if I hadn't been personally invested in everything.

Now I wanted to be on good terms with everyone, if possible, but that was it. Which was why I didn't ask Jace to expand on the family dinners. Instead, I had to proceed with some uncomfortable questions.

"Are any of the heartbreaker rumors true? Sponsors always ask. I can tell them I have no info, but they won't buy it. Anyway, I don't think it would work against you as long as you don't get involved in any scandals. The bad-boy angle works for some."

"Including for you?" The challenging smile was back. It dazzled me, but I didn't lose my wits this time. *Progress.*

"Way to avoid an uncomfortable question."

"I'm not avoiding anything. I just want to

know more about you."

Jace leaned a little over the table, training his gaze on my mouth. My breath caught. I became aware that his legs were touching mine under the table, and the contact singed me.

"But this is all about me getting as much info on you as possible. It's a working dinner." I held up my iPad like a shield. Jace leaned back in his chair, pinning me with those sinful green eyes. His gaze dropped to my neck just for a fraction of a second. Oh, God, my skin there tingled, as if he'd touched it. As if he'd *kissed* it.

"No," he said softly.

"What?"

"You never said it's a working dinner. Since we hadn't clarified that, I have green light to consider this dinner between friends."

That gave me pause. I lowered my iPad, trying to decide on the best way to formulate the next words. Hmm...how did I make boundaries clear without upsetting this sexy god? I didn't want to be rude.

"Jace, I might not have clarified, but this *is* a working dinner. I'm sure you know Dad's rule about friendly versus friends."

"I do."

"Well, I do my best to follow it as well."

Surprisingly, Jace said nothing. Up until then, he'd had a reply for everything. Thankfully, our dinner was delivered a few minutes later, and the sound of cutlery clanking against the plate filled the awkward silence. *Way to make this smooth sailing!* I didn't pussyfoot around, but clearly I'd come on too strong. I hadn't wanted to offend or upset Jace.

We talked about endorsements between bites, and I decided to address the elephant in the room once we were both done eating, but before Jace even finished his dinner, two women approached us.

"Oh my God, you're Jace Connor—"

"I can't believe it's really you—"

"Can I have an autograph?"

Jace stood up, smiling at the women, signing everything they shoved in front of him.

"Can we take a selfie? Or my friends won't believe me."

To make myself useful, I offered to take the pictures.

Jace was good at this. He was friendly and didn't once lose his patience. He'd also mastered the art of evasion—he didn't answer when they asked if he was currently dating someone.

"One, two, three, smile," I said, though I needn't have bothered. Jace was a natural at this. He bestowed that panty-melting smile on the camera, and the girls looked at him as if he was the eighth wonder of the world. I wondered yet again if the rumors about him being a heartbreaker were true.

When the two women left, we sat down again, but Jace's phone rang before I got a chance to speak.

"Sorry, this is my sister. I have to take this."

"Sure!"

He brought the phone to his ear.

"Lori, hi!" He listened intently for a few seconds, first nodding and then swearing. His eyes widened.

"Holy shit! I'll be there as soon as possible," he exclaimed.

After ending the call, he focused on me. "I need to go. Sorry to cut this short. I'm leaving my credit card details with the waiter, so it's all covered. You got everything you need?"

"I did." I still wanted to address the awkwardness from earlier, but now wasn't the time. "Do you need any help with the emergency?"

"No, it's all good. She just needs me there."

I wanted to ask more, but since it was clearly a family issue, I didn't want to butt in.

"Have a great evening." He stood up, and so did I. To my surprise, Jace walked over to me and leaned in to kiss my cheek. He brought a hand to my arm, squeezing it lightly. I sucked in a breath when his callused fingers touched my skin.

Feeling that light five o'clock shadow graze my skin sent little shockwaves through me.

"You too, Jace."

Chapter Four
Jace

"I'm so sorry I gave you all a scare," Lori said, fidgeting in her bed.

She'd had some strong contractions and thought the baby was coming early, but it turned out to be a false alarm. The doctors assured her everything was looking good. Graham called us while they were still at the hospital to give me the good news, so I drove directly to their house. Will was also there.

Val and Hailey were on their way but got stuck in traffic.

"Hey, we're glad it was just a scare," I said.

"They said I need to take things slower, though."

"I've been telling you the same for months." Graham kissed the top of her head, handing her a cup of tea.

"I'm sure your assistants can handle all your bridezillas and their outrageous demands," I supplied.

Lori pointed a finger at me. "Brother of mine, do not pretend you're a wedding hater."

"I never said I was."

"I know you're secretly hoping for a huge wedding yourself."

"Wait, what?"

"You gave yourself away when you said you'd never escape to Vegas, that you'd let me throw you a wedding."

"When did I say that?"

I had a vague recollection, but how exactly did Lori translate those words into me having a secret wish for a huge wedding? Ah, my sisters always had their secret language. The way their minds worked was a mystery to me.

Will grinned. "Jace, I was there and can confirm you said those exact words."

I flashed a lazy smile. "Will, you're supposed to be on my side."

"Time for you to know how it feels when your brother throws you to the lions."

"I already have your theme in mind. Your only job is to find your bride," Lori went on.

She was still shaken from the whole ordeal, and if planning my imaginary wedding took her mind off it, I wasn't going to curb her enthusiasm. By the time the rest of the clan arrived, Lori was already in a much better mood.

Next evening, I stayed at the club until late in the evening, hitting the gym.

I loved working out. Not just to keep in shape and remain at the top of my game, but because there was nothing quite like the rush of endorphins after an intense cardio training, which was why I was finishing off my workout with a run on the treadmill. I was the last one here tonight. The rest of my teammates had left after practice, which was why I was surprised when I heard the gym door open. Was someone from management still here? Everyone employed at the club had access to the gym, but I was usually alone in my late evening training sessions.

I was surprised to see Brooke walk in wearing tight shorts and an even tighter shirt. Her hair was up in a ponytail, not a bun, and for once she wasn't wearing glasses. She was even hotter in workout gear than she'd been in the librarian updo from the first day.

"If it's not my favorite sponsorship business developer," I greeted, slowing my pace on the treadmill.

She quirked up her lips. "I'm the only one."

"Still my favorite. What are you doing here so late? I thought management was gone."

"They are. I had a backlog of emails."

"Working overtime already?" I jumped down from the treadmill and walked a few feet over to the cross-trainer Brooke was considering. Fuck, she was sexy. Her hips made my mouth water. When she noticed I was checking her out, she averted her gaze, exhaling sharply.

"It's always worth going the extra mile in the beginning. Builds credibility."

"True."

I wondered if her insistence on friendly-vs-friends was about credibility as well, or if she'd given me that excuse because she didn't like me personally. I was an optimistic guy, so I went for the former.

"Everything okay with the family emergency?" she asked.

"Oh, yeah. My sister Lori had a pregnancy scare. She's seven months along and had some contractions, but they were a false alarm."

"So they're both okay?"

"Yes. Both healthy."

"What is she having? Boy or girl?"

"A girl," I said proudly.

"Did they already decide on a name?"

"Evelyn."

"Aww, that's so cute and sophisticated." She sighed, and I found her dreamy expression endearing.

As she climbed on the cross-trainer, I asked, "How come I've never seen you at any of our events?"

I racked my mind, but I was sure I'd never met Brooke before Graham introduced her. I would've remembered.

"Daddy never invited my sister or me to any work event."

Ah, yes. Coach's golden rule: friendly, not friends. I wasn't sure if Brooke realized she'd just referred to her father as Daddy in front of me. I'd always been told that people felt comfortable in my presence. While comfortable wasn't what I was looking for—it made me think of pajamas or old sweaters—I'd take it for now. Brooke seemed constantly on edge. Maybe it was the fact that she was new here and the team was skeptical of her, or maybe it was something more. I wanted to show her that we didn't bite, that we were a laid-back group. Life was too short to go to work stressed out every day. I felt protective of her.

"Probably wanted to keep his girls away from this misbehaving bunch."

Brooke chuckled. "You're distracting me from my workout."

I could take the gallant route, but I'd always been more the balls-to-the-wall type.

"Brooke, some honest feedback here: this isn't a workout. You're just dusting off the cross-trainer."

Her pretty pink mouth popped open.

I shrugged. "It's true. You're going at a snail's pace. You're not working out regularly, are you?"

"Well, no, but since we have a gym in the building, I've finally run out of excuses. I'm twenty-seven. This feels like I'm ninety."

"I see."

"I have no tempo."

"That comes with time. Increase speed gradually."

"Yes, boss."

She'd said it jokingly, yet now I couldn't help but wonder... what was she like in the bedroom? Would she relent her control to me, trust me to give her pleasure? Her body was toned, and that outfit left nothing to the imagination: the curve of her ass was highlighted, her small waist, and those breasts were so damn tempting. I was trying real hard to ignore the sight of her perky nipples pushing at the fabric....

I cleared my throat.

"Coach bounced back well after his heart attack last year."

Brooke averted her gaze, glancing at the screen of the cross-trainer. I was betting she was weighing where this fell on the friendly-or-friends spectrum... I knew it was the latter, which was why pride surged inside me when she opened up nonetheless.

"He did. But the few months right after were rough for him. And for us. We tried to be there for him in any way we could, but he didn't exactly let us. I can't help worrying that he's not taking it easy enough."

She was lovely. I knew how she felt. I'd gone through that feeling of helplessness when my oldest brother, Landon, drowned in work after his first wife died. No matter how much I—or everyone else in the family—had tried to reason with him, it wasn't until Landon decided to take action that things changed. Now he was happily married again, but for a few years, we all worried about him.

She increased her tempo on the cross-trainer and was out of breath in thirty seconds flat. She really had no physical conditioning.

"Don't laugh at me."

"I'm not."

I was. Her breath was coming out in sharp bursts as her chest rose and fell. Perspiration dotted her neck. Fuck, that skin looked so soft, so kissable.

I wanted to trace a path up to her ear, suck that earlobe between my lips. I'd hold her with my hips against that wall, feasting on her, starting with her neck, pushing up her T-shirt and running my tongue all over that smooth skin. I looked away from her, but that didn't keep the vision of a naked Brooke under me out of my mind.

Right… I needed some distance, which was why I told her I'd head to the shower. I needed to cool off, get my thoughts straight again.

When I walked back into the gym some twenty minutes later, I saw that Brooke had increased her tempo by at least three speed levels.

"You're going too fast," I commented.

"No, I'm not."

"I bet you won't last longer than ten minutes."

She smirked, and unfortunately for her, chose to increase the tempo even more. She was done for in seven minutes.

"Holy shit, my legs feel like Jell-O," she exclaimed when she stepped on the ground.

"Easy there."

Instinctively, I reached out to steady her, grabbing her arm. The second my fingers touched her, goose bumps formed on her skin. Fuck me, those nipples looked even more perky than before, and I craved to taste them. Brooke freed herself from my grip, licking her lips.

"Okay, so I think this is enough training for one day. I'm going to shower and then finally get around to replacing my flat tire. Noticed it this morning when I parked but wasn't in the mood to change it. I've been dragging my feet about it all day."

"I'll do it."

She paused in the act of drying her neck.

"Thanks, but you're all dressed. I still have to shower—"

"I'll wait."

"I can change a tire."

"Yeah, but you clearly hate to do it. I don't mind."

I walked closer. I was towering over her and she looked up at me, swallowing. We were so close that her breasts nearly brushed against my chest. I was fighting against every instinct not to touch her. Remembering the way she'd reacted to my touch before was almost enough to break my resolve.

"Jace—"

"I'll change it."

"You're sure?"

"Yes."

"Okay. Thanks. I'll be quick."

"I'll wait for you at the front entrance."

To my astonishment, Brooke was ready in ten minutes. The glasses were back on.

"That was quick," I commented as we walked

outside to the parking lot.

"I told you I wouldn't take long."

"Yeah, but when my sisters say that what they usually mean is, sit down and have a drink or watch a movie. We're gonna take our sweet time."

She nudged me with her shoulder, wiggling a finger. "Hey! Don't generalize, Mr. Fancy Forward."

I joined in her game, leaning in closer. Too close, because I practically felt her take in a sharp breath.

"Or what?" I challenged.

"Ohoho, friendly warning. Don't underestimate me."

"Didn't even cross my mind."

She smiled before looking away quickly. Well, well... I had a hunch that Ms. Friendly-Not-Friends here had troubles sticking to her own rules. Behind those black-rimmed glasses was a flirty woman. I couldn't wait to uncover her.

The parking lot was empty as we headed to Brooke's car, a Honda SUV. The flat tire was at the front. I immediately set to work. Brooke brought me the jack, and while I lifted the car, she brought the spare tire. We made small talk while I changed it.

"You often train in the evenings after everyone's gone?"

"Checking if you should avoid the gym in the evenings?" I looked up, winking at her to let her know I was joking. She still became flustered.

"Jace... no, of course not. I meant to talk to you about the other day. I'm sorry if I came across as rude."

"You didn't. You were just making yourself clear. Don't worry. And to answer your question, yes. I am often at the gym in the evening. I like the quiet."

"Wouldn't have pegged you for the type who enjoys the quiet. Especially with the attention you're getting."

"The job's not as glamorous as people think. Lots of training, restrictions on food and drinks."

"Parties are also part of the package."

"I don't enjoy those as much as I used to," I said honestly.

"Why not?"

"Easy there. That question crosses the line from friendly to friends."

Brooke pressed her lips together, looking away. We spent the next few minutes in silence, which was a pity. I liked talking to her. It was easy.

After I finished placing the last lug nut, I rose to my feet. Unfortunately, either the tire or the jack had had grease on it, and I'd transferred it all to my shirt.

"You got it all dirty," Brooke lamented.

"It'll wash off."

"I can wash it for you."

I knew what she'd meant, but I couldn't let the opportunity pass.

"Very creative way of asking me to take my shirt off."

Brooke blinked a few times, playing with the

end of her ponytail between her fingers. "I thought you only took off your clothes for the calendar or your sister's campaigns."

"I make exceptions."

She blushed. "I'm not used to being surrounded by so much testosterone."

I touched her chin, lifting it up a notch, wanting to look straight at her. She drew her lower lip between her teeth.

"How do you like it?" I challenged, resting my thumb on the dimple at the right corner of her mouth. Brooke cleared her throat, and I lowered my hand.

"I've never been around soccer players before. It'll take me some time to get used to it."

"Won't take so long if you spend time with us. Are you joining us at the bar tomorrow?"

We were celebrating our string of victories at one of the bars near the club. We were there so often after home games that the owner usually made it an exclusive event. Tomorrow was bound to be more low-key since it wasn't directly after a game.

"I wasn't planning to."

"Why not?"

"It's just an informal event."

"Which gives you a great opportunity to spend time with us in a relaxed environment. We'll have a few drinks, play darts or pool. Who knows? Maybe you'll like us enough to reconsider the friendly-vs-friends credo."

She shook her head, smiling. "That won't

happen."

I was beginning to think that wasn't true. Coach Derringer was a cold man, rarely speaking more than he had to. Brooke was nothing like him. She was warm and chatty, and his polar opposite in every way, I could tell.

"Does that mean you won't play a game of pool with me? On my team? I haven't lost a game in years." I stepped closer, placing my hand on the car deck, close to her head. I was fighting to bring out her inner flirt. I could tell she was fighting back. I could also tell the exact moment I won her over, because she looked away quickly before refocusing on me.

"Fine. *If* I come, I'll play on your team."

"After we win, I'll buy you a drink and negotiate that credo of yours some more."

"You don't really understand the concept of boundaries, do you?" she asked playfully, her gaze zeroing on my lips before she looked up abruptly. I was barely refraining from pinning her against the car door and kissing her.

I was in her personal space, but I didn't want to push too much. I risked her shutting me down. I owed her honesty, though.

"I understand boundaries, Brooke. I'm just not very good at respecting them."

Chapter Five
Brooke

Next day, I was the first to arrive at the Lords headquarters. I wasn't a big fan of the open-floor office plan. It lacked privacy, and it was a bit too loud, but this early it was just perfect.

I started by sending out an email to all players, informing them that I'd finished reviewing their files and had proposals for each of them that we would be discussing during our one-on-one meetings. I reminded them they could come to me with questions at any time, then proceeded to call a few companies we could approach for sponsorships and endorsements.

When I checked my emails two hours later, my inbox was flooded with replies from the players.

And even though Jace's wasn't the first one, I started by opening his.

Jace: I'm impressed. Ready so quickly? Or did you start with me?

Brooke: That was a mass email.

I'd put everyone in bcc though, so I could see why he'd gotten confused. He couldn't see I'd sent it to every player.

Jace: Damn. And I thought I was special.

Brooke: Aww, sorry to disappoint you. Just doing my job.

Jace: Are you as thorough in your research with everyone as you are with me?

He was calling me out on my scouting activity regarding his shirtless pics. I couldn't admit to giving him more attention than the other players, especially after last evening.

Just remembering how he *looked* at me was enough to make me feel hot and bothered. My entire body was on fire whenever he was close.

Brooke: Always.

I went on to reply to another player's email, but the second the thread with Jace showed another unread email, I went back to it. I couldn't resist.

Jace: You wound me.

Brooke: You'll survive.

Jace: Will I see you tonight?

I'd given the outing some more thought, and Jace was right. It was smart for me to get to know everyone in an informal environment, especially since Dad wouldn't be there.

One of my friends had set up a blind date for me tonight, but honestly... between having to put on a show for a perfect stranger and spending the time with the LA Lords, I preferred the latter.

I'd sent a text last night to my friend to let her know about the change in schedule and had zero regrets.

Brooke: I'll let this be a surprise.

Jace: Come on, have mercy on me. Give me something to look forward to other than the ass-chewing I'm gonna get from coach today.

Brooke: You're going to spend time with your teammates. Aren't you looking forward to that already?

Jace: I already know all of them. You, on the other hand, are a secret waiting to be explored.

I licked my lips, drawing in a shaky breath as I reread the last words, shimmying in my seat. I shot him a noncommittal response. I wasn't looking to keep him on his toes for any specific reasons, but I did think Jace deserved a little punishment for his constant pushing of boundaries.

Brooke: Nah, you don't deserve mercy. Wait and see.

The get-together was taking place at a sports bar two blocks away from the club. Only half the management was attending, and I walked there with two of my colleagues, Veronica and Sheila.

"I've been looking forward to this for days," Veronica exclaimed. "Gives me a chance to unwind."

The two had been with the Lords for three years and were clearly friends. Veronica had been a little frosty with me, but I chalked it up to the fact that I was a new hire.

Veronica and Sheila both launched into a conversation in which they ranked our players by looks. I stayed out of it, even though I was dying to join in the fun, ask them more about themselves. Keeping people at an arm's length wasn't really my forte. I had no idea how Daddy managed it.

The pub was full when we arrived. We spotted a few of the players gathered around a pool table and headed that way.

Jace was sporting an ear-to-ear grin when I approached him. "You made it."

"I did."

"And you left me to wonder all day. You have a mean streak."

"Only where you're concerned."

"Ouch."

"Thought you wanted special treatment."

Jace's grin became, if possible, even wider. I found myself grinning right back at him. Seriously, this man's good mood was infectious.

I had hoped that my reaction to him at the gym was simply a product of seeing him in workout gear. With that shirt stretching thin over his six-pack, he'd looked positively delicious. But right now, I reacted to his gaze the same way as that night. Energy zinged through my veins. My breath caught.

"Come on, let's go get drinks."

When he kissed my cheek, warmth pooled low in my belly. Oh, God. It was going to be a long night.

I ordered a glass of merlot at the counter, Jace soda.

"No alcohol for you?"

"We have a game in two days. I feel better

without alcohol. You want some insider info?" he asked as we waited for our order.

"You'd betray your teammates?"

"Again, assuming the worst of me."

"My bad. Fire away." I took a sip of wine as soon as the bartender put the glass in front of me.

"So, Mark is generally friendly. Luke plays the tough guy, but if you compliment his game skills, he softens. Don't approach Henry after we lose. We're all in a bad mood, but he takes the cake. Even his wife avoids him. Andrew will try to get in your pants."

I nearly choked on my drink. "You can't know that."

"You're a beautiful woman. He'll try, trust me."

He thought I was beautiful? Until now, I'd figured Jace was fooling around because he was a rule breaker in general and didn't think much of work barriers. But what if there was more?

"Gaston is an open book. Be careful though, once he gets started, there's no stopping him."

"Thanks for all the information. I should go talk to everyone."

"Go ahead. But I didn't forget about our pool game."

"I didn't think you had."

Maybe it was the informal ambiance, but the players were more open with me than I'd expected. I'd briefly wondered if Jace had exaggerated anything, but he'd been spot on, right down to Andrew trying to flirt the pants off me.

"Can I tempt you with a pool game later on?" he asked after I'd turned down his offer to buy me a drink.

I'd barely opened my mouth to decline when I realized Jace had stepped next to me.

"I don't think so."

He laced an arm around my shoulders, drawing me closer. I felt the heat radiating off him. His jaw was nearly touching my forehead, and my nose was close enough to his neck that I couldn't ignore the light whiff of his body wash.

"She's mine tonight."

His voice was determined, his stance straight and self-assured, as if he wanted to dominate Andrew, as if he'd staked his claim on me.

I licked my lips, hoping Jace couldn't tell that my pulse had sped up at his words.

"My bad. Should have moved faster. Whenever we have the next outing, I'm calling dibs on those games."

I laughed, going for the diplomatic route. "Easy there. I'm not booking my time so far in advance."

"I'll be the first to ask next time, then."

Andrew pointed his forefinger at me before leaving me with Jace and joining two other teammates who were playing darts.

"Told you there's no stopping him."

"Or you, apparently," I volleyed back good-naturedly.

"So you'd rather I hadn't saved you?"

"Who said I needed saving?"

Jace set his jaw. "You want that game with Andrew?"

"I promised I'd play with you, and I keep my word."

He opened his mouth, but before he could add anything else, two of his teammates dragged him to the darts board.

I admired Jace as he moved through the room. The man was simply beautiful. Not just hot, or handsome... but beautiful. Maybe it was that permanent joy of his that lit him up, but whenever he captured my gaze, I found myself unable to look away.

Apparently, I couldn't look away even when he had his back at me. In my defense though, that back was just as impressive as the front. Muscle-laced and broad, tapering to a trim waist and a very impressive ass. He wore those jeans so well that he should come with a warning sign or ten.

Close to midnight, as the crowd thinned, most of management left, but I chose to stay. I still owed Jace that game of pool. Everyone but the team had left before they decided to start their pool game.

When they gathered around the table, I walked up to Jace.

"Ready, partner?" he asked, handing me a stick.

"Yes."

"Boys, nothing personal against you, but you'll lose," Jace announced to the others. Ah, he had no idea what he was getting himself into.

But he found out exactly four rounds later. I'd missed both times it had been my turn. Jace took my hand, pulling me a little further away from the others.

"Are you doing this on purpose?" he inquired.

"No."

"You just missed those two straight shots?"

"You never asked if I was any good at it."

"And you didn't think to set me straight?"

"Where would be the fun in that?"

"What am I going to do with you?" he murmured. He was so close now that I had to tip my head back to look up at him. Jace's gaze dropped to my mouth for a split second.

"Teach me how to play or learn to lose."

I'd meant it as a joke, but the joke was on me because when we resumed the game, Jace announced he'd be showing me how to play correctly. I'd expected the others to protest, because it essentially meant Jace would be playing the entire game, but they didn't.

They preferred losing to engaging in a lousy game. I couldn't fault them for that. Jace was taking his teaching role very seriously. I was doing everything wrong, from holding the thick end of the stick too high, to leaning forward too much. Correcting my pose and aim meant that he had to put his hands on me constantly.

"This angle here is what you need," he

murmured in my ear, placing a hand on my waist, bending me over the table.

I didn't know if feeling his hot breath on the side of my neck, and the fly of his jeans rubbing against my right ass cheek were messing with my mind, but all I could think about was him bending me over and stripping me naked.

Holy shit!

When he clasped my wrist to correct my grip, I prayed he couldn't feel my erratic pulse. When he brought both hands on my waist to correct my angle, I hoped he wouldn't notice that goose bumps had broken out on my arms. I wanted to glance at him to see if he'd noticed, but I couldn't get away with just checking out of the corner of my eye because he was slightly behind me.

I turned, and immediately realized I'd miscalculated the angle. He was much closer. Our lips nearly touched. The side of my breast brushed his arm. The contact electrified me. Could he feel it? Our gazes locked.

"Eyes on the game, Brooke."

Heat rose in my cheeks as I returned my attention to the pool table. I did notice that Jace touched me less afterward. In fact, he seemed intent on keeping his distance. I must have imagined that current of awareness before. Or perhaps I'd been the only one who felt it, which was fine. Just fine. I wasn't interested in him like that. Of course, I found him hot. Every woman on the planet probably did. But that was all this was.

After we won the second round, Henry and Andrew announced they were done.

"Man, there's only so much beating my ego can take in one night," Andrew said. "Especially with a newbie on your team."

"Beginner's luck," I said jovially.

"Or you could just own up to the fact that I'm a great teacher," Jace challenged.

"I don't know. The jury's still out on that."

Henry laughed when Andrew said, "Ah, my ego's recovering. Keep busting his balls, Brooke. Let's call it a night. Or we'll be no good at practice tomorrow."

The rest of the team had already left, but the three of them hadn't wanted to leave until we finished the game.

Henry and Andrew bid me goodbye, and then they clapped Jace's shoulder. I had assumed they'd all leave together. Jace must have read the question on my face, because after they left, he said, "Come on, I'll drive you home."

"Thanks, but it's not necessary. I'll just order an Uber."

"But I didn't drink anything, and I'm going to drive anyway."

"Jace. It's late. You have practice tomorrow. Go home and sleep."

"I'll take you home."

"No, you won't."

"Then I'll stay with you until your Uber arrives."

I didn't argue, because there were still enough drunk pub-goers around, and I couldn't think of a more efficient way to keep men at bay than having Jace next to me.

"I'm just going to the ladies' room first, okay?"

"I'll wait."

He leaned against the pool table, crossing his legs at the ankles.

When I returned a few minutes later, Jace wasn't alone anymore. A bombshell brunette was sitting on the pool table at a weird angle, showing off her boobs. Jace was keeping his distance. What had the girl done, waited until I was out of the picture to pounce on him?

"Here you are," Jace exclaimed.

The brunette smile's faded when she saw me.

"Ready to go?" he asked, coming my way.

"Yeah. I ordered an Uber. It'll be here in six minutes."

"Let's wait outside."

As we walked out the door, I said, "Listen, if you'd rather stay and talk to—"

"I don't."

"Well, not to be Captain Obvious, but brunette beauty there looked ready to give you her phone number… or even go home with you."

"I'm not interested."

"Why?"

"Easy there. Personal talk goes into friendship territory."

"Ah, I see."

"Personally, I'd say I'm a great friend. Look at you. Stick by my side for one night, and you're already a champion at pool."

I looked up at him, which wasn't the smartest thing because those green eyes were working their magic on me again, and my defenses were already weak tonight.

"What are you doing, Jace?"

"Pushing boundaries." His gaze was scorching hot.

"Why?"

"Because I think you need it."

"You don't even know me."

"You had fun tonight. Will you admit that, at least?"

"Of course I have."

"Good. Because I've watched you around the club. You seem to be constantly tense."

Was it that obvious?

"It's a new workplace. I want to make a good impression."

He was watching me curiously, as if he knew there was more to it than that.

"My previous boss was my best friend. My ex-boyfriend also worked with us. Let's just say that when things went to hell on a personal level, I had to leave."

"So now you're trying out your dad's workplace policy."

"Yes."

"But you're nothing like Coach. And I don't mean that in a good way or a bad way. You're warm and sociable. Everyone's different."

I'd never met anyone who saw through me like this.

"Thanks for sharpening my pool skills tonight."

"We won," he said unnecessarily. The heat of his body was intoxicating. If he came any closer, my knees might weaken.

"I know."

"I believe the deal was that I'd buy you a drink and negotiate the friends-vs-friendly thing."

"Jace…."

"No, no! I don't like the sound of that. You're about to shut me down. I'll rephrase. How about… negotiating that you'll make an exception just for me?"

I didn't know what else to do but laugh. If it were anyone else, I might think that he just saw this as a personal challenge, something to tick off his list. But Jace had sort of taken me under his wing tonight, giving me tips about the players. He didn't have to do that, just as he didn't have to change my tire the other day.

"One drink."

He smiled broadly just as my Uber pulled in. When he bid me goodbye, his lips lingered on my cheek longer than necessary, and it was enough to make all my nerve endings jump to attention.

I had the suspicion that I'd just agreed to far

more than a drink.

Chapter Six
Brooke

Over the next couple of days, I had my one-on-one meetings with all the players except Jace. Since we had that outstanding drink, I insisted we could combine the two.

My job also included making phone calls to existing and potential sponsors, and performing that task when surrounded by noise was especially tiresome. I liked to conduct my calls alone, which was why I sometimes stayed after everyone left, choosing to make some calls during that time. There were plenty night owls in the business.

Which was why, on the evening we'd scheduled our drink, I was caught up at work. I regretfully texted Jace.

Brooke: Can we move our drink to another day? Still have a few things to wrap up.

He didn't answer, and I went back to the contract I was reviewing, feeling a little guilty. Sometime later, I was startled when I heard a sound because I was the last one left. I looked up from the papers.

Jace was a few feet in front of my desk. Those

green eyes were studying me closely. I had the impression he'd been watching me for a while. God, how could he be so gorgeous? I tried to find one single flaw and failed.

"What are you doing here?" I asked as he walked toward me.

"Cashing in on our drink. Threw in dinner as a bonus." He sat against the edge of my desk, his gaze fixating on my lips. The distance between us seemed to simply disappear. When I could no longer stand the tension, I turned my head, looking at the bag he'd set in front of me, but I could still feel the heat of his gaze.

"What did you bring?"

"Chinese and wine."

"Sounds good. Let's dig in."

I relaxed during dinner. We ended up talking about his family a bit, and he told me about an education center his brother Will and his fiancée had set up.

"They're focusing on teaching marketable skills to people who for one reason or another didn't have access to education."

I listened closely, finding the concept more intriguing with every word.

"It's a great initiative."

"I think so too. I'd love to get involved more than just playing soccer, but I'm not sure how."

"How is this financed?"

"Grants, but mostly private donations. My brother Landon owns an investment fund, and he's a big contributor. Everyone from the family chips in. But there are a lot of external donors too. It's smart to spread the risk. I'd like to do more than donate and kick ball with the students, but I don't know how."

I thought this was absolutely adorable.

"Have you thought about approaching some of the companies you have endorsements with to see if they'd like to become donors?"

"That's a great idea, but am I legally allowed?"

"I'll look over your contracts this week, to see if there's any clause regarding that."

Every player and their agent had agreed it was the most productive if they gave me unrestricted access to all their contracts.

"You don't have to do that. It'll take a lot of time. I can ask my agent to look over it."

"I want to."

"Thanks, Brooke." He flashed me a smile. "I promise to keep you company."

"What? No, that's not necessary."

"I'll make myself useful."

"Maybe you'll just divert my focus."

"Well, I could… but I promise I won't." Was his tone flirty or was I making this into more than it was? He drew his chair closer to the table, resting his chin in one palm.

"And how exactly will you make yourself useful?"

"I can do whatever you need me to do, Brooke."

"I bet you can," I murmured. The tips of my ears felt ablaze. Had he meant it as an innuendo or was I imagining things because I just couldn't shut off my body's reaction to him?

Later that evening, he walked me to my car, even opening the door for me. When I was about to slide in, he touched my shoulder, winking at me.

"See you tomorrow, Brooke."

I had to become less susceptible to his charm and sheer masculinity. But how was I supposed to do that when I shuddered from a simple touch?

Oh, yeah. Things weren't looking too bright for me.

I kept my promise of reviewing his contracts, but it turned out to be more involved than I'd anticipated. That translated to long evenings at the club over the next weeks. Jace indeed kept me company.

He'd shown up the first evening with two boxes of takeout and soda.

"What are you doing here?" I inquired.

"Making myself useful, as I promised."

I liked the food and loved the company. It was productive to go over the contracts with him, because he could provide some insider info in each case. We made up a good game plan. We were going to talk to each of the companies he did endorsements for about potentially donating.

Conversation also often veered into personal territory. One evening, I even told him the whole reason behind my leaving the magazine.

"Moving to Europe when my family needed me just didn't feel right," I said, concluding my story.

"Of course not. You wanted to be close to them."

"Exactly." I was deeply touched that he understood me right off the bat instead of telling me that there was nothing I could do for Dad anyway, and I could always talk to my sister on the phone, as Noah had insisted.

Jace slid his thumb under my chin, lifting my head a tad. "Brooke, they didn't value you or what was important for you. It's a good thing they're not in your life anymore."

He was right, but Cami and I had been best friends. Noah and I had been together for two years. I had honestly thought Noah and I might get married one day. The breakup, combined with my sister's divorce, had done a number on me.

"If they couldn't understand why you wanted to be here for your family when they were going through a rough patch, they don't deserve your friendship."

He spoke with such sincerity that I instantly knew Jace would never have asked me to turn my back on my family.

"You really don't have to walk me to my car every night, you know," I whispered later that evening, once we were in the parking lot. He'd parked at the opposite side of the lot and was going out of his way for me.

"Of course I do."

Something had shifted between us that evening after I'd opened up to him. I felt even closer to Jace than before. He bid me good night as usual by kissing my cheek, and I barely resisted the impulse to turn my head slightly so our lips would meet. *No, no, no!*

I wanted him to come even closer, even though I knew I had to put more distance between us.

I definitely was not growing less susceptible to his charm *or* masculinity. Quite the opposite.

I only realized how used I got to spending time with Jace once our contract work was over. My sister tried to needle me for information whenever we went out, but I kept our conversation away from hot soccer players and focused on Dad. Working at the club gave me the advantage of being able to dote on Dad on a daily basis, making sure he wasn't ordering steak or anything with butter for lunch, and that he took all his medication.

It was during one of the team's away games that I realized I felt more relaxed going into work. That was not to say I wasn't determined to do my very best, but some of that artificial pressure I'd put on myself when I started a month ago seemed to have lifted. I was careful not to rub it in that I was Dad's daughter. In that vein, I was also being careful with Jace, because cozying up to the MVP wouldn't reflect well on me.

"I got us tickets," Jace said one evening as we headed to the gym.

"But it was sold out."

We'd discovered we both loved stand-up comedy, and we'd eyed a show in a smaller venue, but there hadn't been any more tickets available.

"Stick with me, and you're set. I told you I'm a good friend."

"I thought you were overselling yourself, Jace, but you are a good friend."

He really was. I wasn't sure how we'd become friends, but I had a hunch that it had something to do with Jace being the kind of person who simply sneaked up on you.

Thanks to my new friend, Jace, I went to the gym every other evening. I'd discovered that all these years I hadn't skipped gym out of laziness. I just hadn't found the proper... motivator. Turned out that watching a hot soccer player work out was all the motivation I needed. Jace always exuded a knee-weakening sex appeal but never more than when he was playing or when he was training. That unshakable focus was hot, and the way his muscles flexed when he lifted weights was even hotter. His shirt clung to him, leaving nothing to the imagination, especially after he worked up a sweat.

So, yeah... plenty of motivation to show up and give my best on the cross-trainer.

"You're getting better," Jace commented. He always started training before I showed up, with the result that he was done way before I was, and he spent the rest of my training time sitting on the abs bench in front of my cross-trainer, talking. That was fine by me. Better than fine, in fact. I liked talking to him. Plus... that view was simply to die for.

"Practice makes perfect, right?"

"I wasn't expecting you to show up here so often." He stood up, coming closer, arching one eyebrow. "Be honest. Is it because of me?"

I rolled my eyes, even though my knees had turned a little weak. "What can I say, Connor? You're definitely helping."

He grinned, leaning against one of the pillars, crossing his legs at the ankles and his arms over his chest. Belatedly I realized I'd been openly checking him out and cast my gaze away quickly, but I was certain he'd noticed.

"Your teammates had grand party plans tonight, and yet here you are, even though I'm pretty sure you would have stolen the show if you'd gone with them. Why is that? You can tell me, now that we're friends and all."

Jace's smile dimmed, and I bit my lip. I didn't want to spoil his good mood.

"I did enjoy the attention in the beginning, but it's just brought around a lot of people who weren't really interested in hanging with me."

"Oh, I'm sorry."

"It's not so bad, I think I was just not used to

it. But thank God we live in LA. My fifteen minutes of fame have passed."

He moved slowly to my treadmill, bracing both hands on top of the console. I lowered my gaze to the cross-trainer's display, which was why I was surprised when he grabbed my wrist. I looked at him questioningly when he pressed his thumb over my pulse point.

"You're overexerting yourself again, Brooke. Slow down a bit."

Right… because that was the only thing that had sent my pulse into overdrive. It wouldn't have anything to do with the sexy-as-hell soccer player standing in front of me.

"Your fifteen minutes might return if you make the GQ list again," I said.

"True. Attention always flares up around that time."

"I bet you'll top the list again."

"Really? So you think I'm better-looking than the rest of the soccer players in the country?"

I thought he was better-looking than 99.9 percent of the population, but I kept that opinion to myself.

This time, Jace flashed me a shit-eating grin, winking.

"I think bias plays a role. You've been number one already, which makes you a favorite."

I'd expected Jace to take offense, but if anything, he looked even more amused than before.

"You're a shit liar, Brooke. You think I

haven't seen you looking before?"

I swallowed hard, trying to muster up an innocent smile. My stomach jolted, as if I'd missed a step. What was I supposed to say? I wasn't sure how to navigate this. Our friendship was still new, and while Jace seemed the kind of guy who spoke his mind, I didn't think that owning up to checking him out was smart. He'd probably laugh it off, but I ran the risk of him thinking I was one of his fangirls. And anyway, I *couldn't* be attracted to Jace. I just couldn't.

I decided to treat this as if it was a rhetorical question and didn't answer it. Instead, I finished the last fifteen seconds on the treadmill, then stepped off. Jace moved right in front of me.

"Cat got your tongue, Livie?"

My eyes bulged. "That's my dad's nickname for me because my middle name is Olivia. How do you know this?"

"I did my research. Asked your Dad a bit about you, without making it obvious."

I wrinkled my nose. That right there was a testament to Jace's ability to sneak up on a person. Dad would never share that with anyone.

"You can't use my dad's nickname."

"You're right. I should find my own nickname for you." He tugged lightly at his lower lip with his teeth. "I have one. Hot stuff."

"What? Jace, no. Come on; you can't call me that when there are others around."

"So I can call you hot stuff when we're alone?

Like now?"

I licked my lips, acutely aware that I couldn't take a step back because I'd bump into the cross-trainer. Jace was towering over me, his shoulders slightly hunched, and that glint in his eyes was dominant.

"How about finding a more appropriate nickname?"

"What are you talking about? This is very appropriate."

I cocked a brow in challenge. If I'd thought this would make Jace back down, I was dead wrong.

"You weren't the only one looking before, hot stuff," he went on in a raspier tone of voice. My pulse intensified. I felt it at the base of my neck and pounding in my ears. But since I'd looked, I couldn't hold it against him that he'd done the same. I rubbed a hand over my face, eager to change the subject.

"Do you want to grab dinner tomorrow before the stand-up comedy?" I asked.

"No can do. Have plans with Milo."

"Oh, you're right. I forgot."

"I'll meet you in front right before it begins. We're going to have a blast, hot stuff."

Chapter Seven
Jace

On Thursday, after dropping off Milo with Lori, I headed straight to the venue of the comedy show. He and I had finalized the grand plans for Lori's party, which was going to be in a few weeks. We hired a band, and then Milo and his friends were performing a play for her. She'd love it.

I hadn't seen Brooke today and was looking forward to a relaxed evening. I loved spending time with her. I'd never met a woman I'd clicked with as I did with her.

She was damn cute the way she kept nagging Coach about his diet, double-checking that he was taking all his pills.

My attraction to her hadn't subsided one bit though. If she wanted to combine our friendship with some benefits, I was all up for it, though for the first time in my life, I thought sex would complicate things, and I liked them the way they were.

The problem was, I couldn't stop wanting Brooke.

When she got out of an Uber a few minutes after I arrived, I nearly swallowed my tongue. She was wearing a tight beige dress and black heels with thin straps around her ankles. It was that strap that fired up my imagination. I imagined her wearing nothing but those heels, wrapping her long, toned legs around my waist.

"Good evening, gorgeous."

She gave an adorable shriek because she hadn't noticed me.

"Sorry for that. You scared me. Am I late?"

"Not at all. Let's head inside. "

I walked slightly behind her, keeping my hand at that point where the curve of her ass began. I'd studied her closely at the gym, but something about this dress was driving me insane. I couldn't even say why. It wasn't too short or too tight or too anything, but I could barely keep my thoughts straight.

I wasn't the only one. I caught a few guys drooling and knew I was the only reason no one had hit on her yet. My arm went around her shoulders out of pure instinct. It could pass as a friendly gesture to Brooke, but I wanted to send out a signal to everyone else: she was here with me.

I liked having her this close, touching her. She smelled delicious. My thigh was brushing her left hip as we walked, and the desire to touch the bare skin of her legs hit me hard. To grip both her hips, then her ass, and lift her up so she'd wrap her legs around me. *Jesus.*

Once inside, I led her straight to the front row.

"First row?" Brooke asked excitedly. She seemed a little breathless.

"Course."

We sat down, and I noticed that the two guys at the next table were leering at Brooke, who seemed oblivious to it all.

"What am I going to do with you, Brooke?"

"What do you mean?"

"Every man here wants to hit on you."

She waved her hand. "No, they don't."

"Every man," I repeated. Me included. She cast her gaze down, playing with her hands, and I thought I saw a tinge of pink in her cheeks.

We ordered drinks, and the show began almost as soon as the waiter brought our cocktails.

Stand-up comedians could be hit or miss. Half an hour into the show, this turned out to be such a miss that I wondered if we'd accidentally walked into a rehearsal. I glanced at Brooke from time to time, searching for signals that she was just as bored, but her gaze was glued to the stage. I'd almost resigned myself to two hours of hellish boredom when Brooke leaned over the small table. I immediately leaned in too.

"Jace... I hope I'm not offending you, but this is terrible."

"Thank fuck. I thought I was the only one so bored I wanted to burst my eardrums so I couldn't hear him. How about we get out of here?"

"Excellent idea."

The room was semidark as we made our way

out. A few viewers huffed with annoyance because we obstructed their view. I slung my arm around Brooke's waist, leading her through the room. She started laughing the second we were out on the street.

"Oh, that was so bad," she said. "So. So bad."

"Awful. And I thought you liked it. Was mentally preparing myself to sit through two hours of torture."

Brooke tilted her head. "You really would have done that if I'd liked it? Awww… you really are a good friend."

No, I wasn't. I was the worst. I moved my arm from her waist to her shoulders, squeezing them lightly. She shivered despite the warm mid-August evening. I pulled her even closer, speaking against her temple.

"Let's do something else, Brooke. I don't want this evening to end so fast."

"Me neither. Hmm… I think we need to watch something good to wash this crap out of our brain."

"We could go to a movie, but I don't know what's playing."

"I do. Looked over the new releases yesterday. Nothing stood out to me. Hey, I have an idea. Let's go to my place. We can watch something on Netflix, or one of my DVDs, and I can make us popcorn."

I wanted to spend time with Brooke more than anything else, but if we were alone… I wasn't strong enough *not* to make a move on her.

She was too alluring. Even now, I was fighting with all I had against the urge to cup her cheek and tilt her head just right so I had access to her mouth. I'd pulled her too close, but I'd be damned if I wanted to let go. She watched me with wide, happy eyes. I just couldn't say no.

"Love that idea. Where do you live?"

"A quiet residential area up north. My neighbors are super nice. Most of them are a little old and like to poke their nose in my business."

"What are your nice neighbors gonna say when you come home with a man?"

She looked up from the screen of her phone. "They're gonna think I have great taste in men."

Brooke's apartment was an explosion of color. Mismatched furniture gave the place a cozy, lived-in feeling, as did the pictures hanging everywhere.

I laughed, pointing at one picture where she was with another woman—her sister, presumably. Brooke was wearing an eye-mask, and the other woman held a cartoon mustache above her upper lip.

"I have a similar picture with Hailey and Lori."

"Taken at a wedding?"

"Yes. My cousin Summer Bennett."

Her jaw dropped. "As in... the one who married *the* Alexander Westbrook?"

Alex was a very well-known actor.

"Yep."

"You're related to those Bennetts that own Bennett Enterprises?"

"The very same."

"Wow. I love their stuff."

"I'm not surprised." Bennett Enterprises produced some kickass jewelry. My gaze landed on another picture, one of Brooke and a woman holding up cocktails and smiling at the camera. I'd looked up Brooke on Facebook a while ago, and she had a few pics with the same woman. It was Cami, her ex-best friend.

"I debated taking it down, but…."

"Why should you? Just because something ended badly doesn't mean you shouldn't enjoy the good memories."

There were no pictures of Noah. I was shocked at the relief I felt.

Brooke shrugged, looking at the picture wistfully. "I miss the friendship. I have other friends, of course, and I get along well with my sister, but Cami was my person, you know?"

I moved closer, cupping her cheek. She looked up in surprise, her gaze searching mine.

"I can be your person if you want, Brooke."

"You don't know what you're getting into. I'm a terrible friend. I'll nag you about stuff, blackmail you into watching the movies I want."

"I can handle it. Besides, I can be equally vicious."

"Hmm… well, if you change your mind at any

point, let me know. How was your afternoon with Milo?"

"We finalized party preparations. Lori's going to love it."

"I bet she will. By the way, I spoke to Hailey on the phone about your contracts and how that could work with the foundation. She had some great ideas."

I'd given Brooke Paige's contact information, but she was also in touch with Hailey, who had gotten more involved with the foundation over the past few months.

"You didn't tell her anything about the party, right?"

"She already knew. But I don't get why you think Hailey can't keep a secret. She said you two always prepared surprises for your mom's birthday and that she never spilled the beans."

"We did, and it's true. Maybe Hailey was better at keeping secrets back then. Or Mom was just really good at pretending she was surprised." I felt oddly vulnerable. Hailey spoke as rarely about our parents as I did, and never to anyone outside the family. Brooke elbowed me lightly, and her easy smile made me pull her even closer.

"You know, Dad had a big role in my soccer career. I used to suck at it as a kid."

"I can't believe that."

"Yeah, I did. But I wanted to be good at it so badly. He and I always bonded over it. He came from Ireland, and soccer is huge in Europe, or football, as they say. He practiced with me relentlessly."

Maybe it was all those evenings I spent with her brainstorming about the center, or the fact that she listened so intently when I talked about my family, but I felt like I could talk with her about anything. But tonight, I wanted to keep things light, and talking about my parents always brought a bout of melancholy I couldn't easily shake off.

"What are we watching?" I asked, to change the subject.

"Are you in the mood for a *Game of Thrones* rewatch?"

"Would be a first time for me."

She stared at me. "Wait… you've never watched *Game of Thrones*? At all?"

"Nope."

"Then you, my friend, are in for a treat." She rubbed her palms together in excitement. "I'm going to make some popcorn. Make yourself comfortable. I'll be back in a few minutes." She took off her shoes on the way to the kitchen. I flopped onto the couch, lying down. When she returned with the popcorn, she glared at me. I was lying on one side, occupying the entire couch.

"Where am I supposed to sit?"

I patted the space in front of me, then opened up my arm.

"Couch is wide enough for both of us to lie down," I said.

She smirked but didn't protest. After turning on the TV, she turned off the light. I'd assumed she would change into something more comfortable, like pajamas or sweatpants and a baggy T-shirt.

But karma hit me in full force two minutes later when Brooke came to lie down in front of me still wearing that beige dress.

With the TV as the only source of light, the room was mostly dark, and the beige color of the dress blended with her skin, giving me the impression that Brooke was naked in my arms. Placing the bowl with popcorn in front of her, she snuggled her body against me. She shifted a couple of times, and her skirt inadvertently rode up her legs. Before she rearranged it, my fingers brushed her thighs. Touching her bare skin sent a jolt straight to my cock, especially when the skin on her legs turned to goose bumps.

On pure instinct, I hooked an arm around her waist, bringing her even closer until her back was against me. This right here? It felt so right that I couldn't get enough of it.

Chapter Eight
Brooke

"They didn't just do that," Jace exclaimed. I snickered. Watching the series with someone who hadn't seen it was more of a treat than I'd imagined.

"We're almost out of popcorn. Want me to make more?"

I made to move, but Jace pulled me back, holding me even closer than before. My heart slammed against my ribcage as I felt those washboard abs press against my back.

"Don't go anywhere."

"Okay."

I snuggled right back in my cocoon. I couldn't explain it, but being wrapped up in Jace like this made me feel safe. I was also hot and bothered. My entire body was buzzing, filled with so much energy, it was slowly becoming unbearable. Each time Jace took more popcorn, I sucked in my breath, as if that would help my chest shrink enough that his arm wouldn't touch my breasts while he reached inside the bowl.

"Ned Stark is my favorite character," Jace proclaimed. I bit the inside of my cheek. This poor man. He'd have his heart broken by the end of the season. "I can't believe I haven't seen it. This show is fantastic."

He sounded mildly surprised, so I pinched his arm, then half turned toward him.

"I wouldn't make you watch something bad, hot stuff."

"Hey, don't pinch me."

I did it again.

"Stop that."

Right… he wasn't really expecting me to stop, was he? Because I absolutely didn't plan to. As I lunged to pinch him again, Jace caught my hand. Then he pushed himself slightly up on his elbow, with the result that his face was hovering a little over mine.

"What are you going to do now, hmm?" he challenged. He was still holding one of my hands captive, and the other was wedged between us, so I couldn't use it.

"Surrender?" I whispered against his lips.

"Right answer. You know, using the nickname I gave you on me constitutes cheating."

"Hmm… I'll think of something better."

He pulled back a notch and his gaze fell to my lips. For a brief second, I was sure he was going to kiss me. Anticipation coursed through me, jolting every cell to life. I became aware of how close we were. My left thigh pressed against his leg. I felt his touch so intensely, it was as if I wasn't wearing anything at all.

A loud *clang* from the screen caused us both to jolt.

"Jesus, I completely forgot about this," I exclaimed.

"Can you rewind?"

"Sure."

As I reached for the remote, which was on the floor, I felt Jace lie back again. The second I finished rewinding, he pulled me against him again.

"Don't make me miss any more scenes."

"Roger that."

Jace laughed softly. I, on the other hand, was on fire. God, the way he was holding me felt so intimate. His hand was splayed on my belly, and it prompted heat to pool between my legs. I breathed in slowly through my nose, willing my body to cool down. I couldn't get used to the smoldering feeling of his body against mine, and when Jace shifted his position a little, his hand moving upward an inch or so, the tension became unbearable. How could he be so blasé about this?

I thought men didn't like to cuddle. I'd been in a few relationships before Noah and had dated after. Men seemed to consider spooning as some sort of commitment. Then again, Jace and I weren't dating. We were two friends watching a movie, which was probably why he felt comfortable enough to hold me like this. Because he knew I wouldn't be expecting anything. The thought made me feel deflated, and in that moment, I realized I truly liked Jace more than as a friend. It wasn't just that I was crazy attracted to him, but I craved more of this closeness. It wasn't in the cards, though. It couldn't be. He was the MVP, and I was a new hire. And I was still not quite back on my feet after the breakup with Noah.

Telling myself all that made lying there with him a little easier. I relaxed in his arms as the bloody scene on the screen captured my attention. I only had to make it through three more episodes, and then Jace would be going home.

I woke up with a groan. I'd lost the feeling in my right leg. A second later, I realized I had bigger problems. Jace and I had fallen asleep in front of the TV, which must have switched to idle mode during the night. Shit. This wasn't the weekend. What time was it? Was I late for work? Had Jace missed his plane? He was flying out for an away game today.

I glanced to the small digital display in the lower corner of the TV. It was five o'clock in the morning. Still plenty of time. I'd doze off for another half hour if I wasn't afraid that I'd sleep in. I couldn't set an alarm, because my phone was too far away for me to move without waking up Jace, and the man was soundly asleep. He was completely wrapped around me. One of his arms was wedged between the couch and my neck. The other was resting on my belly, as it had last night. He'd even slid a leg between mine at some point.

Should I wake him up? It was early, but I wasn't sure how long it would take him to reach his apartment, change, and make it to LAX. I'd decided to let him sleep in a while longer when I felt him stir, withdrawing his leg from between mine. His hand moved a little upward until the tip of his thumb touched my breast. All nerve endings strummed to life, instantly setting me on edge.

***

Jace

"What time is it?" I asked.

"A little after five. Want coffee?"

"Sure."

"I'm going to make some."

She slid out of my arms before I blinked away the sleep, heading outside the room. I immediately missed her. I followed her to the kitchen. After a few minutes, the coffee was ready and I took the cup she handed me. We spoke about the show while we drank.

"Want to pick up where we left when I get back?" I was already eager to be back.

"Sure—oh wait, I have plans that evening."

"What plans?"

Something in her voice tipped me off that I didn't want to know the answer.

"A blind date. A friend set me up. Can't cancel because I already did it once."

Something snapped inside of me. Fucking hell, I didn't want her to go on that date. Or any other date that wasn't with me. I had no plan, no idea what to say. I always had a comeback, a quick joke to ease any situation. I clenched my hands tightly around the cup before setting it on the counter next to hers.

"No."

"What?"

"Cancel that date, Brooke."

She stared at me. "Why?"

"You are not going on that date." My voice was almost a growl.

"Why?" she repeated. I swallowed, searching for the right words at the same time I tried to make sense of things in my mind. Fuck it, I was just going to go with my gut.

"I'm going to tell you a few things. Just listen until the end, okay?"

"O-okay."

I had a burning desire to kiss Brooke until she begged for more and let that do all the talking for me.

"I love being with you, Brooke. I thought I could be just your friend, but I want more. I want you. All of you."

I rested one palm against the kitchen door, just next to her shoulder. I needed to touch her more than I'd ever needed anything else. She looked from my hand to my shoulder, licking her lips. On instinct, I moved closer.

"Oh. I don't know what to say."

"Say you won't go out with that guy." As

soon as I said it, I realized that I needed to hear more than that. "Say you want *me*."

"Jace—"

I moved my hand from the door to her waist, unable to *not* touch her anymore. She sucked in a shaky breath, resting both hands on my chest, and for a split second, I thought she was going to push me away. But then she moved one hand, resting a finger on the top button of my shirt before slipping it through the crack in the fabric.

That slight touch of her fingertip on my bare skin was my undoing. I'd never turned so hard so fast. I kissed her the next second. She instantly surrendered, parting her lips for me. She wanted me, all right. She wanted me bad.

I sucked gently on her tongue, exploring that sweet, delicious mouth. But I needed more than her mouth. I needed to touch her. I skimmed my hands from her waist down to her legs, groaning against her mouth when I reached the bare skin of her thighs. It was smooth and inviting. I pressed her against me, and she whimpered when she felt how hard I was. She parted her legs slightly, accommodating me, and I had to stop the kiss to avoid losing all rational thought. I wasn't looking for a quick lay.

"Why are you stopping?" she murmured. I smiled at the red hue around her lips.

I traced the contour of her mouth with my fingers. "Your lips are gorgeous."

I couldn't wait to taste her again, so I claimed her mouth. Her arms went around my neck.

I pulled her bottom lip between mine before capturing her entire mouth. My hands were roaming, exploring, touching every bit of skin I could find, and then demanding even more. I pinned her against the first wall I found, and then my hands were everywhere. Kneading her ass, touching her outer thighs, and then her inner thighs. I stopped short of touching her panties, but then she rolled her hips forward, silently begging for my touch. How could I not oblige her? I willed myself to slow down and talk first.

But I was so hard that I could barely think. I tore my mouth from hers, and she buried her face in my neck. I lost my train of thoughts when she feathered her lips on my neck. She parted her mouth, licking the spot she'd kissed before, just below my Adam's apple, and I was done for. I cupped the back of her head and growled, "Bedroom. Now."

I felt her knees buckle a little at my command, but I steadied her with a strong grip around her waist. My dick twitched as I realized taking commands from me turned her on.

She whirled around, leading me to the bedroom, stopping in front of the bed. I pushed her hair to one side, placing a kiss at the top of her spine. I hooked an arm around her middle, pressing her ass against my erection.

She whimpered. Taking half a step back, I wedged a hand between her thighs and spoke against her back. "Open them."

She gave me access. I touched two fingers

over the dampened fabric, and she buckled, leaning forward.

"Oh, fuck. Jace!" Her voice was shaking.

The only light in the room was from the sun coming up outside, and when I laid her on the bed, it shone on her thighs. I wanted to see her naked, but I didn't have the patience to take off her dress. Not now. But I had enough patience to simply watch her for one second as I propped one knee on the bed, taking in the rise and fall of her chest, her slightly parted lips.

Her hands were crossed on top of her stomach, and she was fiddling with her thumbs. My girl was nervous.

"Lift your dress up higher, Brooke."

She immediately reached to the fabric, pulling it upward a few inches.

"Higher."

She obliged, lifting it until I could see the silk of her panties.

"Now, spread wide for me."

She opened up, and I kneeled between her thighs. I was so greedy for her that I couldn't decide where to start kissing. Where to start touching. I started kissing that illuminated patch of skin, barely touching my lips to her inner thigh. Her ragged breath filled the room.

She was trembling underneath me, and I knew she was trying to anticipate where I'd kiss next. I chose her neck, working my way up to her chest, then up to her ear.

"Condom?" I asked.

She froze. "I don't have any."

Even though I was close to bursting in my jeans, I liked that answer. It meant it had been a while since she'd been with someone.

"I don't have any either."

That small whimper she let out nearly killed me.

"I'll take care of you, baby. I promise," I said.

I moved the hand I'd had on her breast downward, and she parted her thighs wide before I even reached her navel. Her hands were fumbling with my jeans, lowering the zipper, then sliding into my boxers. I jerked my hips forward when she wrapped her palm around my cock, drawing small circles with her thumb on the tip.

"Fuuuuuck!" I groaned.

I reached the hem of her panties, feeling her suck in her breath as I slipped my hand under the elastic band, and then went even lower. When I touched her clit, her hand squeezed me so tight and good that my muscles immediately locked with tension. I wasn't going to last long. But I was going to take care of her first. I strummed my fingers over her pussy, sliding one inside, nearly losing my damn mind when her inner muscles clenched around me.

"Oh, God, Jace." She dug her heels in the mattress, lifting her ass off the bed, gyrating her hips, all the while pumping along my length. She squeezed me *so good*. Too good.

I was barely holding back my climax, wanting

her to get there first, needing to own her pleasure before I relented to mine.

"Jace, Jace, Jace!" She clenched her thighs, immobilizing my hand as she pulsed around my fingers, shuddering violently.

I moved my hips at a relentless pace into her fist, giving in to my own climax a few seconds later. "Fuck. Baby, oh fuuuuck."

I wasn't sure how many minutes passed until my post-orgasm bliss faded, but I still felt weak.

"Brooke?"

She hummed in response, making me smile. I wasn't the only one feeling boneless.

"Mind's still spinning. Can't feel my body," she whispered.

I chuckled, playing with a strand of her hair, keeping her against me right until my phone rang

"That's my alarm," I said.

"It's six. Will you make it in time?"

"Yes. I pack fast." I climbed over her.

"What are you doing?"

"Kissing you."

She gave me a sly grin and opened up for me as soon as my lips touched hers. Despite being on a tight schedule, I didn't hurry to get out of bed. I wasn't anywhere near ready to let her go.

Chapter Nine
Brooke

The day went by slowly. Given my early start, I was already exhausted by three. The atmosphere at the club was different when the players were away. It was quieter, less exciting. The players spent almost as much time inside the club as management. In fact, whenever they weren't away on a game, they were at the club, either training at the gym or in the arena, or in the video room, watching replays of games or discussing strategies.

The events team had their hands full, because a concert was taking place in the arena two nights in a row.

The arena was booked solid over the course of the year, providing an excellent source of income for the club. In the beginning I'd wondered why the Lords had such a huge arena—more than half of the seats were covered up during the game because they were empty. But because it had twice the capacity of a normal soccer arena, it was excellent for large-scale concerts, which was what Graham had had in mind all along. It was one of the most popular venues in LA.

Since my workload for the day was light, I poked my nose in the events department, helping out here and there. I wondered if later on, after my initial six months had passed, I could take on additional tasks.

I wanted variety. This was one of the things I missed from working at my old job: being a jack of all trades. Booking ads had been my main responsibility, but I'd also taken on many others.

My stomach was in knots as my thoughts veered to Jace. What had last night meant? How was I supposed to act around him? I couldn't figure out if he wanted to pretend it hadn't happened or if he wanted a repeat. I wasn't even sure what *I* wanted. We'd grown so close that the mere idea of losing his friendship had me break out in hives.

Maybe I was worrying about nothing, and Jace wanted to forget all about it. I had to set things straight with him, but I didn't know what to put in a text.

So instead, I daydreamed about our sexy time. I wanted to indulge in a little Jace-appreciation, just to brighten up my day.

Afterward, despite being on the phone for most of the time, talking to various sponsors, I couldn't stop thinking about Jace. Especially after he sent me a snapshot of San Francisco. I only saw the picture and the text for a few seconds before the notification faded. I was very tempted to end the call I was on so I could see what he'd messaged. Sending me pictures of whatever city he was in was our usual modus operandi. I breathed a sigh of relief that things were not awkward between us.

At the same time, I couldn't help wonder if this meant Jace *did* want us to forget what had happened. I shook my head, attempting to shut down that little voice at the back of my mind while I continued the conversation.

When I finally did get to see his message, my palms were a little sweaty.

Jace: You'd like San Francisco. The bay is beautiful.

Brooke: Great view.

I hovered with my thumbs over the screen, unsure what else to add.

Jace: Can't enjoy it too much. Coach is ruthless.

Brooke: Hope he isn't exerting himself. I don't like that he travels so much.

Jace: I'll keep an eye on him for you.

I grinned at the screen.

Brooke: Thanks.

Jace: How is your day so far?

Brooke: Productive :-)

Jace: Mine's not. I keep thinking about last night. About you.

I crossed and uncrossed my legs at the ankles, suddenly aware of a deep ache in my body. Sheila and Veronica were glancing curiously at me, because I rarely texted.

Jace: I can't wait to be back. What do you

want to do on Thursday evening?
Brooke: I have plans.

The next time my phone buzzed, it was with an incoming call. I headed out to the empty hallway so Sheila and Veronica couldn't overhear my conversation.

"Tell me you're joking," Jace said when I picked up. His tone was so strained that I startled.

"About what?"

"About going forward with that date, Brooke."

Understanding dawned on me. "Oh. No, I canceled that. But I still have something planned."

"Okay. What are you doing?"

"I've cleaned up some of my old things and am taking them to a soup kitchen Paige mentioned to me."

"Which one?" he asked. After I told him the address, he added, "Why don't you bring them to the education center?"

"She said they had enough supplies."

"Who is going with you?"

"No one," I answered, confused.

"Brooke, you're not going there alone."

"Jace—"

"It's a sketchy area. I'm going with you."

"You're exaggerating."

"Brooke, I'll go with you. I can help you carry your things and keep an eye out for anyone looking for trouble."

His tone was determined, bordering on

dominating, but I loved his protectiveness. I loved that he wanted to be part of this.

"What time do you want to go?" he asked.

"Does six o'clock work for you?"

"I'll be in the parking lot waiting for you."

"Okay. Thanks, Jace."

"So your day is productive, huh?" His tone changed, moving from serious to flirty.

"Oh, yeah. Got a lot done. My mind has been laser focused."

"I see. Nothing hijacking your concentration?"

"Nothing at all," I teased.

"Let's see what I can do about that when I return."

I licked my lips, remembering our night. My entire body ignited, as if he was touching me. I leaned against a wall, fanning myself.

"You're so bad for me," I whispered.

He let out a low laugh. "I can't wait to be back."

Just then, Veronica poked her head into the hallway, and I had no choice but to bid Jace goodbye. He was on my mind the entire afternoon. Yep, the daydreaming was officially continuing.

Brooke: I'll have you know that twice I almost sent an email to the wrong person. I think our phone call has something to do with that.

Jace: Music to my ears.

I smiled, shaking my head.

When I arrived home in the evening, I was ready to call it a day even though it was only eight. I'd already gotten into bed when I decided to check my messages. I had a new one from Jace.

Jace: How was your gym workout?

Today was usually a gym day.

Brooke: Didn't go.

Jace: Knew you were only going there for me.

What could I say? He'd found out my secret. Just like that, I wasn't feeling sleepy anymore.

***

Jace

"Are you sure your ribs don't still hurt?" Hailey asked for the hundredth time the next day.

"One hundred percent."

My sisters usually doted on me, but even more so when I was playing outside of LA. I almost never admitted that something hurt simply because I did not like them worrying for no reason.

"Do you have some time for your dearest sister on Saturday? I could use some help repairing that old shed."

"I'll be there. I'll call Will and Landon and ask them if they have time too."

"You don't trust my skills?"

"No, I don't."

"Hey!"

"Just being honest. Whenever we're working on something, I do most of the work."

"But I keep you entertained."

I laughed. "True, but I also need help doing the actual work, so I need reinforcements. How is work going?"

"Oh, you know. The usual. Love some clients, want to throttle others. Everything is in balance."

She sounded content, though even if she weren't, she wouldn't outright say it. Hailey was a bit like me. I always considered things internally, without voicing my thought process. Probably why Val and Landon had gotten so good at needling information out of someone.

"And speaking of clients I want to throttle, one is calling right now. Talk to you later?"

"Sure."

After hanging up, I dove right into the apple pie in front of me. I was with the team in one of the hotel's conference rooms, enjoying a short break from watching yesterday's game.

I loved having Hailey back in LA. Before taking this job, she traveled a lot as a business consultant. She was usually in LA during weekends, but sometimes I was away for games, so there were stretches when I hadn't seen her for weeks. Even though she was two years older than me, I'd always considered myself in charge of her, probably because I'd always been much taller than her.

I still had a few minutes left of the break and used the opportunity to send Brooke a message.

She and I had texted constantly over the last couple of days. I was mostly sending her small updates, asking for the same in return. She always answered right away, as if she was looking forward to my messages as much as I was looking forward to hers.

"Boys, five minutes left of the break," Coach barked. Even though we'd won the game yesterday, he wasn't going easy on us. I had no doubt that he wouldn't be thrilled about me and Brooke. Unfortunately, Coach had had a front row seat to my personal life over the past few years, at a time when I'd enjoyed parties and no-strings trysts. But I'd never shied away from a complicated situation.

I couldn't wait to be back in LA, to pick things up with Brooke where we'd left off. My phone lit up with a message.

Brooke: Sometimes you're the hammer, sometimes you're the nail.

I'd asked her how her day was, and my girl was clearly not having a good time, so I excused myself from the room and called her.

"What's wrong?" I asked as soon as she picked up.

"Oh, nothing in particular, just a so-so day. Can't wait for it to be over."

"You're watching *SNL* tonight, right?"

"You remember that?"

"Of course. I'll call you, and we'll watch it together?"

She laughed softly. "Why would you do that?"

"Because I want to spend time with you. Even if just on the phone. Besides, I have a great record of entertaining you."

"Well, I can't disagree with that." Her tone was playful, and fuck if I didn't miss her even more than before. I wanted to see her. I needed her. "Tell me what you're wearing right now."

"Jace," she chastised.

"Tell me."

"No! I'm at the club."

"Tell me. I want to know what you're wearing," I insisted.

"A skirt and a blouse."

"And under those?"

"Panties and a bra," she whispered.

"Describe them. In detail."

She made a small sound, like a groan. "Black. Silk and lace."

"Babe…"

"I'm not telling you anything else."

"We'll save it for tonight." I smiled, imagining her blush.

"Oh, Jesus."

"Have to go back anyway, before Coach comes out to drag me in the viewing room. Talk to you later."

"I can't wait." She sounded far more excited than when she'd picked up, and knowing I was responsible for the change filled me with euphoria. I couldn't wait to spend one hour of quality time with her. I also wanted us to have a serious conversation about where we were and where this was going, but I'd wait until I was in LA and we could talk face-to-face.

I wasn't a fan of away games. Being on the road was tiring, and no matter how often I'd played in a rival arena, it still felt foreign. I also had very little time on my own. Back in LA, soccer talk ended when I left the club, but during away games, the boys and I were joined at the hip.

However, this time we were in San Francisco, where I actually had family: my Bennett cousins.

After coach finally released us, I headed to Pier 39, where I was meeting Pippa for a quick brunch before flying to Michigan where we were playing a friendly game with a local team.

Out of all our cousins, we were closest to the Bennett clan. I was sort of regretting there weren't any more weddings to be had on their side of the family, and none planned on ours, because over the past couple of years, we'd mostly seen each other during weddings.

Pippa was already sitting at a table, bent over a piece of paper, sketching. She was the head designer at Bennett Enterprises, and she liked sketching by hand.

She jumped up upon seeing me.

"Why do you never stay with us when you're in town?" She gave me a kiss on the cheek before we sat down at the table.

"I don't want to impose."

"Nonsense. We'd have more time with you."

"Cousin, I have full confidence in your abilities to lure every single piece of news out of me in the hour we have today."

She gave me a small smile. "Well, that's true."

Of course, half an hour in, we were both up to date, which was when Pippa brought up the subject of my love life.

"You know I'm always happy to lend a hand."

"Pippa...."

She liked to dabble in matchmaking, especially during weddings. But instead of insisting, she sat up a little straighter.

"Wait a second... you're up to something."

Pippa could read people like no one else. She glanced at my hand, which was on my phone. "Hmmm... you've checked your messages quite a few times, and you're not proclaiming as usual that you're happy with your *single* status. Dear cousin, are you telling me officially that my meddling isn't necessary?"

I was in a pinch. Whatever I told her would go straight back to my sisters, and things between Brooke and me were so fresh that I wanted to keep everything to myself for a while.

"Can I go with *no comment?*"

She gave me a knowing smile, and I was certain she'd inform my sisters about this right away. "That just answers my question. Someone has you all tied up in knots."

As usual, Pippa was right. By the time I

returned to LA on Thursday, I needed to see Brooke badly.

Chapter Ten
Brooke

On Thursday, the team and Dad returned in the morning. I arrived first at the small coffee shop where I was having breakfast with Dad and Franci, but they arrived within ten minutes. Dad was the only morning person out of all of us, but since he wasn't very talkative, Franci and I filled in the silence. He'd always been like this, content to sit back and listen. I used the opportunity to assess him, and I was relieved to find that he didn't have any dark circles under his eyes and he seemed well-rested.

Predictably, Dad became a little chattier when the conversation turned to my job.

"None of the boys giving you trouble, right?"

"No, Dad. It's all good."

"I know those devils. They like pretty girls like you. Though I think they're all smart enough to know you don't shit where you eat."

I avoided his eye as I sipped my coffee.

Once I reached the club, I practically ran upstairs, stopping by my office to grab my legal pad to make notes, then darting into the large meeting room where the entire management team was gathered. I was relieved that I'd arrived a whole seven minutes before the meeting was scheduled to start.

I sat next to my boss, who said, "When Graham asks for our department's input, I want you to speak up, okay?"

I nodded, feeling a flutter of excitement. I'd volunteered to bring forward the department's inputs at many a meeting, but this was the first time my boss had conceded. I'd just had a feedback session yesterday, and it had gone fantastic.

Usually, I disliked meetings with more than ten attendees. They tended to be unproductive, with each person fighting for airtime, derailing topics, and going off on tangential problems that weren't on the agenda at all. Today's meeting, however, was the complete opposite. It helped that we had a mediator who made sure no one was interrupted or went on for too long.

I was especially happy when Graham asked for my input.

"The club's image is extremely well defined. I'd say that if we stretch it in too many directions, it might dilute that image, confuse the consumers."

Graham nodded. "You're right. That was my gut feeling too, but it's good to have confirmation."

It felt great to be appreciated.

"What do you suggest?" Graham went on.

"Well, our boys are already covering a rather large palette of industries between their sponsorship contracts. I'd suggest that instead of adding more industries, we work on raising the team's profile on a national level. I know it's not easy. We're not the only team in this country, but a few of the boys have achieved national recognition, which will help raise everyone else's profile. I've contacted several national magazines and heard back from a few. They're interested in in-depth spreads."

The PR department usually took care of this, but I had a green light from them and Tina.

Graham whistled. "I knew you could pull it off, Brooke."

Tina smiled at me, and I barely bit back a grin. Yep, I was most certainly ditching the image of *coach's daughter*. They were finally seeing me as a competent professional. I inwardly cringed, imagining what they'd think if they knew about me and Jace.

Why did I have to go ahead and muddle things? It was one thing to relax around my coworkers and be friendly with them, and another thing altogether to get so personally close to a player.

Had I not learned anything from my breakup with Noah? If I hadn't been dating him or been best friends with Cami, I'd still be at the magazine, spearheading the LA office.

I didn't even know what Jace was after. For us to be friends with benefits? From what he'd told me about his personal life, he hadn't had serious relationships, which was okay with me. After believing for a few years that Noah and I were going to have it all, I just didn't have it in me to even consider dreaming again, not when the fallout had left me in such a disastrous place, both emotionally and financially.

We'd been living together in a gorgeous apartment that I wasn't able to afford on my own, so after the breakup I'd been lucky to find the rent-controlled apartment I currently lived in.

As the meeting ended, I asked Tina and Graham for a few minutes of their time.

Once everyone else filtered out, I said, "I didn't want to bring this up when everyone else was here because it's a detail that doesn't concern them, but I've been trying to work out a timeline with Fashion W. They want a photo shoot with the entire team, and the only blocks of time when all the boys are free is either in two weeks, or the three-day break before the final game. I'd rather they fly out to New York in two weeks so they can rest before the final."

"That sounds reasonable," Graham said, "though some are likely to protest having to cancel their plans on such short notice."

"I'm counting on that, but if that timeline's okay with both of you, I'll communicate this to the team in person. It'll be easier to respond to their complaints and reassure them that this won't happen often, but it's an opportunity we can't miss."

Tina shuddered. "This one's brave. I wouldn't want to face the boys and tell them they have to cancel their plans."

Graham grinned. "Better her than us."

I rubbed my hands. "Wish me luck. I'm going out on the pitch. Their practice is about to end."

"Thanks for taking one for the team," Tina said.

I chuckled as I left the room, heading straight to the pitch, still on cloud nine that my contributions to the meeting had been valued.

Practice was still going on when I arrived, so I sat in the stands, purposefully not going to the coach's corner. Dad was on the field, shouting directions at the boys, but I still didn't want them to see me there.

I relaxed, taking in the activity on the field, appreciating their game. Oh, who was I kidding. I wasn't appreciating their game. More like the sexy-as-hell testosterone Jace was exuding.

I couldn't take my eyes off him. I loved seeing him like this, laser-focused on his game, giving one hundred percent to every move. How could he be so laid-back in real life, and yet so balls-to-the-wall on the field?

When Dad blew the whistle, the boys ended the game, slowing their pace, then performing a few stretches. I stood up, waving so they could see me as I descended the steps to the pitch.

They formed a semicircle around me.

"What's up?" Andrew asked.

"I wanted to communicate something to all of you, and I prefer to do it in person." I swept my gaze to each player, willing myself not to linger on anyone in particular. I failed, of course, especially because

Jace was pinning me with the same heated gaze from the morning when he went all alpha on me, asking me to cancel my date. I cast my glance away, looking at no one in particular while I spoke.

Out of the corner of my eye, I saw Dad heading directly to the changing rooms. I'd thank him for that later.

"As I told you when I first took the job, I'm aiming to get some new sponsorships. To that end, getting the team national coverage is helpful. I'm happy to tell you that Fashion W is interested. They want a photo shoot and an interview with every player. However, finding time in everyone's schedule has been a challenge. Their headquarters is in New York, and a round trip would take at least three days. I cross-checked everyone's calendars, and you are all commitment-free in two weeks between the home game and the Phoenix game."

Half of the team started to protest at the same time.

"Some of us also have a personal life," Levi said in a tense tone.

I rolled my shoulders. "I am aware of that. Believe me, if I had a better alternative, I wouldn't be springing this on you. But if we don't take advantage of this opportunity, they'll just move on to the next soccer team. I can't make up for the lost personal time, but I can ensure that your time there will be as pleasant as possible. I've preemptively made reservations to the Box."

Through the wave of complaints, I heard a

few appreciative whistles. The Box was a very coveted and exclusive bar.

"Heard the wait list to get in is at least two months," one of the boys said.

"I pulled a few strings." I tried not to look too pleased with myself.

"Are you bribing us?" Jace asked lazily. It was the first time he'd spoken since my announcement. Amusement flickered in his eyes.

"Yes, yes, I am."

Jace gave me a thumbs-up. Andrew grinned at me. "You know what, throw in some tickets to the basketball game that weekend, and you have my support."

"Done." I clapped my hands, looking at everyone else. I felt bad for springing this on them and ruining their plans, but honestly, the opportunity was too good to waste it.

"Are you coming with us?"

That came from Jace. He'd asked the question casually, but I didn't miss the sly note and the way he was looking at me... hot damn. He had to stop doing that, because I felt as if my panties were about to burst into flames.

"Yes, of course."

The right corner of his mouth lifted in a half smile, as if he had something in mind for me.

"I'm in." Jace turned to the rest of the team. "Come on, don't be sticks in the mud. New York is fun. You can turn back to your regular routines in our other off days."

I loved that he had my back. I'd reward him later for that. In the end, the entire team agreed. Some were more enthusiastic than others, but that was the best I could have hoped for.

Jace went to sit on the bench along with a few others while I discussed some details with Andrew. Over the captain's shoulder, I had a direct view of Jace. He had his training bag on the bench and winked at me as he took out his phone, tapping his thumbs on the screen. I knew he was texting me even before I felt the vibration in my tote announcing an incoming message.

My pulse went haywire during the rest of my conversation with Andrew and rose to a full-blown staccato when I read Jace's text.

Jace: Meet me in the gym at ten to six.

Chapter Eleven
Brooke

Six o'clock couldn't come fast enough. Unfortunately, at around three, my scheduled phone call was pushed back to six.

Brooke: Change of plans. I have a phone call at six, so I'm going to run my errand real quick now. Call will last about two hours. See you tomorrow?

Since I'd be spending the evening at the club, I wasn't feeling guilty about taking a break now. Jace didn't answer, but I wasn't expecting him to. The team was having a practice.

I jogged to my car and checked that all the boxes with supplies were secured in the trunk and the back seat. When I was about to open my door, I heard Jace's voice behind me.

"Brooke!"

I whirled around. "What are you doing here? Everything okay?"

"We agreed we'd go together."

"I know. But you were in a training session, and my schedule changed. Wait a second, you're still supposed to be in training."

He came to a stop in front of me. "Took a break card."

My eyes bulged. I knew Dad's rule: each player had three break cards during each season, meaning they could skip practice. Family emergencies were covered outside of that.

"Dad says you never take one."

"Until now. Get in." He opened the car door, stepping so close to me that I had to tilt my head back to look up at him. His eyes were glinting dangerously. The mix of bossiness and protectiveness was intoxicating.

"Paige said she and Hailey often do this."

"Did Paige also tell you that Will always goes with her? Or that I go with Hailey?"

"She might have mentioned it."

"Don't fight me on this, Brooke. I just want you to be safe."

"We can go another time. You don't have to give up practice."

"Already took the break card, so let's go."

I relented, climbing into the car. I felt guilty that he'd blown practice for me but also oddly happy.

As soon as we reached our destination, I was beyond grateful Jace was with me, because the area did seem dangerous. I dropped off the boxes with the contact person Paige had given me. Jace shadowed me, and whenever he wasn't carrying a box, he put an arm around my shoulders or my waist, tucking me into him. His protectiveness humbled me.

"Thanks for coming with me. You were right, coming here on my own wouldn't have been smart," I said once we were back in the car. He nodded. I liked that he wasn't giving me an I-told-you-so speech. We spoke about the center during the ride.

"We have to talk," Jace said as I pulled in the parking lot of the club.

"I know. It's five. I still have an hour before my conference call starts."

"Okay."

I tried to imagine how the conversation would go, but after working myself into a frenzy, I decided to just take things as they came along. Jace was leaning casually against the chair, smiling at me.

"Brooke, stop fretting."

"I'm not fretting."

He pointed to my lap. I caught myself fiddling with my thumbs.

I blushed. "You're right."

"Why are you nervous?"

"Because... I don't know, Jace. I was afraid— I still am afraid that our friendship will change. That we could lose it."

Jace lifted one corner of his mouth, then the other. God, he was simply gorgeous. I allowed myself a moment to drink him in.

"We won't lose anything. Look at us, going through our same old friendly routine. You're ogling me like you want me to strip naked. I pretend I don't notice."

"Oh, Jesus," I muttered.

"So, we got that out of the way. What else is on your mind?"

"It's early days at the club for me. I feel like everyone is finally seeing me as an employee, not just Coach's daughter. The management meeting today was incredible. I felt valued, and I'm afraid that if we... you know... I'm afraid they'll stop taking me seriously."

Jace said nothing. My chest tightened as the silence stretched, because this was so unlike him. Finally, he unhitched himself from the chair.

"Would you feel the same in a few months?"

Wow. Whatever I'd expected him to say, it wasn't this.

"You... you'd wait?"

"Yes."

"Why?" He could have his pick of women, from models to actresses and anything in between.

"I love being around you, Brooke." His eyes crinkled at the corners. "I will of course do my best to shorten the waiting period...."

I groaned.

"Consider it. I don't want to put you on the spot."

"And yet you're cornering me."

"No, I'm not. If I were cornering you, I'd have you in my lap, kissing you until you said yes."

"Yes to what?"

"Everything I ask for." Jace leaned in, his shoulder slightly rolled, dominating the space in the car, dominating me.

I swallowed hard, hearing the blood rush in my ears. My entire body reacted to those words. My nipples tightened; the muscles in my lower belly clenched.

"I still haven't ruled that out," Jace went on, and I lowered my eyes to the radio display, trying to calm my erratic breathing. I needed to change the subject.

"We're still on for watching *Game of Thrones* on Sunday?"

"Yes, Brooke. We'll still have that. And I'll still change your tire, fix whatever you need fixing. None of that changes."

"Okay."

I looked back up.

"But you won't mind if I openly flirt, will you? Kiss you when you look at me like this?"

Before I could chastise him, someone knocked at my window. It was Veronica. I lowered it, and she glanced between me and Jace.

"Hey, you two. Brooke, can I ride with you today?"

"I'm actually going up to the office. I have that conference call."

"I'm leaving now," Jace told her. "I can drop you off wherever you need to go."

"Thanks, you're a life saver. Sorry for interrupting."

"No problem. Just caught up with Brooke to ask her a few things." He focused on me again. "About that thing I mentioned, you won't mind, will you?"

I narrowed my eyes at him. Clearly, I couldn't call him out in front of Veronica. All I could say was, "Of course not."

Chapter Twelve
Jace

Friday was an eventful day in the Connor family. Since Lori's birthday had been the day before, we were supposed to have the party for which Milo and I had been preparing for months today. We ended up celebrating it at the hospital, because Lori went into labor at eleven o'clock in the morning.

At three o'clock, we welcomed a beautiful baby girl into our family. Evelyn looked a bit like Lori, who was the only blonde in the family. The rest of us had brown hair ranging from light to dark, and except for Will and Hailey, who had brown eyes, everyone had green eyes. The entire clan was gathered around my sister in the hospital room, which made the place too crowded.

"I swear to teach her tricks and shenanigans," I informed my sister.

Lori smiled. "I don't doubt you will."

"I'll do my best to keep him in check," Will added.

I clapped his shoulder. "Buddy, you're welcome to try."

Lori all but kicked us out at five o'clock, insisting that only Graham stay, and the rest of us headed to Val's house, where the would-be birthday party for Lori was supposed to take place.

On the way, I checked my messages and noticed one from Brooke.

Brooke: Dad says you skipped practice today because Lori went into labor. Is everything okay?

Jace: Perfect. They're healthy. I just left the hospital.

Brooke: Do they need anything? Is there something I can do? Do you have a picture with Evelyn?

I chuckled as I typed back, wishing I had taken a pic so I could send it to Brooke. I liked sharing details of my life with her, and that was new to me, but Brooke made it so easy.

Once we arrived at Val's house, I noticed Milo was a bit more silent than usual. He'd been excited and all smiles at the hospital, but now something was weighing on him. My suspicion was confirmed when Hailey exchanged a few words with him, but he simply shook his head.

"Can you talk to him?" she whispered when we entered Val's house.

"Sure." I followed him into the backyard, sitting next to him on the grass.

"Milo, what's wrong?"

He hesitated.

"Come on, you can tell me. Man to man."

"You promise not to tell anyone?"

"I promise."

"Do you think now that little Evelyn is here, Graham won't want to be my dad anymore? Like my other dad?"

I felt as if someone had punched me straight in the face. I had no idea Milo had these fears, and I was not sure how to tread. Telling him his biological father was simply a scumbag who couldn't handle responsibility was not the way forward, so I chose to focus on the positive.

"Milo," I said softly, "that will never happen. Graham is your dad no matter what. Even if you have ten more sisters or brothers, it won't mean he won't be your dad, or that he'll love you any less. Okay?"

Milo pondered that for a few seconds before nodding.

"How is it to have a sister?"

"Buddy, I have a lot to say about that. I can give you extensive advice on everything, from annoying your sister to protecting her. Ready to take notes?"

"Ready," he declared with a grin.

Dinner was delicious, as usual. We made plans for repairing Hailey's shed the next day. I'd convinced Will and Landon easily, and they said they'd bring over Paige and Maddie as well.

Now, Val announced she'd stop by too, with her gang.

"I'll bring some perfume samples too," Val said. "You can all try them out."

My brothers and I carefully avoided looking at each other. Trying out samples was not our favorite activity. I, for one, simply couldn't pick up on the finer notes. The things we did for our sisters.

"I convince you two to shoulder some work, and this is how we're rewarded." I shook my head mockingly. Will gave me a thumbs-up.

"Careful, don't anger Val before dessert," Landon said.

"I will pretend I have not heard a thing," Val assured us. "Besides, we're all going to shoulder some of the work."

Will raised his eyebrows. "Oh… like that time when we were painting Hailey's living room, and Jace and I ended up doing all the work."

"That was just one time." Val grinned sheepishly before looking to Landon for support.

"Don't look at me, I wasn't here for a few years." He glanced at me. Traitor. Throwing me under the bus, huh? I could butter up Val, but that was not my style.

"I'm with Will on this one. It's usually gossip central between you girls while he and I work."

"No, it's not. You'll see tomorrow," Val said.

I couldn't help myself. "Anyone up for taking bets?"

Val and Hailey narrowed their eyes. Will took me up on it. Landon chuckled, taking his daughter from Maddie's arms.

"Jace, I'm surprised you don't have any plans tomorrow evening. Dry spell?"

"You wound me. You know I'm always up for helping out my sisters."

"Hmm... sure, but I sense there's something more here. Anything you want to tell us?"

I'd been subjected to enough interrogations, ambushes, and interventions to know Val wasn't just fishing for info. Pippa had talked to her.

"No. Nothing at all."

Val watched me suspiciously but didn't press the matter, though I knew better than to think she was giving up. She was just waiting for the right time.

After dinner, we all moved into the living room. I sat on the couch next to Hailey.

"What did Milo say?"

"Just asked me what it's like to have a sister," I said vaguely. The little man had asked me to keep his secret, and I planned to do just that.

"Oh, okay. By the way, I have an idea: why don't you ask Brooke to come to my house tomorrow too? I've spoken to her a few times, but I've never met her. She'd love sniffing samples."

"She has plans with her family."

"Right. Well, you can... wait a second, what's with that face?"

I tried with all my might to look innocent. "What face?"

"That expression here. Your left eye is twitching a bit. You're jumpy."

"I'm not."

"Started when I mentioned Brooke. Is something wrong??"

"No, Hailey."

She took a long look at me. "Something's off with you. I just can't tell what."

"Just been a busy week."

Hailey grimaced. "And now you're placating me. Holy shit, something *is* off. Anyone bothering you with absurd claims again? Just tell me, Jace. I'll take care of it."

Oh, crap. And now she was going to start worrying about me. My plan had been to leave her in the dark. I was closest to Hailey. I'd always been, and growing up we'd been in competition with each other as to who gave Landon and Val more white hair. But now I realized that if I didn't at least tangentially tell her what was going on, she was going to construct her own scenarios and worry for no reason.

Everyone else was engaged in their own conversations, not paying me or Hailey any attention, so in a low voice, I filled her in.

Hailey's eyes widened. "I can't believe Pippa was right."

"Oh, you've already talked to her."

"Yep. I thought she was just being overly optimistic, as usual. But holy shit, Brooke, huh? Hmm… well, I don't know what advice to give you. But I'm sure Landon and Will have plenty to share. You can ask them for tips, at the very least."

"How about I do my own thing?"

Hailey flashed me an apologetic smile. "Your chances of failure increase?"

I wasn't going to allow anyone's lack of confidence to deter me. Which was why on Monday morning, I went to the club earlier than usual. My plan was simple: arrive before anyone else, sneak into Brooke's office, place the stress ball on her desk and hang the painting on the wall behind it.

She'd shown them to me yesterday online, which was why I woke up earlier today and stopped at Target to buy them.

We'd had a laid-back afternoon yesterday, and I hadn't touched on the topic of *us*. Despite what I'd told her, I didn't want her to feel pressured. I was prepared to wait... for a while.

I placed my toolbox on the floor and worked on hanging the painting. It took me all of fifteen minutes. After putting the stress ball right in front of her keyboard, I rushed to bring the toolbox to my car.

Then, instead of heading to the gym or the locker room, I went back to the upper floor. While waiting for management to arrive, I made myself a coffee. No one would question my presence here, since everyone was welcome to the kitchen and we all often had lunch together here. But I wasn't just lingering for the coffee. I had a specific purpose. I'd never been a fan of the Lords office remake, which went from separate offices to an open-plan office space for each department. They were separated by glass partitions.

Now, however, I could appreciate the benefits. From where I stood, I had a direct view to Brooke's desk. I just wanted to see her reaction, that was all. Did I risk her getting mad at me? Probably. Even though I'd been careful. Everyone else would probably assume Brooke herself had brought the stress ball and hung the painting.

Two girls from the PR department arrived first. Finally, at eight thirty, the elevator doors opened and my Brooke strutted out. She was flustered and a little out of sorts. Had she overslept?

She whizzed past the kitchen without seeing me and stilled when she reached her desk. For a few seconds, she had no reaction at all. But then she lifted the ball with both hands, and turned, noticing the painting. Even though I was far away, and I could only see her profile, there was no missing her reaction.

That smile right there? Yeah, it had been worth getting up at five o'clock.

Chapter Thirteen
Brooke

I was still staring at the painting with a grin. It was my favorite from the website—a depiction of a rainforest. When on earth had Jace done this? Had he come here yesterday? Or this morning?

Sitting at my desk, I shot Jace a message to thank him, positioning the stress ball so I could look at it all day. Did I have time for daydreaming? No, I did not. Was I going to do it anyway? Yes, I would.

I still needed to sort out some details for the New York trip... specifically, make sure the boys would be in the VIP area of the bar. I might have gotten ahead of myself when I'd told the team this was a done deal, but I was insistent.

The bar's general manager was an old friend of mine from college, and I knew I'd wear him down eventually.

My phone beeped with a message while I was talking on it, and oh, how I had to fight the impulse to end the conversation early just so I could read it.

But I behaved, focusing on my task until Ryan threw in the towel. "Persistent woman."

"Thanks."

I was feeling very smug as I ended the conversation, immediately reading Jace's text.

Jace: Loved seeing you smile this morning.

Brooke: You were here?

Jace: Yeah. Was having a coffee :-)

Brooke: Ready for the game tonight?

Jace: Stakes are high, but we're working hard.

I took that to mean that he was nervous, and while the boys were watching tapes later that afternoon, I headed downstairs and slipped a note in Jace's locker wishing him good luck. It was perhaps a silly thing to do, but I wanted to lighten up his day as he'd done with mine.

Half an hour later, he called me.

"Fuck, Brooke. You're sweet."

I walked to the supplies room, grinning and whispering, "It's just a note. But it did brighten up your day, huh?"

"You bet it did. Come watch the game. I want to see you there." He'd lowered his tone, and it was sexy as hell.

"Yes, boss," I replied playfully.

I did watch the game that evening, cheering for the Lords along with everyone else, but over the next few days, I saw a lot less of Jace than I was used to. I couldn't make it to the gym in the evening and most of my phone conferences were around lunchtime, which meant I had to resort to buying quick sandwiches to eat at my desk either before or after. As a result, a few days later, I had Jace withdrawals. I missed him. And yet, the prospect of facing him head-on was unnerving. Then I was frustrated with myself, because my big fear was that our friendship would ultimately suffer. Yet because I couldn't get my bearings together, I was creating a barrier between us.

Which was why, two days before the New York trip, I sent him a message.

Brooke: Are you still at the club? I want to talk to you.

It was late, but I'd heard Tina mention an hour ago that the boys were still here, analyzing a game.

Jace: Yeah, but preparing to leave. I'm in the locker room.

Brooke: Is the rest of the team there too?

Jace: Just me.

Brooke: I'll be there in a few minutes.

I sent an email with the New York itinerary to the entire team before leaving my desk.

My hands were damp with perspiration as I descended the staircase to the locker rooms.

Come on, Brooke. You're just asking your friend Jace to sit down and talk over breakfast tomorrow. There's no reason to be nervous.

I tried to cool down and calm my pulse as I opened the door to the locker room, but I suspected I was fighting a losing battle. I wouldn't just waltz in if the team was here, but since Jace said he was alone,

I didn't see a problem.

Except that he was wearing only a towel and a smoldering smile.

"Hey, Brooke."

"Hi."

I stood rooted in front of the door, unsure where to look. That towel kept catching my attention, but I didn't allow my gaze to roam below waist level. The problem was that his chest was no less distracting. That six-pack just seemed unreal. Remembering how those abs felt beneath my fingertips sent a jolt of heat through me. Right. I needed to maintain eye contact.

I'd kept a respectable distance between us, but Jace seemed to decide it wasn't necessary. He walked toward me with determined strides, stopping only a few inches away from me.

"You said you want to talk to me."

"I wanted to ask you to have breakfast with me tomorrow." I inhaled deeply, and the scent of his body wash was impossible to miss. It was so potent and masculine that the muscles in my lower belly clenched tight.

"Can you put clothes on?"

Amusement flashed in Jace's eyes. "No, I don't think I will. I don't want to wait until breakfast. Let's talk tonight. Right now."

I licked my lips. "But—"

"No buts. Just you and me. Laying out our cards. Nothing more."

"Well, that's why I wanted to have breakfast

with you."

"A lot of things can happen between now and tomorrow. Don't want to risk you getting cold feet."

He put one palm on the wall, next to my head. His arm was almost brushing my right cheek. And those green eyes were relentlessly trained on me.

"I won't let you get away with a no."

"Of course you won't."

He was so close that I had a hard time focusing, but I gathered my wits.

"Okay. We'll talk tonight. But let's go upstairs, have some dinner."

"Sure."

"I'll wait for you to change, and then we can go grab food."

Jace smiled triumphantly. "Be right back."

I waited next to the door, trying hard not to think about the fact that Jace was naked on the other side of the lockers. He came back a few minutes later, training bag slung over one shoulder.

"After you, Brooke."

He gestured toward the door, and I felt him watch me all the way out of the club. The food truck across the street was simply amazing. There was a line when we arrived, but it moved quickly.

"I know you really want a burger and fries. Don't hold back on my account," Jace whispered when our turn came. I grinned. Of course I couldn't hide from Jace.

"I want to be a good friend. I know they're not on your meal plan."

"I can deal with you eating a burger. Besides, there are other ways you can be a good friend."

When our turn came, I ordered a burger with sweet potato fries and guacamole dip.

I liked the club best late in the evening, because it was quiet. We sat side by side at the kitchen table, chairs turned slightly toward one another. Neither of us spoke as we ate, but the anticipation was building with every passing minute until it seemed as if the air was thick with fog.

When Jace finished his wrap, I felt every muscle in my upper body contract.

"Relax, hot stuff. Why are you so nervous?"

I straightened a little, stopping in the act of reaching for another fry.

"Okay, well, first things first. You can't call me hot stuff anymore. You might slip and call me that when there are others around."

Jace pulled his chair closer to mine until his left knee touched my right one. The contact point burned white-hot.

"We'll talk about that nickname another time."

He leaned forward, resting his forearm above his knee. His gaze was hard and intense. He balled his palm into a fist, as if that was the only way he could keep himself from touching me.

"I understand that you want to solidify your position here, Brooke. I know what it means to have to prove yourself. It takes hard work and dedication, and any time others doubt you, it sets you back."

"Yes, exactly."

"I know what that pressure feels like. I deal with it on a daily basis."

I immediately knew what he meant. As a pro player, that pressure was ongoing. In a regular job, once you'd reached a certain acceptance from the team, things became easier. People were more understanding when mishaps occurred. But as an athlete, your value was constantly recalculated based on your latest performance. Every mistake was blown out of proportion, with fans, managers, and coaches alike wondering if it was a sign that a player had passed his peak.

"Honestly, I have no idea how you deal with it."

"By giving every game my best shot. The only thing I can control is my performance. So, if you feel like you need some time before we take this step, I understand. I'll wait."

I sucked in a breath when Jace took one of my hands, turned it palm up, then feathered his fingers on my wrist, trailing them up my forearm, then back down. "I just need to know if you want the same thing, Brooke."

He stopped the movement of his hand, looking straight at me. I gave him a small nod, even though I wasn't sure exactly what he wanted, or what I was agreeing to. Friends with benefits? Something else?

"That was easy. See? No reason to be nervous."

"It's good we spoke tonight. Now I won't be fretting until the morning."

When Jace rewarded me with a warm and happy smile, I decided to stop with mental questioning. Jace brought my hand to his mouth, kissing it. That soft touch set me on edge. When he looked up at me again, the heat in his gaze was so strong, it was almost palpable. I leaned back in my chair. It didn't help. I was on fire, and Jace was relentless. It was as if now that we'd agreed on waiting, he wasn't holding back any longer.

Clearing my throat, I stood up to throw away my wrapper in the bin, with Jace on my heels. Afterward, we took the staircase, descending to the ground floor. Jace was one step behind me, and when we reached the last one, he hooked an arm around my waist, feathering his nose down the side of my neck.

"Just one more thing…. How do you feel about naked sleepovers in the meantime?"

I pulled out of his grasp, turning fully until we were face-to-face. Or well, more like face-to-chest, since Jace was standing on a higher stair.

"No sex, Jace."

"You're being cruel." He grinned as he launched the accusation. I was fighting to keep a straight face.

"I'm serious."

Jace descended one step. He still towered over me, but at least I didn't have to tilt my head back so much to look at him.

I had other problems now. Such as Jace's lips almost touching mine.

"I know you're serious. But I don't think you want to be."

I squinted. "Jace, this is a hard line for me, and I'd like for us to be on the same page before we fly out to New York."

He cupped my chin, stroking his thumb over my cheek. He was too masculine, too handsome... simply too much, and I couldn't help but react to him. My breath caught, and I licked my lower lip.

"We're on the same page, don't you worry."

Chapter Fourteen
Brooke

I loved New York, especially in the second half of September. One way or another, I made a trip to the city that never sleeps at least once a year. Most of my visits had been work-related, just like this one. Except, I couldn't exactly call this work: I was going to oversee the boys pose in semisexy pics, and then I was going with them to one of the fanciest bars, in the VIP area. Oh, and I was flying business class. *Pinch. Me. Now.* Could life get any better? I really didn't think so. On the day of the trip, I woke up early to pack. I didn't need much, just a suit and something to wear at the club in the evening. The latter was a bit problematic. Theoretically, we were going there after-hours to relax, so I was off the clock. Still, I couldn't wear what I normally would, which was either a short dress or jeans with a glitzy top. The boys wouldn't take me seriously.

On the drive to the airport, I was giddy, feeling as if I was heading on a vacation. But then, while relaxing in the back of the cab, I checked Facebook and came upon a picture that made me nauseous.

Noah and Cami were a couple.

I dropped the phone in my bag, pressing a hand on my collarbone before closing my eyes. *A couple.* When had that happened? When I was still with Noah? Seeing the picture stung like hell.

By the time I joined the team at the airport, it was already boarding time. I tried to pull myself together, but it wasn't easy. Over the past two months, the sense of deep hurt after the breakup and loss of Cami's friendship had started to heal, but now it felt raw again. I had the overwhelming urge to climb in my bed and stay there the entire day, but I had to soldier on.

"Good morning." I flashed everyone a smile. Guess who wasn't fooled? Jace. Cocking an eyebrow, he motioned with his head toward the back of the room, but I did not acknowledge it. Did he let that deter him? He did not. When the flight operator announced they were ready to board the business class passengers, Jace waited for the entire team to line up in front of the counter, and then sat next to me.

"What's up? You look unhappy."

"It's nothing."

"Try again." He leaned slightly into my personal space, and I licked my lips, looking away. It was too early in the morning for all the testosterone Jace exuded.

"Just saw this morning that Noah and Cami are a couple now."

"I'm sorry."

"I don't know why this affects me so much. It's not like I still have feelings for him. But I feel betrayed and replaceable. Even a little worthless."

"You, Brooke Derringer, are worth everything. If someone else doesn't recognize your worth, that doesn't mean it's not there. It just means they don't see it."

Jace put a hand on my upper back, rubbing it gently up and down. The comforting gesture turned sensual when he flashed me his killer smile, looking at my mouth.

The tension was broken when Jace said, "We should get in line."

I felt marginally better when I stepped inside the plane, and my mood improved even more when I noticed there was no one sitting next to me. I got two first-class seats all to myself. I felt like royalty, and as soon as the seat belt sign was deactivated once we were in the air, I toed off my shoes and stretched my legs on the other seat. Several minutes later, the flight attendant brought me a glass of champagne, even though they hadn't even started to serve drinks.

"I didn't order this," I said in amazement.

"One of your flight companions did."

I didn't have to look up from my drink to know who that was, but I raised my gaze anyway. Jace was sitting one row in front, on the opposite side of the aisle. He winked at me, and I returned to sipping my champagne, suddenly a little out of breath. My drink did wonders for my state of mind. Turned out there was internet on the flight, so I whisked out my laptop, deciding to use the few hours on the flight to get ahead of the day. I wouldn't get much work done once we reached the studios.

My inbox was like Sisyphus's task. No matter how fast I went through my emails, there were always new ones coming in. I'd just pressed *send* to a reply to a longtime sponsor when the count of unread messages moved from forty-three to forty-four.

I typically only eyed the subject of the newest emails, to check if something was urgent... with one exception: Jace.

I opened his email so fast, I nearly broke a nail.

Jace: You look smoking hot today. I can't stop picturing you naked.

Holy shit, was he serious? He couldn't write that to me. On my work email, nonetheless. To make my point, I simply replied with his name, followed by a dozen exclamation marks.

Before I even had a chance to move to another email thread, the unread count went up. He'd replied.

Jace: I have a direct view of those gorgeous legs. You can't fault me for thinking about how fucking sexy you were with them wrapped around me.

A wave of heat crushed into me, making me aware of a deep humming in my body. I didn't take my legs down. If Jace couldn't keep his thoughts straight, that was his problem. Actually, I planned to tease him like it was my job. Yep. That was my revenge plan. Why did he have to go and send that email? Now all I could think about was the way he'd made me feel that morning.

I spent the next few hours hiding behind my laptop and ignoring the new unread email from him, even though curiosity gnawed at me.

Once the plane landed at JFK, I took my sweet time gathering my things, waiting for the boys to leave the plane. I was betting that Jace was staying behind too. One stolen glance at his seat confirmed my theory.

After all business class passengers had left the plane, I stood up. Jace was already on his feet, his jaw set.

He retrieved my bag from the overhead bin before gesturing for me to walk in front of him. I felt him right behind me as I walked out of the plane and onto the tunnel connecting us to the airport.

"You can't ignore my emails," Jace said into my ear.

"You can't send me that kind of email," I shot back.

"I don't remember anything in our agreement about not dirty writing to you."

I half turned, glaring at him. "I'm adding that now."

Jace took in my glare before grinning. "You can't change the agreement, Brooke."

***

"Nothing quite like the Empire State Building," I whispered to myself while sipping my coffee, watching out the window. This was the first break in four hours. It was only going to last five minutes. I'd interned here during a summer, and the second I'd entered the building, I'd been transported to those days.

I wished I could tell my younger self not to fret so much, that things would work out. On the other hand, I suspected that the uncertainty had been exactly what had driven me so hard.

The boys had one-on-one interviews with Edith, one of the top in-house journalists. After finishing my coffee, I strutted right back into the interview area. It was a comfortable and informal setup. Edith sat on a couch with each of the boys, a recorder between them. I had stood by silently during each interview, speaking up only if Edith asked something inappropriate. She could be pushy.

The boys could very well speak up for themselves, but that tended to create tension. If I played referee, the players didn't have a chance to get pissed off.

It was Jace's turn now. Edith was just as ecstatic as the photographer had been when she'd gotten to snap pics of Jace.

"Do you need water? Or a coffee? If the couch isn't comfortable enough, we can find you a chair."

Jace threw me an exasperated glance. It had been clear since we'd arrived that the magazine was mostly excited about Jace. The rest of the boys had laughed this off, except for Levi, who only displayed contempt from that point on. His interview had been the most difficult to referee.

I thought his frustration might be partly because he wasn't having a great season. His stats had started strong but had worsened considerably over the past few months.

Jace had taken everything in stride, but I could tell that the constant attention was slowly starting to suffocate him.

"Couch is good, Edith. Don't need water, or coffee. Let's get started."

I had kept my distance from him until now, not wanting to give him the chance to lay out all the other things I hadn't *explicitly* mentioned in our agreement.

I'd made an exception during the photo shoot, of course, because well… I was human. I couldn't very well let this opportunity pass. I listened closely during his interview. Edith began with a standard set of questions, including:

"Has soccer been something that always came naturally to you?"

"I've been into it since I was a kid."

Jace cast his gaze toward me for a split second before focusing on Edith again. He didn't mention his dad. Had he shared that only with me? I was certain he knew what I was thinking about because vulnerability flashed in those deep green eyes. It made me want to come up with an excuse to steal him away and hold him close.

As the interview progressed, Edith pushed harder, culminating with a question I had made clear was not allowed.

"Are you single, Jace?"

I spoke before Jace even opened his mouth.

"Edith, skip that question. I told you the team's personal life would not be a subject of the interview."

"Off the record, then? Everyone here is dying to know."

I took a look around. The technical assistants were practically eye-fucking Jace. I wondered how many of them would show up at Jace's door tonight if he said he was single.

"Edith!" I warned.

"That's okay," Jace said good-naturedly. "I can answer that. I am single, but I won't be for long. There is someone special I'm fighting for."

Chapter Fifteen
Brooke

Oh, wow. Wow. I couldn't believe he'd said that. As the interview wrapped up and we bid everyone goodbye, I could feel Jace watching me. We headed straight to the hotel afterward, and I was having a hard time keeping my eyes off Jace.

"Who's hungry?" Andrew asked after everyone checked in. The team answered in a chorus of "Me!" Sometimes I forgot they burned—and needed—more calories than the average person. I had been counting down the minutes until the moment I'd be alone in my room. I planned to nap right until I had to take the boys to the bar.

But instead, I whipped out my phone and said, "What do you want to eat? I can call and make you reservations."

Everyone started talking at the same time, but I got the message: they all wanted different things.

Jace pulled me a little further away from the group.

"Brooke, we can get our own food. You've been running around all day. Get some rest. Want me to buy something for you?"

"Thanks, but I'm not hungry. If I change my mind, I'll buy something later."

Jace nodded. "Hats off for the way you put everything together today. It was honestly one of the best-organized interviews I've had."

"Thanks."

I was exhausted when I reached my room. So of course, the second my head hit the pillow, instead of falling into a dreamless sleep, adrenaline kicked in.

I was in New York. What was I doing wasting my time sleeping? I could rest back home. So instead of having the beauty sleep I'd been fantasizing about for the past two hours, I slipped on jeans, a T-shirt, and sneakers. As I fixed the belt on my jeans, I glanced at the little black dress for tonight. I regretted now bringing that vanilla outfit. The boys wouldn't have judged me if I showed up wearing something more edgy. Why had I been so hard on myself? On the bright side, I now had the perfect excuse for shopping. Honestly, I was glad the players had gone out without me. I needed a few hours to myself.

Once I stepped out of the hotel, I closed my eyes for a few seconds, smiling from ear to ear. Traffic and honks were part of my daily life in LA as well, but I could swear New York sounded different.

Where to go first? I was only three subway stations away from my favorite shopping area. As an intern, I'd been on a tight budget, so cabs had been out of the question. I didn't see the need to waste money on one now either. I slurped an iced coffee and people watched in the subway until I reached my station. Then I skidded up the stairs and into shopping heaven: Macy's.

Again, being an underpaid intern at a fashion magazine in New York had taught me a valuable skill: shopping on a budget. I had a knack for finding treasures. Three hours later, I had two bags full of clothes I didn't need (but absolutely couldn't resist), yet still no outfit for tonight.

I stopped at the sight of a red dress. Hmm… I already had the right shoes for it. With the right belt, it would look fantastic. Ten minutes later, I was whirling around in the changing room, admiring the dress from all angles. Jace was going to swallow his tongue when he saw me.

I couldn't wait to see his reaction. I also bought a sexy corset to wear underneath it.

I was bursting with excitement while handing the cashier my credit card. Now I was ready for the evening.

By the time I returned to the hotel, my feet were killing me. But did I rest? No. Instead, I went on to the next level of preparation: hair and makeup. Since I was wearing a dress with personality now, I needed a matching hairdo, so I got to work.

I smiled at my reflection in the mirror before leaving the room. I'd slicked a sheer gloss on my lips, and put all my efforts into highlighting my eyes. I'd used a mascara that promised extravagantly long lashes. The product had more than fulfilled its promise, especially because I'd also used an eyelash curler. My hair was pulled back in an updo that looked naturally messy, but had taken forty minutes to get right.

The elevator was packed, as was the lobby. The bar was in the underground of the hotel, and those who hadn't made a reservation had to line up in front of the entrance.

I glimpsed the team right away, tucked away in a corner of the lobby, and waved at them. Andrew gestured to the rest of the boys to head toward me. Jace had been typing on his phone but looked up at Andrew's nudge. Even from this distance, I didn't miss the appreciative once-over he gave me. As the two approached, Jace seemed to be undressing me with his gaze.

Well, hell. I was already fanning myself. How was I supposed to get through tonight?

We all headed together inside the bar. I told the hostess our name, and she walked us to our private area. Andrew took the lead. Jace and I were at the rear.

"Just a warning, I'm gonna spend the entire evening next to you," he whispered.

"Why?" I asked, mystified.

"Because someone's bound to hit on you if I leave you alone, and then I'm going to do something that will blow our cover."

"Jace, no one's going to hit on me."

"See? You can't even tell how beautiful you are. You definitely need me as a bodyguard. And chatting with you on work nights isn't against the agreement."

I glared at him, but far from backpedaling, Jace looked as if he was very close to pinning me against the nearest wall and kissing me senseless.

"Well, bodyguard. Let's take a look around."

I could immediately tell why the place was so coveted. The diffuse lighting cast the place in a slick and elegant glow. Everything was decorated in shades of warm brown. The space was divided in several smaller booths, with wood paneling displaying a lace pattern dividing them, stopping the sound from propagating across the room. A small dance floor was wedged between the booths. I planned to ignore it the entire evening, as I wasn't much of a dancer.

Our booth was close to the bar, but it turned out I needn't have nagged Ryan so much to give us one of the ultra-VIP spots, because the players were out and about the entire time, mingling with others.

I, on the other hand, planned to take full advantage of the cozy booth. It was comfortable and relatively quiet. I gulped down the complementary peanuts and almonds before the waitress even came to take my drink order. Now I was debating ordering everything there was to eat on the menu. In all my excitement to shop and get ready, I'd forgotten to eat.

I ordered grilled prawns to start with but was

still lost in the menu when the couch caved next to me. I knew it was Jace before I even glanced sideways. No one else would be cocky enough to lean into me the way he did.

"Do me a favor and keep me from ordering the entire menu before they bring my order," I said.

"Will do."

"How do you like the bar?"

"Gives me an excuse to sit right next to you, so I love it. You look incredible."

Clearly, Jace wasn't going to turn the flirting down. Maybe it was time to switch tactics. As he took the menu from me and started flipping through it, I said nonchalantly, "This shirt is perfect on you. The only way you could look hotter is if you took it off."

He stopped in the act of turning the page, his eyes bulging.

"What's the matter, Mr. Connor? Can't win at your own flirting game? Good to know I can render you speechless after all."

He did look incredible, wearing jeans and a black shirt with long sleeves rolled up to his elbows. The dark color contrasted with his green eyes.

My grilled prawns arrived before Jace could reply, and I dug right in.

"Oh, God, I'm so hungry. Completely forgot to eat."

"What did you do today?"

"Went shopping. You?"

"Ate a steak with Andrew, then hit some

stores. Milo asked me for some Knicks memorabilia. He wanted a specific shirt from the seventies. Didn't find it, but I got him a few other shirts instead."

"Oh, no. I actually know a store that sells vintage memorabilia," I said after swallowing half a prawn. I loved that Jace had gone shopping for his nephew when he could have simply sent someone to do that for him.

"We could go together tomorrow."

"Of course."

He looked down between us, then placed his hand over mine on the couch. "We haven't spent much time together lately. I've missed you."

"I've missed you too."

He snapped his gaze back up, looking at me with hope, interlacing our fingers. "Spend the entire day with me tomorrow?"

"But you have tickets to the basketball game early in the afternoon."

"I don't really give a fuck. I just want to be with you."

It was amazing how such simple words could affect me so much. His flirty side never got to me the way his sweet side did.

"One day. Just us." He watched me with an intensity that simply demanded from me to say yes. We were leaving very late in the evening tomorrow. One whole day with Jace? Hell, yes.

"Okay."

When the waitress came by to ask if we wanted to drink something, I ordered a Martinez cocktail

Jace cocked a brow.

"What? I have a bodyguard. I can go wild."

I only drank that one cocktail, but the atmosphere around us made me lower my guard, and inhibitions. Away from the Lords offices, I felt more relaxed than I had in the months since I'd started working there. Jace and I talked the whole night and we were among the last ones to leave.

We happened to reach the elevators at the same time as a large group of partygoers, so we squished like sardines inside. I managed to wedge my hand between two women to push the button to my floor, as well as Jace's. I knew the team was three floors above mine.

Jace was holding an arm on my waist, glaring at the guy in front of me, who was openly leering at me. I looked up at Jace at the precise moment he glanced down and noticed my corset. His palm, which had been resting on my back, curled, his fingers pressing into the fabric of my dress as if he wanted to yank it away right this second.

I'd never got aroused so fast in my life. The ache between my thighs only intensified when Jace let go of my waist to take my hand. *Oh, God.* He was checking the room number on the card cover I was holding, then looked up at the display showing on which floor we were.

Desire slammed into me, wiping away every other thought. His shaky breath landed on my temple. When the elevator came to a stop, the entire group got out, leaving us alone. Jace flipped me to face him as soon as the doors closed, and then his mouth was on mine and his hands were touching me desperately. He only stopped kissing me long enough to growl, "Your room. Now."

Chapter Sixteen
Jace

I was a goner. I'd known it for a while, but tonight I'd had all the confirmation I needed. Taking her hand, I led her from the elevator to her room. Brooke's hand shook slightly when she slid in the card.

We'd barely closed the door behind us when I started touching her again, pinning her in place with my hands on her waist. I ran the tip of my nose up and down the back of her neck. She started to shake slightly. Then I flipped her around, needing to see that fire in her eyes, to taste her. I kissed her hard and deep, exploring her until she pressed her hips against me, seeking friction. I was painfully turned on. I kissed her even harder, swallowing up her moans.

I was greedy for her sounds of pleasure, to taste the rest of her. I explored her mouth all the way to the bed, feeling her give in to me more with every lash of my tongue, every stroke of my hands. She was undoing my belt before I even reached for her zipper.

"Wait a second, baby," I whispered.

"No. Why wait?"

I hurried to the bathroom, opening the personal hygiene kit, retrieving the condom. I'd noticed it earlier when I'd inspected my own kit. I placed the packaged condom on the bed before pouncing on her again, kissing her with even more urgency than before. She worked on my belt again. I yanked my shirt over my head, pushing my jeans and boxers out of the way before removing her clothes.

I lowered her zipper, pushing her dress down, and nearly came when I saw that corset she was wearing. It was stunning and sexy.

"You look beautiful, Brooke."

"Thank you."

"It's a good thing I didn't realize you were wearing this when we were in the bar." I traced her clavicle with my fingers as I spoke, feeling her skin turn to goose bumps, her breath becoming more labored.

"Why not?"

"We wouldn't have made it to the room."

I moved behind her, starting to undo the tie at the top, pulling it out of the eyelet.

After every eyelet, I parted the fabric, kissing the skin I'd uncovered. When I reached the middle of her back, I sat on the bed, pulling her between my legs. That gorgeous, round ass brushed against my inner thighs, testing my control.

Once I'd undone the last of the eyelets, Brooke made to turn around, but I stopped her. "No. I want you like this."

She stilled, and I could tell she was holding her breath, waiting to feel where I'd touch her next. I moved two fingers between her legs, stroking her over the silk. Brooke moaned, pressing herself into my fingers, reaching with her hands behind her back, clearly greedy to touch me. I removed her panties, then turned her around, holding her exactly where I wanted her, sucking on a nipple until I felt her want to pull away because she'd become too sensitive. I didn't allow it. I kept her firmly in place with one hand, while I stroked her clit with the other.

"Ooooh, Jace. God—"

Her words became unintelligible when I slipped two fingers inside her, curling them until she buckled, and her thighs started shaking. I'd found her sweet spot. I kept her like that, licking her nipple, pumping my hand between her legs until she braced her hands on my shoulders and came hard. She nearly lost her balance, but I steadied her, placing an arm on her waist, the other on her thigh.

"Sit on me, babe."

She plumped her sweet ass on my thighs the next second, resting her knees on the bed, lacing her hands around my neck. Her breath was still shaky. I glanced down between us. My erection was pressing against her pubic bone, and when she brought a hand down, rubbing her palm against the tip, I tilted my head back, letting out a deep, guttural sound.

"Fuck. Fuuuuck."

I moved us both on the bed, bringing Brooke underneath me and putting on a condom. And then I slid inside her—not too much, because I wanted to give her the time to stretch around me. Brooke fisted the bedsheet with one hand, pressing her hips into me, taking all the rest in.

"You feel amazing." I lay like that, without moving, simply enjoying this amazing feeling of being wrapped up in Brooke, feeling her arms around my neck, her inner muscles pulse around me. I'd been certain I would be rough tonight, but when I started pumping in and out of her, I *needed* to do this slowly, to explore her as gently as possible, to savor every tiny sensation she spurred inside me. I wanted to lose myself in her, draw this out for as long as possible. I skimmed my hands over every bit of Brooke I could touch, smothered her face and neck with kisses.

My orgasm built up slowly, starting with a pull behind my navel, a tension clenching in all my muscles. I held out until she climaxed, but not a second longer.

I moved away from her only enough for me not to crush her with my weight, but I kept an arm around her waist as we both fought to regain our breath. I had to let go all too soon, walking to the bathroom to take care of the condom. I chuckled, realizing I was still semihard.

When I looked in the mirror, I saw Brooke in the doorway glancing at my ass appreciatively. A second later, she realized I was watching her, and shrugged.

"What? It's a nice ass. Can't blame me for

looking."

"Wouldn't dream of it." I held out my hand for her, pulling her my way until she was flush against me.

"Hmmm… I sense someone's looking forward to the rest of the night."

"That's an understatement."

I pulled her into the shower, where we made out more than cleaned up, with the result that I was rock hard by the time I carried her to bed.

I placed her on the mattress, skimming my lips from her navel up to her sternum before moving on to a nipple, pulling it into my mouth. Brooke gave a low gasp, and by the way she clenched her thighs together, I was sure she was ready for me again. Moving between her thighs, I rubbed the length of my erection against her entrance. She was so slick for me, it was maddening.

"Jace, this is…." Her words faded in a gasp.

"I want you to still feel me when I'm not inside you. I want you to miss me."

"Just so I'm prepared, are we going to get any sleep tonight?"

I smiled against her skin, down her chest.

"Probably not. But you can rest tomorrow. You already agreed to spend tomorrow with me." I stopped my descent, looking up at her. My muscles locked down while I waited for her reaction. Would she backtrack, because things had changed between us since we'd made plans a few hours ago? I was prepared to push back if she did. There was no way I wasn't spending tomorrow with her.

"I know. I can't wait."

I returned to kissing her, even though I had an inkling she'd only agreed so fast because we were in New York.

***

Brooke was sleeping with her head on my chest when I woke up next morning. For the past fourteen years, the first thing I'd done upon waking up was to head out for a run. Right now though, I wouldn't move from this bed even for a million bucks. I was just going to wait for Brooke to wake up... even though, if she needed much longer, I might run out of patience and take matters into my own hands. I had plans for us today, and sleep was getting in the way.

Brooke began to stir about half an hour later, and I saw my chance.

"You up already?" she mumbled, lifting her head to look at me.

"Yep."

"And cheerful. My head feels like it's weighing a ton. Why are you so fresh?"

"I usually get up at this time."

"Oh, that's right. For your run."

"First morning in fourteen years when I didn't go for a run."

She squinted. "Is this supposed to make me feel special?"

"Yes."

Brooke didn't look too impressed. I changed tactics. I twirled us in the bed, climbing on top of her, and running the tip of my nose up and down the side of her neck. She squirmed under me, letting out a shriek of laughter. The side of her neck was a ticklish area. Good to know. I didn't want to be cruel this early in the morning, so I moved lower, kissing between her breasts.

"What are you doing?" she inquired.

"Showing you how special you are. Wouldn't want you to operate under a misconception."

I was about to resume all that kissing when I noticed her grin. "What?"

"Nothing. Carry on. I need lots and lots of proof before I believe you."

"I'm more than happy to provide it." She laughed, but the sound quickly turned into a moan when I lowered a hand between her thighs, lazily drawing a circle around her clit.

"That's a shortcut," she pointed out playfully.

"I'm full of tricks."

Afterward, when we both came out of the shower, I became aware of how hungry I was.

"Let's order room service."

She poked my abs. "Blasphemy. We're in New York on a weekend. Do you know how many breakfast and brunch places are around?"

"I don't actually. I don't go out much when I'm here for a game."

"Well, today, you have your very own guide." Brooke lifted her arms, pointing her forefingers at her head. The towel she'd wrapped around herself slid a few inches lower, and she caught it just in time, grinning sheepishly.

"Wouldn't mind if you'd let it drop."

"Of course you wouldn't. But then we'd be right back where we started, and you would still have no breakfast. Come on, no time to lose."

We met in the lobby of the hotel twenty minutes later, after I'd gone to my room to change.

Brooke was already there, talking to Andrew.

"Hey, man," Andrew greeted. "Brooke here tells me she'll show you a store where you can buy that vintage stuff for Milo."

"Yes. She's saving my ass. Won't have to show up with that lame shirt I bought yesterday."

Andrew nodded. "See you at the game?"

"Not sure I'll make it. You know I'm not a big fan. I'll catch up with you at the hotel afterward."

Afterward, Brooke and I headed out onto the street. "Where to?"

"How much do you trust me?" She was grinning from ear to ear.

"One hundred percent."

"Then follow me."

Her excitement was contagious. She'd been spot-on about New York having a wealth of options for breakfast. The problem was that everyone else seemed to know that too. The first two joints we tried were at full capacity. The third and fourth had a long waiting line.

"I'm sorry, I wasn't expecting this," Brooke said with frustration.

"Babe, I really don't care what we do. All I want is to spend time with you."

"Let's make a deal. Just grab whatever on the street, and then we can go buy Milo's gift."

"Okay."

We ended up eating hot dogs, but I honestly didn't mind. Brooke chatted the entire time, telling me about her life as an intern here, how it compared to her stint in Washington, and then in LA. I liked learning about this side of her. I admired her for having the balls to do things her way and take chances.

Midway through our stroll, she called Coach, giving me an apologetic smile.

"I promised I'd check in with him."

Since we were walking next to each other, I heard everything she said, and couldn't hide my smile as she gently asked him if he'd gone to his doctor's appointment yesterday.

Coach usually didn't like anyone getting into his business, but I suspected he was different when it came to his daughters. Then again, who could resist Brooke?

The store where she brought me was one of those I'd found on Google but then couldn't locate on the map. It was a hole in the wall, but a gold mine. It had everything I was looking for.

I usually went alone on my shopping trips for Milo. I'd always liked keeping family things separate from everything else, but I was glad Brooke was with me today, and that she was having fun with me. I loved that she enjoyed the things in my life that I valued, instead of scoffing at them.

Lately, I'd been surrounded by people who were only interested in fame or money, but even before that, I'd never felt so *complete* around someone the way I did when I was with Brooke.

"What were you going to do today before I asked you out?"

"Shopping."

"Let's do that too."

"We're shopping for Milo."

"I want to buy you something."

She shook her head. "Trust me, you do not want to see me with shopping mode switched on. Once I start, I can't stop."

She wasn't asking for anything for herself, but that just made me want to buy her everything.

The one thing I discovered about myself while we were choosing items for Milo? I was incapable of telling Brooke no. She was well on her way to convincing me to buy him the entire store.

"I'll take the shirt and the hat," I told the cashier.

"What do you think you're doing? We're not nearly done shopping."

"Yes, we are."

"But he'll love this. You told me about his

collection of cards. It will fit right in."

She remembered that about Milo? How?

"I know it will, but Lori will berate me until the end of time for getting him so many things."

Brooke held up the card deck, looking at me with puppy eyes. "No, she won't. She just had a baby. Anyway, blame it on me. Say I talked you into it. Look, it's even on sale."

I bought it, of course. Somewhere between watching Brooke champion my nephew's cause and thinking about Milo's reaction (and ignoring Lori's), my defenses collapsed in a pile of ash.

"Can't believe you talked me into buying all this," I said once we returned to the hotel. We went straight to her room.

"Can't believe I had set out some very clear rules, and you made me stomp all over them."

"I made you, huh? So you had nothing to do with it?"

Brooke was with her back to me, sorting through her luggage when I snuck up behind her, wrapping my arms around her waist. Resting my nose in the crook of her neck, I had the strangest thought. I didn't want to go back. I knew I had a tough game ahead of me next week, but for the first time, I wanted to blow it off.

I moved one hand from her waist upward, cupping a breast. She wasn't wearing a bra, and I took full advantage of it, flicking her nipple with my thumb until it turned into a hard nub.

I moved my other hand downward.

"Jace!" She gasped when I pressed two fingers over her clit. Even through all the layers of clothing, she felt enough friction to respond.

She gripped my wrist, and I stopped.

Pulling out of my arms, she turned to face me. "We should talk."

"I know. I'd say I'm sorry for breaking my promise of waiting, but I'm really not."

She threw her head back, laughing. "I wasn't expecting you to be. I would lay out a new agreement, but I have a feeling that you'd just make me break that too."

With a low groan, I snaked an arm around her waist, pulling her close.

"No matter what happens, we're friends, Brooke. Let's just take this one day at a time. Let's start by being friends who are having fun. Do what feels right, when it feels right. You put too much pressure on yourself."

"I know. You're right."

She nodded, melting against me as I kissed her.

My teammates were still heatedly discussing the game they'd watched when we boarded the plane. Brooke was sitting alone again, and it crossed my mind more than once to just sit next to her, but I didn't think I could be that close to her and not give us away.

So I remained in my seat next to Andrew,

trying not to be too obvious in checking out Brooke when she got up from her seat to take her laptop out of the overhead bin.

"Dude, did you score last night?" he asked.

Out of the corner of my eyes, I saw Brooke wince.

"What are you talking about?"

"Knocked at your door this morning to go for a run, but you didn't answer. Figured you didn't sleep there."

"Then I was out running already."

"Yeah, right."

I cocked a brow at Andrew, who immediately dropped the topic. Brooke had already slipped into her seat, and I couldn't see her face, couldn't tell what was going through her mind. I wanted to put her at ease. Did she really think that if something happened, she'd have to fend for herself? Even if it meant I'd make life harder for myself at the club, I'd fight for her.

Chapter Seventeen
Brooke

The LA Lords headquarters was a flurry of activity over the next week. We were nearing the end of the season, which concluded on October 31. The teams with the most points would then go on to compete in a sequence of playoff games for the MLS Cup.

Everyone was on edge, torn between cheering for our boys while also not putting pressure on them.

I'd taken a close look at Jace during lunch today. I hadn't spoken to him more than a few words because we were surrounded by coworkers, but once I was behind my desk, I shot him a text. I knew he was watching tapes this afternoon.

Brooke: You looked very tense during lunch.

Jace: Pressure is high. Are you offering to help me relax? :-)

Brooke: Of course. What can I do?

Jace: I have a few ideas.

Brooke: Why didn't I see this coming? :-))

Jace: Tonight, I'm going to the education center to play ball with some of the students, but I want to spend time with you too. Come with

me? I know you don't want people at the club to know about us, but I want to see more of you outside the club.

I hesitated, but the truth was, I needed more of Jace too. As long as we were being careful around here, I couldn't see the risk. Besides, I wanted to see the center with my own eyes.

Brooke: I'd love to.

I grinned when he texted me the address. We drove there separately in the evening. Jace was behind me right until we reached an almost empty boulevard, and then he drove past me. I sped up, driving past *him,* grinning at him in the rearview mirror.

Jace had a competitive bone, but so did I, which was why we chased one another right until we pulled up in front of the center.

We climbed out of our cars at the same time, and Jace strode right to me.

"You like speed. I learn something new about you every day."

"I can drive like a Tasmanian devil," I confirmed, wiggling my eyebrows. Jace leaned in, feathering his lips on my cheek before moving to my mouth. *Oh, fuck,* how he kissed me. My knees buckled. He brought his hands to my waist. His fingers pressed into me greedily.

On a groan, he pulled back. "Let's go inside before I change my mind and whisk you away. I said I'd be here, and I don't like to disappoint."

I nodded, still recovering from the kiss.

"Paige, Will, and Hailey are waiting for us."

"Did you tell them I'm coming too?"

"They know we're friends. Hailey might suspect we're more."

"You can't look at me like this," I whispered.

"Like what?"

"Like you want to make my clothes disappear."

He caressed my cheek with his thumb, before moving it lightly over my lips. "I'll do my best, but I can't make any promises."

When we entered, a pretty brunette hurried to us and kissed Jace's cheek. She extended her hand to me.

"Brooke, nice to finally meet you in person. I'm Hailey. Jace, you should hurry. Everyone's waiting for you."

Jace immediately headed to the backyard for the game. Hailey gave me a tour.

"So, are you teaching as well?" I asked.

"I will start a course that teaches people to be personal shoppers, or style advisors at department stores."

"But you don't work in fashion, right? I remember you said something about PR on the phone."

"I am in PR, but I worked at Macy's as a style advisor during college."

I could see that. Hailey wore high heels and a

dress with lace at the collar and on her sleeves. It might look pretentious on anyone else, but she rocked it.

"I've also worked as a business consultant, and I've thought about creating classes surrounding that, but all jobs as analysts or PR require a college degree, while this stylist stuff doesn't, though the fashion world is a little hard to break into."

"I might be able to help with that. I used to work for a fashion magazine. I have contacts."

"That would be great. Paige was actually talking about taking this to a new level and trying to find work placements for the students."

I spoke to her about my contacts in the fashion world as she gave me the tour. Once she'd shown me all the classrooms, we went downstairs. The classes were over, since it was so late, so most students were in the backyard, either playing soccer or watching. She introduced me to Will and Paige, who were on the sidelines, cheering.

Seeing Will, I realized those potent genes were a family trait. He and Jace looked nothing alike, but they both had this magnetic pull surrounding them.

I filled Will in as well about my network in the fashion industry while we were watching the game. I was focusing on Jace, who was having a blast. I could tell that even though the game was easy for him, he was tired. He'd had a long day and still showed up here, giving his best. He was so affectionate with everyone.

In New York, Jace had said we were friends

having fun, which honestly had been exactly what I'd hoped he would say, because I was still reeling from the news about Noah and Cami, too raw to consider anything else. But this gorgeous and utterly charming man wasn't going to make it easy for me to think about this as just some fun between friends, was he? I sighed. All signs pointed to no.

"Whatever they told you, it's not true," was the first thing Jace said when he joined us, pointing between Will and Hailey.

"Jace, I'm offended," Paige said. "You think I can't keep these two in check?"

"We just talked shop," I informed him. "But what exactly did Jace think you'd be saying about him?"

Will rubbed his hands. "How much time do you have?"

"No time at all," Jace offered, glaring at his brother.

"Ha! That's what *you* think. I have plenty of time," I volleyed back. Hailey instantly laced an arm around mine. Jace looked as if he wanted to break up this party before it even started, but then he was roped into soccer talk by some of the students.

"He's got one big weakness, and that's our nephew Milo. Which is probably why Milo always goes to Jace for advice for nefarious plans."

"Hey, he comes to me too," Will said indignantly.

"Nope, there is a difference," Hailey went on. "You indulge Milo's ideas, but Jace actively comes up with his own ideas. I like busting our baby brother's ass, but fair is fair."

***

Jace

I was glad I'd brought Brooke here tonight, even though it meant my siblings would grill me about her. Hailey already knew, of course, but to give credit where credit was due, she hadn't said one word to anyone.

When Brooke moved to talk to some students, Will caught up with me, immediately asking, "So... what's the story with Brooke?"

"She's helping me with some of the sponsor contracts, and I told her about the center. I thought she'd like seeing this place."

Will gave me a shit-eating grin. "You expect me to buy this? With the way you look at her?"

"What are you implying?"

"That you're in this deep. Oh, I bet Val and Lori will catch up on this in no time. Expect an ambush at the next Friday dinner."

I chuckled. I expected it much sooner.

"Just putting it out there, but life changes when you meet your match. For the better."

I bit back a smile. Will never talked just to *put things out there*.

"I'll keep that in mind."

Before, whenever my family said things like these, I brushed them off easily, because I honestly hadn't understood where they were coming from. Now I was starting to.

Paige asked for Will's help at the bonfire just as I saw Brooke jog into the building. I ventured inside before Hailey or anyone else got a chance to catch up to me. I wanted a few minutes alone with her. I found Brooke in the kitchen.

"I'm so thirsty," she said in between large gulps.

"What do you think of this place?"

"It's great. By the way, Paige said they are looking to set up a work placement network, and I offered to put them in contact with some people. And I had an idea. We could probably approach some of the companies you signed deals with and ask if they're interested in this. I mean, donations are great, but work placement is the next step, so everyone has a chance to actually start somewhere."

I was too stunned to say anything. I liked that Brooke seemed to understand the things that were important to me without needing me to say them out loud.

"What do you think?"

"That you're incredible." I walked over to her, cupping her cheek.

She shuddered a little, licking her lower lip. When I pressed my thumb on the spot she'd wet before, she inhaled sharply.

"Absolutely incredible."

She blushed, looking down. "It just makes sense."

"I like that you're so passionate about this."

"Anyone would be."

"You're wrong." At her inquisitive frown, I added, "Some of my dates seemed to think that donations were a waste of my money."

Her gaze hardened. "They thought this place was a waste of time?"

"Sort of. Even before, I've always donated to various charities."

"Can I ask you something? Did you ever have a serious relationship?"

"Not exactly. For the longest time, I went with the flow, you know."

She gave me an easy grin. "Hot soccer player surrounded by women? Can't see why you wouldn't. I can only imagine how much work you gave PR."

I grimaced. "That's an understatement."

"Now I'm curious."

"I don't remember every incident, but there was a memorable one where someone wrote to the club saying she was pregnant, that it was my kid and she'd go to the press if they didn't give her my contact info."

"Jesus!"

"Yeah. Took us a while, and Hailey's help to prove it was a lie. I didn't even know her."

"Is that what made you want to change your partying ways?"

"No. It was before that. About a year ago, I decided to turn over a new leaf."

Brooke pouted. "From your tone of voice, it

sounds like it didn't quite work out."

"I started going out with this teacher. She seemed genuine… turned out she wasn't. She'd just been hoping for a break into the music industry, and that she'd get it through me. I introduced her to a contact of mine. They hit if off real well. In the studio, and in bed."

"Jace, I'm sorry," she said softly.

"But now I have you, so none of that matters."

She smiled shyly, kissing my jawline. "Shall we head back outside? I promised Paige I'd let her pick my brain a bit more."

"Sure. We can go wherever you want afterward."

She tilted her head, smiling. "Well, somewhere we can be alone so I can help you get rid of all that stiffness I saw today, as I promised, Mr. MVP."

Fuck, could she be any sweeter? Brooke made to move, but I kept her in place, bringing my lips over hers, kissing her deeply, until she arched her hips forward, pressing herself against me. I tore my mouth away.

"Let's get back out there, hot stuff, and hurry up with Paige. Countdown starts now."

Chapter Eighteen
Brooke

Between the renegotiations with sponsors and helping out the events team, I was working overtime.

But then, so was everyone else. No one knew their elbow from their ass. Which was why, Monday morning, when a bouquet of flowers was delivered to my desk, Sheila and Veronica didn't notice at first, despite their desks being close to mine. Then they pounced on me.

"Wait a second. These weren't here earlier," Sheila mentioned.

The girls from PR a few tables away also looked up from their computers, having noticed the commotion through the glass partitions.

"You've got an admirer—"

"Oh my God, you've got a guy who sends you flowers? Who is he?"

Before I could say anything, Veronica snatched the card.

"*Have a great week, hot stuff.* That's it? No name?"

I couldn't hide my shit-eating grin, but in all fairness, I didn't try very hard.

"My lips are sealed," I informed the girls.

"You're mean," Sheila said.

"I don't want to jinx it." That was true in more ways than one.

"Hmm, so that means it's just starting."

"Yep." Also true.

"Well, girl, if you decide you don't want him, I'll take him. I'd love a man who sends flowers just so you have a good week," Veronica said, and I detected a little jealousy in her voice.

No chance in hell. I'd thought about chastising Jace, because this wasn't a safe move, but I couldn't bring myself to do it. It was too sweet and thoughtful, even if a bit daring. I sent him a text to thank him.

After everyone minded their own business again, I set the flowers right next to the stress ball. A strange warmth filled me. I had a full day ahead of me, and I started by talking to Carl Hill. His company produced footwear, had been one of the team's main sponsors for years, and he'd wanted one of the boys to be the face of their newest line.

He was torn between Andrew and Jace. Levi had been heavily hinting that he wanted to snatch up this opportunity. Carl had considered him too, but his interest had subsided because Levi had fully embraced the wild side of the soccer player lifestyle: partying and drinking. As a result, his performance on the field suffered.

Secretly, I was keeping my fingers crossed that Carl would go for Jace, but I presented both players impartially.

I had devised a rating system using various criteria: social media influence, consistency throughout the season, and so on.

I'd also mentioned the foundation in conjunction with Jace, because I firmly believed it was a plus point, and it turned out I was right. Carl thought it would make him look good.

"I'll think about it over the next few weeks and get back to you, all right?" he said.

"Sure. I'll be in touch."

I was certain he'd go with Jace, and it made me immensely happy. I couldn't wait to share this with Jace, to see him light up at the prospect.

I loved that he put so much passion into everything, and that he was always ready to go the extra mile. I was right there along with him, ready to do the same. God, I was already so deeply involved in this. I stopped typing, drawing in a lungful of air. After the way things had ended with Noah, I thought I wouldn't be able to open up again, and yet, I could feel it happening. I was a little scared.

In the evening, I managed to convince Sheila to hit the gym with me instead of going with the PR girls to the next-door bar for happy hour, as we sometimes did. She was a fun workout partner, but she was no Jace.

There was nothing quite like a sweaty, muscle-flexing Jace to motivate me to push myself past my limits.

Halfway through our workout, the universe granted me my wish because Jace strode into the gym. He walked right up to us. The edgy glint in his eyes gave me goose bumps.

"Hello, ladies."

"Jace, don't tell me you're going to work out after all the games you're having," Sheila exclaimed.

"Believe it or not, this is how I relax."

Sheila rolled her eyes. "Well, I usually relax with a cocktail, but Brooke here convinced me to give the treadmill a try. I'm going to the bar afterward." Looking at me, she said, "Are you sure you don't want to join us?"

"Already have plans. Sorry."

"Meeting Mr. Mysterious?"

"Oh?" Jace prodded. I narrowed my eyes. I was meeting *him* afterward.

"Yes," I replied, keeping my voice even.

"She got flowers today from some guy she's started dating. She smiled like a lunatic the whole day."

"Did she now?"

The tips of my ears felt on fire. I realized Jace might have taken the lack of chastising as an encouragement to push boundaries even more than usual. I kept my eyes on the small screen for the remaining twenty minutes, not even glancing at Jace, even though I felt the tension gathering in the room like a thick fog. Could Sheila feel it?

"Ugh… I give up," Sheila exclaimed when there were ten minutes left. "I'm gonna shower and hurry to catch the others at happy hour."

I shook my head. "Have fun. Don't drink too much. I'll see you tomorrow."

Even as Sheila walked out of the room, I stuck to my workout, focusing at the screen as if the video was fascinating, and not the one hundredth repeat of *How I Met Your Mother.*

My entire body tensed when I heard Jace move through the room.

"Brooke, are you ready to go?" he asked when he stepped in front of me.

"I need a few more minutes. What are we doing tonight?"

We'd just agreed on meeting but didn't make an actual plan.

"Do you want to go to my place? I'd love to spend the evening and the night with you. This week is going to be crazy. Who knows when we'll have the chance to just enjoy each other?"

I was going to bring up the flowers, but at the warm, happy expression in his eyes, I couldn't bring myself to, so I let it slide.

"Okay. I need fifteen minutes to shower and change, but you can leave now if you want. We're driving with separate cars anyway."

"I'll go ahead. See you at home." The happiness in his eyes dimmed somewhat. My stomach churned, but before I had a chance to ask what was wrong, he left the gym.

When I entered Jace's house, I was surprised

by the delicious food smell greeting me. I was even more surprised to find out that the source of the aromas wasn't takeout. His house was amazing. I'd been here twice. I had expected something huge and extravagant, given his status, but while it was spacious with three bedrooms and a gorgeous backyard, it wasn't opulent. It was comfortable and low-key. The walls were painted in shades of cream, paired with light brown tiles. I loved the huge windows most.

Decorations were scarce, but Jace said he didn't spend much time in his house anyway. The few items I'd noticed had all been bought by his sisters.

I'd never seen him in his kitchen, cooking.

"What is this?" I asked in amazement.

"What does it look like?" Jace gave me a cheeky smile before returning to dice some herbs.

"What are you preparing?"

"Pasta. Wanna help?"

"If you insist."

Jace laughed softly. I did help him, sneaking a few kisses in between.

"Brooke," Jace cautioned, when I'd gotten too caught up in the kissing part.

I was standing behind him, arms wrapped around his middle, peppering kisses on his upper back, then pushing myself on my toes and kissing the back of his neck. Turned out that area was a sensitive spot for him, because I heard him draw in a sharp breath.

"I'm behaving, I'm behaving," I said quickly. "Don't you go ruining our dinner on my account."

"Well, I've done my part. This needs to simmer for twenty minutes. Do you want to go change into something more comfortable?"

"Like what?"

He disentangled himself from my arms, turning to face me.

"I don't know. Whatever you find. A shirt, some shorts. Nothing at all."

"Are you trying to get me naked already? You haven't even fed me yet."

"I was merely laying out your options."

"Uh-uh."

Before I even realized what was going on, he'd lifted me off my feet, placing my ass on the counter, spreading my thighs wide and stepping between them. My pulse raced when Jace slowly drew his gaze over me, as if he couldn't decide where to touch first. When our gazes locked, I felt as if I was about to hyperventilate. That bedroom stare was simply delicious... and I wouldn't mind starting dinner by indulging in Jace.

He lowered his mouth to the nook between my neck and shoulder. I felt his hot breath first, and then his mouth. I jerked my hips forward an inch when I felt his tongue, my arms automatically lacing around his neck and my legs curling around his.

"Mmm... I'm trapping you here forever," I informed him.

"I wouldn't mind."

"You say that now. Wait until you see what I have in store for you."

"I'm happy you came here tonight, Brooke."

"Well, you should have told me you were cooking. Great selling point."

"I'll keep that in mind."

"I can't believe all you've ever fed me before was takeout or popcorn."

I felt him smile against my skin. "My cooking repertoire isn't too varied. Ten dishes, tops."

"Oh, snap. How will entertain me after you run out of those ten?"

"I can think of a few things."

He moved his mouth, feathering his lips over my clavicle before descending toward my cleavage. Before I realized what he was up to, he'd pushed me slightly on my back and pulled down the fabric of my dress, enough to reveal a bra cup. A second later, he yanked that down too, freeing one breast. He placed small, quick kisses all around it before teasing the nipple with his tongue. I pushed my ass forward a few inches, greedy for more contact. How could he turn me on so fast?

No matter how much he gave me, I was always ready for more. But when I made to pop open the button of his jeans, he caught my hand. "Babe, no. Dinner first. And then I'll sink inside you so good and deep."

Holy shit! I soaked my panties through, already aching for him. He was expecting me to be patient until after dinner when he'd been teasing my nipple like that? How much foreplay did he think I could take?

"You're not playing fair," I informed him.

"I just wanted a taste of you. You're the one who wrapped herself like a vise around me."

"I thought you didn't mind."

"I don't. Just pointing out that you're the one who's unfair."

Narrowing my eyes at him, I let go of my arms and straightened my legs. He covered my boob again.

"Now I'll have dinner all hot and bothered."

"I'll take care of you afterward."

When he stepped back, I hopped down from the counter. We set the table while the pasta sauce finished simmering.

To be honest, I was expecting something decent, but the pasta was out-of-this-world good.

"Oh, God, this is so delicious." I closed my eyes, savoring the tomato sauce. "Jace, this is amazing. So, what other recipes do you know?"

"You'll have to stick around and discover that yourself."

"A dangerous thing to say. You might not be able to get rid of me."

"It's as simple as cooking for you? I'm a lucky guy, then."

While we ate, I asked him about the upcoming games.

"I'd love it if you could join me on some of my away games."

"You want me there?" My heart seemed to double in size.

"Yeah."

I deflated as I considered all implications.

"It wouldn't be smart, though," I murmured.

"Right, wouldn't want everyone to know."

"Jace...."

"I got it." His jaw tightened, but he nodded. I realized now what his reaction at the gym had been about, and my stomach bottomed out.

"Jace, I'm sorry this is complicated. I'm not.... It's not that I don't want people to know, I just think they might not value my work as much."

"I understand."

It was clearly bothering him, and I didn't want to make Jace unhappy.

"It's just for a little while," I said in a low voice.

"I know. I told you I'll wait."

Yet part of me couldn't help fearing that he'd get tired of that. Jace was used to having whomever he wanted, whenever he wanted. Women were falling over each other trying to land him. His Twitter account was proof of how many were clamoring for a chance to get in his bed. What if he eventually decided he'd had enough of this hassle?

I shook my head, pushing those thoughts away. Just because Noah hadn't wanted to work on our relationship, instead turning to Cami, didn't mean Jace would choose the easier way.

Jace was a real man in a way that Noah had

never been.

But the fear lingered at the back of my mind, uninvited and unwelcome.

While we cleaned up, I brought the conversation back to his cooking.

"Where did you learn to cook?"

"Val. I've stolen a few of her tricks, though I'm only able to replicate easy recipes. Good to know you like it. I've only ever cooked for my family. Never knew if they really meant it when they said they liked it, or just took pity on me."

My stomach flipped, then flipped again. Damn, he was making me feel special.

"Well... I've met some of your family. I seriously doubt Hailey wouldn't tell you straight to your face if you were feeding her crap."

He barked out a laugh. "True, though I can't be sure. She's always choosing her battles. But yeah, Will is always the ultimate test. He doesn't mince words. Val says I was the only one of the boys who stuck around the kitchen, testing everything Mom was cooking. I don't remember that. I miss it somehow, though."

I stopped drying the plate, focusing my full attention on Jace. He rarely spoke about his parents, and when he did, the sadness in his eyes was unmistakable, so I didn't bring them up.

"I know it's weird. How can I miss something I don't even remember, right?" His voice caught a little, and he shook his head, as if he were trying to push away the thoughts. I moved to hug him from one side.

"You just miss your parents, Jace."

He kissed my forehead, murmuring, "I do. Sometimes I get mad at myself for remembering so little about them. I had nine years with them. I have sporadic memories, like Mom tending to a scraped knee, Dad teaching me how to fish. Why don't I remember more?"

My heart ached for him. I wasn't sure how to comfort him, but I wanted to try. "Nine is a young age, Jace. I don't remember much from when I was a kid either."

"I know. But I don't have memories from later with them, which is why I would've liked to remember more from earlier. Nothing major, you know, just a birthday, or Mom reading me a bedtime story, things like that."

He tightened his arms around me. Jace had been holding back more than the fact that he cooked great pasta. He was a deeply sensitive soul. Considering that he always walked around with a smile on his face, I'd always thought everything just bounced off him. I couldn't wait to uncover all sides of Jace.

Chapter Nineteen
Jace

"Oh, by the way, I forgot to tell you. Spoke to Carl Hill today. He still needs some time to think, but I think he'll go with you. He was also interested in the foundation," Brooke said.

"That's great news. When do you even do this?"

"It's just a few emails and phone calls here and there."

"Thanks for everything, Brooke."

"My pleasure. I think this can be really great. I talked to Hailey and Paige—they said that some of the contacts I gave them agreed to conduct a few interviews at the center. This could turn out wonderfully, Jace. I'm excited."

She spoke with so much passion that I couldn't hold back. I cupped the back of her head, tilting it slightly backward before dipping in to kiss her, greedy for all that fire. I'd never thought someone who got me so completely even existed.

I moved my mouth from her neck to her shoulder, pushing the straps of her dress away before undoing her zipper. I needed her naked. When her dress fell to her feet, I held her hand as she stepped out of it. Then I walked us to the couch. She was right in front of me, and I was one step behind, already hooking my thumbs in the elastic of her thong.

I couldn't be this close to her and not touch her. I lowered her panties, palming both ass cheeks and giving them a squeeze before undoing her bra and laying her on the couch on her back. She was looking up at me with so much hunger that I barely had enough self-restraint to get rid of my clothes and put on a condom. Settling between her legs, I rubbed two fingers between her thighs. Fuck, she was wet. I kissed her stomach, moving up to her collarbone, rubbing the head of my cock along her entrance. Even though I was blind with need, I wanted to prolong this, to increase the anticipation. I looked down between us, watching her chest rise and fall in rapid succession, her hips lifted just slightly off the couch, ready for me.

I entered her in one quick move, watching her eyes widen before capturing her mouth in a kiss, and interlacing my hands with hers. I wanted to be connected to Brooke in every way possible. I needed it.

She felt out of this world good, even better than in New York. Nothing ever felt this fucking perfect. She was pressing her thighs against mine before hooking her heels just under my ass, urging me on.

The faster I moved, the more she demanded.

My mouth was moving from her shoulders to her mouth, then back to her body. I wanted to worship every part of her, but I wanted her to be more comfortable.

I slowed my thrusts before pulling out of her. She blinked, confused, looking at our interlaced hands as if the only way she could make sense of anything was if we were connected.

"I need you in my bed."

She smiled happily, bringing an arm around my neck as I lifted and carried her to the bedroom. The moment she was on her back, I leaned over her, taking one nipple in my mouth, touching her waist and hips. I didn't enter her. First, I wanted to memorize every curve. She whimpered, running a hand through my hair before rolling her hips, and I gave in.

I entered her the next second, burying myself inside her to the base. I needed to chase my release more than I needed to breathe, but more than that, I wanted to prolong the moment.

I rolled us over so we were lying on our sides, and ran my fingers over the leg she kept on top, hooking my elbow under her knee, pulling her at the angle I wanted her. And then I started fucking hard, thrusting deep. Brooke bit her lower lip, fisting the pillow as she moved her hips in a relentless rhythm. I'd never tire of this: watching her, bringing her pleasure. I wanted to know this woman inside out.

"Touch yourself, Brooke. I want to watch."

She did as I asked, no hesitation. She climaxed

spectacularly, and the sight made me come apart. I kissed her slowly, rocking into her at a lazy pace, wringing out every drop of pleasure before pulling out and keeping her in my arms.

She rested her cheek on my chest, feeling warm and soft against me. I kissed the top of her head, knowing I had to take care of the condom but not wanting to let go.

"Shower, lazy girl?"

"Mpf."

"What was that?" I chuckled. She poked two fingers between my ribs. "What did I do to deserve that?"

"Laughing at me when you're the one who brought me to this state."

"I see. So I shouldn't do it again?"

She lifted her head, pouting. "I did *not* say that."

After we cleaned up, we returned to the living room. It was still early, and I wanted to make the most of our evening together. Brooke talked about a short trip she'd be taking with her sister to buy some gardening supplies during an annual flower festival in two months.

"I can join you," I suggested.

"Jace, you'd get bored."

I couldn't tell if she really meant that, or if she simply didn't want to make plans for us so far in advance. But I wanted her to be certain about one thing. "I disagree. I find everything you do fascinating."

"You do?"

"Yeah."

She smiled shyly, and I remembered she'd been through a disappointment not too long ago. I wanted to erase any hurt, any bad memories, make sure she wouldn't go through either again.

"By the way, I'll watch your away game with my sister. She'll probably shoot me for making her watch a soccer game, but that will only last until I tell her all about you, and then soccer-watching will turn into Jace appreciation. It'll take her mind off her troubles."

"You're using me," I said in mock indignation.

"Totally."

We debated flicking through TV channels before deciding I still had a lot of *Game of Thrones* to watch.

As we settled on the couch, I pulled her close and asked, "What are you doing tomorrow?"

"Working."

"In the evening, smartass."

"No plans yet, why?"

"Spend the evening with me. After the home game." I scrutinized her expression, my heart pounding insanely fast. I didn't know how much pushing was too much, if she even wanted to spend as much time with me as I wanted to spend with her.

"I like the sound of that."

"Where do you want to go?"

"Nowhere. How about I cook something for you? I happen to know far more than ten recipes, and I can't wait to impress you with them. You'll be too exhausted to go out. I'll take care of you."

I nodded, dipping my head to her neck, kissing it before speaking against her skin.

"I'd like that."

I couldn't remember the last time someone I wasn't related to said that to me, and her words brought on a feeling that was so new to me, and yet so unexpectedly fulfilling that I didn't know what to do with it, except pull her even closer, settling in for a night in with my girl.

Chapter Twenty
Brooke

On the evening of Jace's away game, I had popcorn, guacamole with chips, and wine ready. In other words: everything that was bad for our hips but oh-so-good for our soul.

Franci arrived before the game began, and we carried the goodies to the living room together.

We called Dad, as usual, to wish him luck.

"How are my girls?" he asked.

"Ready to cheer for the Lords," I said. "Go get 'um."

We never spoke more than two or three minutes, because Dad was a man of few words. Yet, these calls were important to him.

"We're really watching soccer, huh?" Franci wondered after Dad hung up.

"Well, no. We'll be watching Jace... with some soccer on the side."

I'd told her about him on the phone, but now I was going to give her all the dirty details. We sat cross-legged on the couch as we'd done when we were kids. The two of us had developed a love for binge-watching even before the era of Netflix. I had missed Franci terribly once she'd left for college, feeling a little lost without my older sister there.

"Remember when Dad would try to rope us into watching?" Franci asked.

"Oh, God, yes. And Mom would come to our rescue. She was quite resourceful, coming up with excuses." My heart tugged as I remembered my conversation with Jace, about how he felt as if he didn't have enough memories with his parents. My parents had divorced when I was a kid, but I had many good memories before that, and even afterward they both did their best to be good parents to us.

"You know, I think Jace is even hotter than last year." Franci parked her chin in one palm, sighing at the screen. "That should not be legal."

"I agree."

"Well, hot or not, I am going to be impartial. Is he treating you right?"

"Oh, yeah."

"Does he know his way under the covers?"

"Hell, yeah."

Franci wiggled her eyebrows. "When can I officially meet him?"

"Officially? Don't be so old-school. I don't know. We're very relaxed about things."

"Relaxed. Uh-huh."

I grinned, even though I knew this would only bring another round of teasing. It was good to see my sister cheerful, even though she was having fun at my expense. Her divorce had been finalized three months ago, but she was still not over it. I couldn't ask how she was, because she'd agreed to join me for soccer night on the condition that I didn't ask about her. Maybe that was for the best. There was such a thing as over-discussing a topic. Maybe what she needed was just some fun with her sister.

"Hmm… that Levi guy is a close second on the hotness scale," Franci commented as the game went on.

"I guess."

"You guess?"

"I don't like him. He's a bit arrogant and is jealous of Jace."

"Interteam competitiveness is normal though, right?"

"To a degree, yes. But Levi is being an ass about it."

Over the past week, he'd stopped by my desk a few times, inquiring about Carl Hill. I told him that Carl was considering only Jace or Andrew, but Levi wanted me to push him more. He wanted to be back in the running.

I told him his game had to improve first, because not only was Hill not even considering him anymore, other sponsors were worried about Levi as well.

Franci giggled before eating a mouthful of popcorn.

"What?" I asked defensively.

"You're protective of Jace. It's cute."

Of course, I was. Not that Jace needed it, but I just couldn't help my instincts. He didn't need any crap from his own teammates. The strength of a team consisted in them being able to rely on each other.

"Ugh, I can't wait for him to be back. He's got another game away after this one."

I jutted out my lower lip like a small kid.

"Ohoho, wait a second. I thought you said it was all very… relaxed."

"That doesn't mean I can't miss him."

"So, let's see. You two text during the day, regularly make plans, and don't see other people, right?"

"Yes."

Franci smiled but didn't say anything else, which immediately had me on alert. Franci was one of those people who always voiced their opinions, and I appreciated her for that.

"What?" I prodded.

"It sounds like the two of you care about each other a lot."

I sighed, bringing my knees to my chest. Of course, I cared about Jace. I wasn't sure if it was because he and I had grown close before, but I could feel my attachment to him deepening, transforming from a friendly bond to something else. The shift was happening so fast that I didn't even know how to find my balance.

If things didn't work out, how were we supposed to go back to being just friends? My muscles strummed tight, as if my entire body was rejecting that scenario.

I was only half watching during the first

halftime, but by the end of the second one, I was completely into it. The score was 1:1, and the Lords needed this victory. Our forwards were good (I'd go with excellent, but I might be biased since I had a soft spot for the MVP) but so was the opposition's defense.

The last few minutes were brutal. Every move or scheme the forwards tried, they were blocked. When there were just two minutes left, the unthinkable happened: Jace scored... and then went down as two of the other team's forwards smashed right into him.

"Oh my God." I felt my heart crawl up my throat. I moved closer to the TV until I practically had my nose pressed against the screen. Everything around me faded as I tried to gauge how seriously Jace was hurt: the rest of the game, the presenters' commentary, even my sister's reassurances.

***

Jace

Victory was worth a few bruised ribs. I'd taken one elbow above the spleen, and a knee straight to the kidney. I'd had worse, and I had time to recover before the next game.

"Nice game, man," Andrew congratulated as we entered the lobby of the hotel. "Meet you at Jim's Irish in ten minutes?"

"I'm not coming tonight."

"You're hurting?"

"No, just not feeling it."

Jim's Irish was a sports bar just across the hotel. We went there after every game here, but tonight I wasn't in the mood.

I bid Andrew good night before heading to my room. The first thing I did was charge my phone, since the battery died sometime during the game. As soon as the screen lit up, I had to grin. I had about one million messages from my family, asking how bad my injury was. I replied to each before discovering Brooke had also messaged me.

Brooke: Are you okay? I couldn't tell on TV.

Brooke: Are you hurting?

Brooke: Jaaaace, don't leave me hanging like this. Are you hurt?

I smiled as I stretched on the bed to call her. I felt oddly happy that she was so worried about me.

"Oh, thank God. I was starting to panic."

"Starting? Sorry to tell you, but you panicked before you even sent the first message."

"Smartass. How are you feeling?"

"Looked worse than it was. I'll have some bruises, but there's nothing broken or torn."

"Then why do you sound so strained?"

I'd straightened to rearrange my pillow, and I'd automatically sucked in a breath—it was easier to deal with the pain that way.

"I am in *some* pain but nothing major."

"I don't buy that."

I wanted her here. The thought of Brooke

being in my hotel room after a game... I liked that. One of the reasons I hadn't gone to Jim's Irish tonight was that I just didn't like the general vibe, which included women coming onto us.

But this, lying in bed and talking to Brooke... this was just what I needed. I wanted to give her what I hadn't been able to give anyone else—and I'd better be able to do it.

I almost asked her yet again to fly with me to a few away games but stopped myself just in time. I was pushy, but I remembered how wary she'd been last time I brought this subject up. I didn't want to come on too strong and scare her away.

"Bet those lips could make me forget any kind of pain."

"You're so predictable, Jace Connor."

"What can I say? I'm easy to please. Brooke, seriously, don't worry. I'm gonna be good as new before our next game."

"You're playing in the next one?" She almost screeched the sentence. Something heaved in my chest. Was it bad that I liked how indignant she was on my behalf?

"Yep. As I said, not much damage done."

"Will you stop saying that? The more you say it, the less I'll believe it. It's like when someone keeps telling you they're fine to hide that they're not."

"I'll have you perform a full-body check when I'm back."

"That's in five days." We were flying to San Diego to film a promo spot.

"Would you like to do one via video chat? It'll be less fun, but I'm adaptable."

She laughed and didn't stop for a few seconds. "Oh my God. What am I going to do with you?"

"Be very thorough in the checkup when I'm back. I'm warning you, I'll be very demanding."

"You always are, Jace."

"I don't remember hearing you complain."

"Mmmm… that's because I like it. You make me discover new things about myself. Listen, my sister's here. I have to go back to her. Can we talk later?"

"Sure. Tell her hi from me."

"I will."

Despite the pain, I smiled as she hung up.

I couldn't wait to be back in LA. Damn away games. I couldn't believe I had to wait another five days until I saw her. We spoke every day and exchanged texts. I liked sending her short messages throughout the day, even if it was just to share a funny picture, or to tell her what I was having for lunch. Her replies always cheered me up, made me feel as if I wasn't so far away.

I called Val next.

"Tell me nothing's broken" were the first words out of her mouth. The hushed voices in the background were loud enough for me to realize I was on loudspeaker.

"Nothing's broken."

"I told you," Will said. "He's tough."

"Yeah, but that looked bad," Hailey supplied. Someone agreed with her, and I thought it sounded like Paige.

"Dinner going on so late?"

"Landon and Maddie already left, and so did Lori and Graham."

"Next time, call right after the game, man," Carter said. "Val was crazy worried."

"I will. Sorry, Val. Didn't want you to worry."

"Want to have dinner together when you come back?" Hailey asked.

"Can't. I have plans with my girl."

There was a pause, and I imagined my sisters exchanging furtive looks.

"I want details," Hailey demanded.

"You don't deserve to know any details. Payback for your lack of faith in me."

"That was *not* lack of faith. Merely a strategy to increase your chances of success, but hey, I get it now. You have your own style."

"Damn right I do. You still don't deserve too many details."

I moved through the room to the small fridge. We always asked hotels to store ice packs. I retrieved one, putting it on my sore ribs after lying back on the bed. I couldn't wait for Brooke and me to go public. Except for Graham, my family knew, because Hailey had spilled the beans, but I wanted everyone to know. I wanted everyone to see how proud I was of Brooke, and just how wrapped up I was in her.

"But how about the rest of us?" Val pressed.

"Brother, be smart and don't open this can of worms," Will advised.

"I'll take your advice."

"Now you're taking Will's advice?" Paige asked incredulously. "He's outnumbered. I'm with Val and Hailey."

I laughed, giving in to the interrogation. They'd leave me no choice anyway.

Chapter Twenty-One
Brooke

"I hate update meetings," Sheila said, typing furiously on her keyboard.

"It won't be so bad," I told her.

In the days leading up to the quarterly update meeting, it occurred to me that I might have bitten off more than I could chew. I'd renegotiated seven major contracts, intending to walk into that room and impress everyone... but I was running the real risk that three of them might not be finalized in time, which would defeat the whole purpose. Burning the midnight oil on this wasn't helping. The ball was in the other parties' courts right now, which meant I spent half my time on the phone, nudging them.

The bright side of being busy every single minute was that I didn't have that much time to miss Jace during the day. The negative side was that as soon as I had a few spare minutes, or was in bed at night, it hit me in full force. The first time I was going to see him was during the meeting. Nothing was being discussed in detail, but every department presented their highlights, and then the captain went through the team's statistics. Graham insisted this was a way for management and players to remember they were all in this together, working toward the same goal. I thought it was the perfect opportunity to cement my position here.

By the time Wednesday rolled around, I'd managed to get everyone to sign on that dotted line.

When the team stepped onto the management floor, I was certain anyone could look at me and tell how much I'd missed Jace. I gave him a small smile, even though his magnetic pull was almost too much to bear.

Jace was being careful too… right up until we walked side by side into the meeting room. He perused me shamelessly, as if he was already visualizing taking off every item of clothing. I was already on edge, and the way he looked at me felt so intimate that I was burning up on the inside.

He stopped in the doorway of the meeting room, saying, "Does anyone know where the legal pads are stored? I want to take some notes but don't have one on me."

"In the supply room," I said.

"Where exactly? I can never find anything in the supply room. Or can you come with me real quick to show me?"

My heart thundered in my chest. Could anyone pick up on his true meaning? I was going to berate him for this. I could just tell him to go get it himself, but I was sure Jace would find another way to push the issue, and then it would really become awkward.

"Sure. Come with me."

Jace walked behind me in the corridor, but even though he kept a respectable distance, I could swear I felt the heat of his body. I didn't look at him as I entered the supplies room, which was as large as an office. I headed straight to the closet where we kept the legal pads.

I didn't even glace his way when I heard him close the door, even though my entire body fired up in anticipation. I was about to bend and open the drawer when I felt him at my back, his thighs pressing against my ass. Then I felt his lips on the back of my neck. My skin turned to goose bumps as I straightened up.

"We're—"

"Shh, I know we're not supposed to." He brought both arms around me, resting his hands on my stomach.

"That's an understatement."

"Just wanted a few minutes alone with you."

"You could've texted me to meet you somewhere."

"Didn't know how badly I needed you until I saw you."

Some of my annoyance melted, but there was still enough left.

"You could've waited until after the meeting."

"Not unless you wanted everyone to be able to tell just how much I'm dying to be alone with you."

He lowered one hand from my stomach to my

belly, pressing me against him. *Oh, God.* Even through the jeans, I could feel that he was semihard. I stood rooted to the spot, feeling my center pulse with need. He turned me to face him, and I barely had time to register his expression before he brought his mouth to mine, kissing me feverishly. I became more aroused with every stroke of his tongue and was barely keeping my hands in place on his shoulders. If I gave them free rein, I wouldn't be satisfied with just stroking him over his clothes. I'd need skin on skin contact.

"Brooke, fuck, baby," Jace whispered. He brought his lips to my forehead, resting one hand on the small of my back. "You feel so good against me."

"Jace—"

"Just let me hold you."

I mellowed, enjoying the way his strong body felt against mine. A minute turned into two, and Jace moved his lips over my cheek down to the side of my neck, torturing me with small kisses.

"Go back out there before I forget where we are and just take you home. I can't believe I have a game tonight. But I can't wait to see you afterward."

I smoothed my hair and clothes, reality closing in. We were at the office!

"Jace, you can't do this at the office." I crossed my arms over my chest, willing myself to calm down.

"I know. I just…."

"We don't have time to talk now. I need to get back."

"You're mad."

"You think?"

I left the supply room without another word, heading into the meeting room and taking a seat. Jace arrived a few minutes later. Could anyone pick up on the sexual tension between us? I breathed in and out a few times, telling myself I was overthinking this because the pull I felt toward Jace was so strong.

When it was my turn to present my highlights, I stepped in the center of the room and looked everyone in the eye as I enumerated the contracts I'd renegotiated. I explained my reasoning for opening them up in the first place, and the benefits I'd reaped for the Lords.

I looked at Graham and Tina last. I hadn't told either of them about these last three contracts, just in case I wouldn't be able to close the deals before this meeting. They were both looking at me appreciatively, and I suddenly felt lighter, as if all this tension I'd been carrying around since I'd started here had lifted a little. I was part of the team now.

I also looked at Jace, and my heart swelled at the pride in his eyes.

"I have an announcement to make before we finish," Graham said. "I will be taking parental leave for a year. I will come in for the quarterly meetings, but otherwise, I'm taking a huge step back. Tina will be taking over my responsibilities, sending me reports twice a month."

Everyone at the table cheered, congratulating Graham. Tina was beaming as well. She would effectively become general manager in his absence.

When the meeting ended, everyone filtered out of the room quickly, except Jace, who remained seated, typing on his phone. I knew he was really waiting for the room to clear so he could be alone with me, so I stayed back too, wanting to clear the air.

After everyone left, he came up to my seat.

"You're seriously mad at me?" he asked.

"Jace, someone could have put two and two together when we returned. Or walked by the storage room. That was just irresponsible."

Even to my ears, my voice sounded unnecessarily harsh. His gaze turned hard. Wait, he wasn't even going to apologize? If he was expecting me to be fawning all over him just because I missed him and he was Jace Connor, he was in for a surprise. I didn't say anything, merely levelled a glare back at him.

I'd missed him like crazy. Even now, all I wanted was to drag him out of the club and spend my day with him. But he'd also pissed me off.

We both looked at the door at the sound of footsteps approaching. Andrew was back.

"Oh, I didn't realize you were still here, Jace. Everything okay?"

"Yeah. Just discussing some details."

"When do you have a free moment, Brooke? I want to run something by you."

"Jace and I have just finished up everything.

We can talk right now."

Andrew must have sensed Jace and I weren't on the same page, because he told him, "If you still need time—"

"I don't. We're done here."

Chapter Twenty-Two
Brooke

That evening, I went to watch the game live. Every Lords employee was welcome in the VIP box, and tonight, it was a full house.

I was looking closely at the pitch, searching for number eleven. I sent him a quick message to tell him I was watching, even though I knew he'd only see it at halftime.

I didn't know what made him look up as he strode onto the pitch, but I felt as if he gazed straight at me. I couldn't be sure, of course, what with the other thousand watchers, but when that gorgeous smile made an appearance, my breath caught. I looked down at my hands so no one else could see my matching smile. I wiggled my fingers and toes, unable to sit still. I couldn't believe I was having this reaction just because he'd smiled when he'd noticed me, as if I was the only one who mattered.

I was beginning to understand why he inspired Twitter hashtags and die-hard fans. I messaged him right before the game finished, asking if he still wanted to meet. I wasn't sure where we stood after our fight. He'd been out of line earlier, but so had been my reaction. I wanted us to be able to talk things out.

I was in such a frenzy that after the game, I even scrolled through Twitter.

I shouldn't have.

The endless snapshots of Jace were hot enough to make me fan myself, but the captions reminded me of how many women wanted Jace.

I waited quietly in the lobby of the club, wondering if he'd read my message. Maybe he was caught up with his teammates. Or maybe he had seen it and just didn't care to reply. I shook my head, trying to dispel the ugly thoughts and trying not to feel like a fool because I was waiting for him here and he might not want to see me tonight at all.

When my phone vibrated, my hands shook a little as I unlocked the screen.

Jace: Loved seeing you in the stands. Can't wait to make it up to you for earlier.

My knees almost buckled from the wave of relief seeping through me. I couldn't text back fast enough.

Brooke: Meet me in the lobby?

Jace: I'm going to need another hour or so. Coach wants us to go through some scenes now while they're fresh in our mind. Why don't you go home, and I'll meet you there?

Brooke: Okay.

I smiled at the screen before clutching it to my chest. I had it bad for him.

Once at home, I discovered I was nervous. Jace arrived ten minutes sooner than expected, which didn't help with my nerves at all. I was too caught up in the smile he was flashing me to notice that he was carrying a small paper bag.

"What's this? What are you doing?" I asked.

"Apologizing."

My heart gave a mighty sigh as I took the little bag from him.

"You've… wait… where did you get this?" I asked once he'd stepped inside and closed the door behind him.

"Pulled some strings."

"Used your charm to find a store open so late?"

"Something like that."

"Dad wasn't really giving you a speech, was he?"

"No, but it seemed like a good excuse."

I took out the small box of chocolate truffles, immediately popping one in my mouth. It was delicious.

"Jace, thank you." My voice didn't sound quite right.

"I'm sorry about earlier." He tugged my earlobe between his thumb and forefinger, kissing my cheek, then just resting his nose against my skin, bringing his arms around me. "I didn't mean to make things difficult for you. I just saw you and… I knew I wouldn't get a chance to catch you alone after the meeting, and I didn't think it through. Forgive me?"

"You're so good at apologizing. How can I say no?"

I felt him smile against my cheek. "I really did well with the chocolate, didn't I?"

"You didn't have to buy me a present. I love the truffles, don't get me wrong. But I wasn't expecting—"

"Brooke, I didn't buy these because I thought you were expecting them. I just thought they'd make you happy."

Oh, wow. Jace could make me *swoon*.

"They do."

"I've missed you."

"I've missed you too."

He blinked a few times before looking away, but not before I noticed the surprise in his eyes. My heart clenched for him. Why wouldn't he think I missed him too?

"Yeah? How much?"

My next words were unintelligible, because Jace was kissing my neck, torturing all my sweet spots.

"Didn't hear that clearly," he said on a chuckle. I playfully pinched his arm. Jace gasped in surprise. A few seconds later, he lifted me off my feet.

"Jace, what are you doing?"

"Moving on to the second part of the evening. Showing you how much I've missed you."

"Ah, you think you're done apologizing?"

"I'll do both at the same time. I'm a great

multitasker."

"Braggart."

I laughed when he lowered me on the bed, climbing on top of me. He rested his knees at either side of my hips, trapping me underneath him.

"You owe me a full-body check, Brooke."

"Hmmm… I think I'll let you get on with that multitasking of yours first. You have to earn the bragging rights."

"And I will."

He leaned slightly forward, bringing one hand to the top button of my blouse. He drew a circle around it with his middle finger. Heat speared me. I clenched my thighs, as if he'd drawn that small circle on my center. Jace didn't miss my reaction. He smiled lazily as he undid the button, before moving lower. He repeated the motion with each button, until I was so turned on, I felt that I might lose my mind. Once all buttons were undone, he yanked my blouse away, leaning over me to kiss my torso. He seemed intent on exploring every inch of my upper body, skimming his lips from my navel upward on my ribs, then my chest. I was barely keeping myself from writhing underneath him. My center pulsed. My nipples were so sensitive that they were aching at the contact with the silky bra.

I grabbed the hem of his shirt, awkwardly pulling it over his head. I gasped as I came face-to-face with a huge bruise on his left side.

"Does it hurt?"

"A little."

"Should we be doing this?"

"Babe, even if I was covered in bruises, I'd still be all over you."

"Well then, I must reward you for your effort, right?"

I wiggled from under him, barely refraining from pinching him when he gave me a smug smile. I undid his belt, taking it out completely before getting rid of his jeans. I also did away with his boxers, fastening my palm around his erection, licking the tip.

"Brooke," he growled, jerking his hips forward.

I was sitting with my legs curled up next to me, one hand propped on the mattress for support, the other tightly wrapped around him. I sucked in my belly in anticipation when Jace reached down, slipping one hand under my skirt. He pulsed in my mouth when his fingers touched my panties and he realized how ready I was for him. He slid his hand inside my thong, giving me two fingers at once and curling them inside me so good that my vision faded. My inner muscles spasmed around his fingers.

"Babe…." He brought one hand to the side of my head, gently guiding me back until he was out of my mouth. And then he pushed me on my back, positioning himself over me. He tugged down one cup of my bra, as if he was too impatient to take it off, as if he needed me too much to bother with logistics. He pulled a nipple into his mouth, driving me crazy with the gentle suckling.

I reached behind my back, awkwardly undoing the clasp. Jace groaned when my bra came off completely, moving to the other breast. His hips were nestled between my legs. I became painfully aware of the fact that he was naked and I still had panties on when the tip of his erection pressed against the fabric. I wanted him so much that my entire body was aching with need.

"Oh fuck, Brooke."

He reached one hand under my skirt, grabbing my thong and yanking it down, past my knees, down to my ankles. Then I kicked it away.

Jace reached blindly to the nightstand, and one second after sheathing himself with a condom, he rolled us over until I was on top of him. I lowered myself on him in one quick move, pinching my eyes shut. I'd never felt so utterly and completely full. I wouldn't last long. I felt an orgasm already forming, exquisitely and slowly, spurred by the feeling of him inside me, the lashes of his tongue alternating between torturing my nipple and my mouth.

I came so hard that I needed to hold on to him tightly. Jace took control, gripping my hips, moving me up and down his cock, prolonging my wave of pleasure until he reached his own climax. He kept his arms around my waist afterward. His hot, shaky breath tickled my collarbone, but I didn't want to move. I loved feeling him all around me like this.

"I forgot to congratulate you for today's victory," I said a while later. We were cuddling in my bed after a quick shower. I spoke in between peppering small kisses on his shoulder and chest.

"Thanks. Great day for both of us, huh?"

"You could say that. Did you see Graham's face in the meeting? He seemed impressed."

"Everyone was. You're great at what you do."

Jace brought a hand to the side of my head. I looked up at him, surprised to see him frown.

"What's wrong?"

"I know we said we'd wait, but... I'd like everyone to know we're together. I saw how much everyone appreciates your work, Brooke."

"I know. I think they trust that I'm competent by now."

"Does that mean you'll consider it?" He brought me higher, until our faces were almost level.

"I've been thinking about this the entire day. It's important to you, and I think it's time."

He smiled, wrapping his fingers in my hair, tilting my head back slightly. "Thank you. I can't stop missing you whenever we're not together, Brooke. I want to be able to spend time with you when we're at the club too. During lunch, or other breaks. I want to take you out on dates and bring you to Friday dinners. I want you to be part of my life in every way possible, and I want to be part of yours too. I want everyone to know I'm your man."

"Jace, I want that too. All of that. All of you." My heart was thundering in my chest. I leaned in to kiss him. Everything he'd said just humbled me.

I hadn't ever felt so adored, and... safe from

heartbreak. I couldn't believe how much Jace meant to me, how far I'd come from the woman who thought love just wasn't in the cards for her.

I was still a little nervous about Jace and me sharing a workplace. But with this sexy and amazing man on my side, I trusted we'd figure everything out.

Chapter Twenty-Three
Brooke

I talked to Dad first, and then I planned to approach Tina.

My dad took the news about as well as I'd expected. I took him out for breakfast, and after a hefty negotiation where he said a bit of butter wouldn't hurt and I vehemently disagreed, I sprang the news on him.

"Livie, are you sure that's a good idea? I've known the boy for years. He's got a reputation." My dad only used my nickname when he was worried for me. "It's true that his behavior has been different over the last year or so. But I'm going to keep an eye on him. Mixing your professional and personal life is never a good idea. Remember what happened at your old job."

"It's not the same situation."

"I know. But you wouldn't have had to leave your workplace if you weren't close personally to either Noah or Cami. I just want you to be happy, Livie."

I gave him a small smile. The last thing I wanted was to let Daddy down.

Later that afternoon, I was tapping my foot repeatedly as I sat in front of my boss. We'd gone through the agenda for the next few weeks, and now that we'd discussed all the open topics, I wanted to bring up Jace. I was a face-to-face kind of gal, and I wanted to clear the air as fast as possible. I was confident in the work I'd done here over the past three months, and I hoped my personal life wouldn't overshadow my accomplishments.

"Tina, I'd like to talk to you about a personal thing."

"Sure."

"Jace and I are seeing each other. It's not going to interfere with my work in any way, but I wanted you to know."

Tina, who'd been reviewing one of the contracts as she spoke, looked up suddenly.

"Jace Connor?"

"Yes."

"Okay. Okay. Well, there's no policy against coworkers dating at the club, so there's that. But I would've expected better of you, honestly." She pursed her lips, looking at me with clear disappointment.

I was too stunned to say anything more before leaving her office. I had *not* been expecting that reaction. I would just have to buckle down and put twice the effort into everything. I was determined not give her one reason to doubt my work.

I was alone at my desk until lunch, when

Veronica and Sheila returned from an offsite meeting. I'd asked Veronica for a sandwich, and I could have kissed her for joy when she set it in front of me.

"Thanks."

Veronica looked at me funny as she sat opposite me.

"Everything okay?"

"Tina told me about you and Jace. Congratulations."

Something was off, because Veronica looked as if she wished she could stab me rather than congratulate me.

"Thank you. It's not been going on for long." I had no clue why I was being defensive.

Veronica smirked. "Right... those flowers were from him?"

"Yes."

"Smart girl."

"What do you mean?"

"Well, I guess that if there will ever be personnel cuts, they won't let go the MVP's girlfriend and Coach's daughter. The opposite is true for promotions."

I felt my throat tighten. I set my sandwich down, looking straight at Veronica.

"I'd never use my personal connections to get any kind of advantage."

"Maybe, but they'll help anyway. That's just the way the world works. When I applied for your job, Tina said I wasn't a good fit, yet you being

Coach's daughter seemed to do the trick."

"My work experience qualified me." I hadn't known Veronica had applied for my job. "Jace is a player. My dad is the coach. Neither of them has a say in management decisions."

"Except that Jace is Graham's brother-in-law. As I said, smart girl. I mean… until Jace gets bored, at least. We all know he's not relationship material."

I also hadn't realized Veronica had a bitchy side until now.

I hadn't expected her to question my work ethic or warn me off Jace. The surprise over the latter turned into a simmering anger. She didn't know Jace. Not the way I did. Sure, she'd been at the club far longer, but I knew enough about Veronica to conclude that she didn't know any of the players on a personal level.

She hadn't seen Jace at the foundation with those kids, or heard him talk about Milo or even his siblings. She didn't know how strong Jace's love could be, or his devotion. She was judging him based on the image the media had built about him, and it wasn't fair.

For the rest of the day, I buckled down to work, trying not to take it personally when Veronica and Sheila went on their afternoon coffee break without inviting me. Frankly, I'd imagined Veronica and Sheila joking with me about Jace, maybe peppering me with questions as they'd done when I'd gotten the flowers. I'd begun to think of the girls as my friends, but clearly I'd been wrong. For the first time since I started at the Lords, I couldn't wait for five o'clock to roll around.

My temples were already pounding. The only light at the end of the tunnel was that I'd made plans with Jace for tonight. I couldn't wait to see him.

At four fifty-nine, I skidded down to the parking lot. Jace was waiting for me already, leaning against his car, his legs crossed at his ankles, and giving me a big grin.

That grin right there was worth all of it. He held out his arms, and I walked into them without hesitation but only gave him a quick peck on the lips.

"How did it go?" he asked. "If it makes you feel better, I got an ass chewing from Coach, but I was fully expecting him to give me the talk."

"Sorry about that. He kind of gave me the talk too, but that was the easiest part of the day. My boss was disappointed, and my colleagues think I'm gonna use this to advance my career or that you'll break my heart."

Jace jerked his head back. "Babe, I'm sorry. I'll talk to Tina."

"No, she'll come around. I think she was just blindsided."

At least, I hoped so.

"I can vouch for the other thing. I'm not going to break your heart. Not now or ever. It's my job to take care of it. Of you."

I blinked, everything inside me going soft.

"You know what I think?" he continued.

"What?"

"That we need to hurry to Friday dinner. Listen to Hailey and possibly Landon. They'll sing my praises. I'm not sure where everyone else will stand."

"Think your own family will warn me off you, Connor? That's rock bottom, isn't it?"

"No," he said seriously. "It's just that no one's ever seen me in love until now."

"You're in love with me?" I whispered.

"I'm head over heels."

"Jace, you're…." I couldn't say more, because I was a little overwhelmed with emotion. Clearing my throat, I tried again. "I love you. I'm not even sure how it happened, or when. But I do."

He smiled widely, bringing a hand to the side of my face, leaning in for a kiss. I gave him a quick peck before pulling back. He cocked a brow.

"Right. We need rules," I said.

"Rules?"

"Yes. No excessive PDA at the club."

"Define excessive."

"Anything more than this." I pointed between us. Jace cocked the other brow too. "Don't look at me like that. Also, no sex around here."

Jace didn't argue, which I took as a sign that he agreed with me. One second later, I realized I'd been deeply mistaken, because he cupped my jaw, pressing his thumb along my lower lip. "When have we ever kept to any rule?"

Chapter Twenty-Four
Brooke

I'd lie if I didn't admit that I felt a little anxious about joining the Connors at Friday dinner. I'd hung out with a few of them at the foundation but never all together. Plus, I knew from Jace that Friday dinners were a long-standing tradition. No pressure.

"Oh, wow. This is amazing. Like a private park," I exclaimed as we entered Val's yard.

"Maddie, Landon's wife, designed it a few years ago."

The gang was all there, milling inside the house. I greeted Landon, Maddie, and their daughter Willow first, then Will and Paige. Val lived with her fiancé, Carter, and his two nieces, Peyton and April.

I'd feared that meeting Graham in such an informal setting would be unpleasant, but he put me at ease right from the start.

"Brooke, let's make a deal. We're not going to talk about the Lords at family gatherings. We're not coworkers right now. And anyway, you report to Tina."

"That sounds easy."

"It is. This is my wife, Lori. And our daughter, Evelyn."

I smiled at Lori, then couldn't help cooing to the baby. She was adorable. Opening my tote, I retrieved the onesie I'd bought for the occasion.

"Ah, you continue spoiling my kids," Lori said.

"Guilty."

"Milo is still over the moon about all the goodies Jace brought him from New York." She glared at her brother.

Jace held up his palms. "Brooke talked me into it. I'd just gone to buy a few things. She convinced me to buy half the store."

"I did."

"What am I going to do with you two?" she scolded playfully.

As if knowing we were talking about him, Milo sprinted into the house. Jace had shown me pictures, and I recognized him instantly.

"You must be Milo."

"Yes, ma'am."

"Nice to meet you. Hope you liked the player cards."

His eyes lit up. "Oooh, yes. I'm just missing a few."

I chatted with Milo right up until Val offered me wine.

"Chardonnay is my favorite," I told her as she filled my glass.

"We have a system. We drink Chardonnay

when we celebrate something and Pinot when we're sulking," Hailey explained.

"Hey, that's a great system. I might adopt it too."

"We're so happy you came by tonight. We were wondering when Jace would finally man up and bring you around," Hailey went on.

"I heard that," Jace called from a few feet away.

"Pretend you didn't," Hailey volleyed back smoothly. "If this has you up in arms, you're going to be brooding by the end of the evening."

"I thought you were supposed to be on his side," I said.

Jace winked at me. Hailey caught our exchange and smiled to herself.

"I switch sides from time to time. Just to spice things up."

"As a sister should do," I declared.

Val placed an arm around my shoulders, squeezing me in a side hug. "I like you, Brooke. You're just what Jace needs."

I grinned from ear to ear. If there was one person who knew Jace best, it had to be Val.

"We should give her some input on our dearest brother," Hailey said.

Lori elbowed her. "Hailey! We don't want to scare her away."

"Oh, no worries. I'm not easily scared."

Man, I was enjoying this. No wonder Jace stuck to his iron-clad rule of not taking on any social commitments on Friday evening. I sat on the couch surrounded by the girls, who had no shortage of stories to share while we sipped wine.

"Jace was good at giving scares," Lori said. "Remember when this guy showed up to take me to a movie, and Jace gave him the talk? I wanted to be mad, but instead I was trying hard not to laugh because my thirteen-year-old brother was scaring the crap out of a sixteen-year-old."

"Wait a second, Jace gave the guy the talk?" I asked incredulously.

"Yep. It was so efficient that the guy never asked me on another date. He's got an overprotective streak a mile long," Lori went on.

"I would've paid serious money to see this." I was enjoying their stories so much that I would've gladly skipped dinner just to hear more. He rarely spoke about himself, but his sisters' stories were like pieces of a puzzle. The more I heard, the closer I felt to Jace.

During dinner, the girls kept the storytelling to the minimum, but guess who filled in the gaps? None other than Will. "Careful with this one. He's a troublemaker. Spent half my teenage years chasing him and Hailey around."

Hailey rolled her eyes. "And you spent the other half causing trouble, so don't try to convince Brooke you were a saint. Jace and I weren't that bad."

"Interesting. Now you're on Jace's side, huh?" I called her out. "When Will is also throwing you under the bus?"

"I know when to have his back." Hailey grinned before winking at Jace.

Midway through dinner, the conversation turned to the foundation.

"I can always wire more funds if they're too low," Landon offered.

"Thanks, Landon, but we've just signed up a few more donors," Will said.

"Jace and Brooke have been a great help," Paige added.

Jace took my hand under the table, squeezing it lightly. I loved watching his interactions with the family. His tone of voice changed slightly when he spoke to Val and Landon—even when joking, he talked the way I would to my parents.

After dinner, we all went back to the couch area.

"I really need an additional couch," Val commented as everyone tried to wedge in on the existing one, plus the armchairs, ottomans, and two bean bags. I had offered to help her bring some drinks from the kitchen.

"Jace said you bought a new dining table a while ago."

She nodded excitedly. "Yes. Family's getting bigger every year. I knew it was only a matter of time before Jace brought you to our dinners."

"You did? How?"

"I could tell from the way he talked about

FIGHTING FOR YOU

you."

Jace had talked about me? I really wanted to ask for more details but wasn't sure how to go about it without being too obvious.

"Plus… you did speak with Hailey a few times. She's always an excellent source of information."

"I'll keep that in mind."

When we returned with the drinks, I searched the room for Jace and found him sitting on an armchair. Milo was curled up on the arm, and the two of them had their heads together, whispering. They were cute.

"What are you talking about?" I asked, approaching them. The two abruptly stopped talking.

"Judging by their guilty faces?" Will supplied helpfully. "Jace is teaching him to be up to no good."

Milo turned a little red. Jace wasn't fazed.

"Someone has to. Otherwise he might grow up to be a grumpy ass."

Will and I both laughed, especially when Jace earned a dirty look from Lori, presumably for saying "ass." She was cradling her newborn girl in her arms.

I sat with the girls again but gazed at Jace from time to time. After Milo switched uncles, Willow hopped into Jace's arms, first playing with a teddy bear and then falling asleep on his chest. Holy hell! Up until now I thought that Jace working out at the gym was my favorite sight. I changed my mind. Jace holding his niece was now in the top spot. I wasn't sure what was hotter: the way his biceps flexed whenever he repositioned her tiny head when it lolled sideways, or how he kept kissing the top of her head while he and Landon chatted in low voices. Hmm... a tough decision to make, and Mr. Chardonnay was not helping; quite the contrary. It made everything Jace did appear hotter.

After Landon took Willow away, I saw my window of opportunity and headed to Jace, sitting on the arm of the armchair, refilling his glass of wine.

"You're having fun," he said.

"Oh, yeah."

"Anytime you want me to rescue you, just wink at me."

"I don't want to be rescued."

Jace grinned. "The evening's not over yet. They're getting feisty."

"Have some faith in me. I can be just as feisty."

"Trust me, I know... but you're outnumbered."

"That just makes it more fun."

***

Jace

I loved Friday dinners. I always had, even though as a teenager I'd rolled my eyes at Val whenever she repeated that I couldn't go out with my friends on those evenings.

"This is a lovely evening," Brooke exclaimed

when the two of us were alone in Val's kitchen, about to bring a new round of dessert. "And the food is amazing. Thank you for taking me with you."

I wrapped my arms around her middle from behind, skimming my nose up and down the side of her neck.

"I love having you here with all of us. I'd tell you that next week will be less overwhelming, but I don't like to lie."

"You want me here next Friday too?"

"I want you here every Friday, babe."

"You're sure? It's family time."

I wasn't sure if she was rebuffing me or if she was simply concerned. I felt her belly contract under my palm. Every instinct in me wanted to put her at ease, but I had little practice expressing my feelings.

She was incredible. I couldn't believe she'd even brought a present for Evelyn. She hadn't told me anything about it.

"And we each bring our better halves. You're mine."

She whirled around, flashing me a big smile. "That's sweet. Remember that when you have fangirls all around you, okay?"

She'd said it in a teasing tone, but I could see a sliver of unease in her expression. Her ex's betrayal still hurt. I wanted to assure her that I'd never hurt her in any way.

"Brooke, I don't pay attention to any of that. I love you, babe."

I felt her shudder against me, her eyes

widening. I moved my hands from her lower back onto her ass, pressing her against me. She bit my neck lightly, sending a heated jolt straight under my belt. I pulled back a little, wrapping a hand in her hair and tilting her lips up. I skimmed my mouth along her jaw, enjoying the way her breath hitched, her hips arching slightly against mine. Her entire body was anticipating the kiss. I crushed my mouth against hers, stroking her tongue with mine until she rose up onto her toes and wrapped both arms around my neck.

"Been waiting to do this the whole evening," I said.

"What kept you from doing it earlier?"

"The kids."

"Oh, right. Playing the role model, are we?" She made to tickle me, but I caught on to it and immobilized her wrists in one hand, tickling *her* with the other.

"Why did you do that?" she demanded.

"Because you tried to tickle me first. And you seemed to doubt I could be a role model."

"That is absolutely not true."

"It's okay. I doubt it too, but that's why they have a dad. They can be the voice of reason. I'd suck at it, but Landon, Will, and Graham are doing a great job. I'll just teach the next generation of Connors shenanigans. Someone has to."

That had been on my mind for a few years, when I watched Will and Landon with Milo. Our nephew had needed a father figure, and they'd both stepped up to the plate—Will even more so than Landon, who'd been away at the time. Being a dad came naturally to them, but not to me. I'd tried mimicking Landon's style, since it had been effective on me as a kid, without much success. As such, I'd fully embraced my role as the troublemaking uncle, even though I had often wished I could step up to the plate and be that father figure Milo had needed at the time.

"I personally think you'd be a great dad."

"What makes you say that?"

"I've seen you with the teenagers at the education center. You're a good voice of reason when you want to be."

I thought she was just appeasing me, but as the evening went by, she kept watching me whenever I played with Milo or Peyton, and I realized she believed that.

She saw something in me. I hoped that *something* was really there, and not just a wish she was projecting. Scratch that. Even if it was the latter, I would fight to become everything she wished for and deserved.

Chapter Twenty-Five
Brooke

Yes, yes, yes.

I glanced at the email I'd received from Carl Hill, smiling. It had taken him weeks to answer, but he finally had, and Jace would become the face of his company.

This was big, big news. Not only was Jace going to give his entire paycheck to the foundation, but Carl also had agreed to make a hefty donation himself and discuss with Paige the possibility of hiring some of the students.

I sent Jace a quick message to let him know.

It would take a while for him to reply, because the team was on a plane, returning from their away game, which also marked the end of the season. The Lords had finished at the very top and were now moving on to the playoffs for the MLS cup.

I also sent Andrew an email, explaining the outcome. I knew he'd take this in stride, because Andrew was a laid-back guy. Plus, I had secured some other excellent sponsorships for him.

Since I was on a roll, I also wrote to Levi.

Honestly, it had also been the most difficult to find opportunities for him, what with his worsening stats. I hoped his agent was having better luck.

I went to make myself a coffee, needing some reinforcement for the afternoon.

Veronica and Sheila were at the machine too. They fell silent the second they saw me, which made me think they'd been talking about me.

"Hello, girls. Any espresso capsules left?"

"Think I saw a few," Veronica said. She and Sheila went on to talk about some car problems Sheila was having.

"I know a really good mechanic," I offered. "He's a bit on the expensive side but does the job quickly."

Sheila smirked. "Thanks, but I'll stick with mine. Can't afford an expensive one. Unlike some, I'm not dating rich soccer players."

I pondered my next words as I took my full coffee cup from the machine.

"I don't appreciate this attitude. You made your opinion clear, but this day-to-day hazing is beneath you, frankly. Let's act like the grown-ups we are."

They looked stunned, and I rolled my shoulders confidently. I wasn't going to take anyone's crap.

Everyone else in management had taken the news well, but I worked with these two daily. If things didn't improve, I was going to have to do something about it; only I wasn't sure what. I just didn't want it to come to the point where I would dread coming to work.

As soon as the workday was over, I practically flew out of the office. I was meeting Franci at one of our favorite ice cream shops.

She was already ordering when I arrived. I bought a cone with pistachio and cookie flavors.

As we sat down at the round, old-fashioned tables, I tried to gauge her mood so I could tell if she needed cheering up, but Franci was looking better than she had in months.

"You have a new haircut," I remarked, taking in her elegant bob.

"I'm reinventing myself. I have a date later on."

I was shocked. I hadn't expected her to take this step for another few months.

"Don't look at me like that. Date is perhaps was the wrong word. I just need some action between the sheets. I've given up on anything else."

"Who knows? Maybe it'll develop into something more."

She gave me a small smile.

"What?" I inquired.

"Well, just a few months ago, our roles were reversed. And look at you now."

"You're right."

It wasn't that I'd consciously chosen not to have expectations, but between the collapse of my sister's marriage and my own mistakes, I'd been on the defensive.

"Am I wrong in believing a certain soccer god played a role in changing your mind?"

I grinned. "What do you think?"

"I like Jace even more right now."

She'd been a big fan from the beginning, but even more so after she'd officially met him two weeks ago.

"Well, it's a good thing, because I'm completely in love with him."

"I'm so happy for you. Are your coworkers still giving you trouble?"

"They're not the friendliest bunch, but I'm not letting them intimidate me."

Of course, not being intimidated was not the same thing as being on civil terms, and that was what I strived for.

"You always amaze me."

After finishing our ice-cream, we strolled further down the street, passing one of my favorite stores for interior decoration. The picture frames in the window display caught my attention.

"Can we go in there real quick? Jace is coming back tonight, and I want to surprise him."

Jace had a lot of family photos pinned to a corkboard in his kitchen, but he'd mentioned once that he wanted to exchange it for something better. This would fit perfectly.

Franci smirked.

"What?" I asked.

"You've fallen hard for him."

I smiled to myself as we headed inside the

store.

***

Jace

"Looks like someone's waiting for you," the Uber driver remarked when he pulled in front of my house. Brooke was getting out of her car, waving at me. I climbed out quickly, eager to get to my girl.

First thing I did was kiss her hungrily, not particularly caring that we were out on the street for all my neighbors to see. She tasted like vanilla and pistachios.

"I missed you," she whispered, and fuck if I'd ever get tired of hearing these words from her.

"Did you forget your key?" I asked. I'd made her a copy a few weeks ago.

"Oh, no, I just arrived."

Taking her hand, I led her inside the house. A paper bag dangled in her hand. I assumed it was takeout, but once we were inside, she made a come-here motion with her finger, leading me into the kitchen.

"I got you something."

She took out a huge photo frame. Upon closer inspection, I realized it was multiple smaller frames built into one, like a puzzle. She pointed with her thumb to my corkboard of pictures.

"Thought we could put your pics inside here."

"Babe, I love this. Thanks."

"Want to put them up now, before we order

something to eat? Or you want to talk about the game first?"

"You really want to hear about the game?"

"Only if it helps you unwind."

"You're amazing." I placed my palms on either side of her face, kissing her forehead. "Let's arrange the pics."

She was much better at it than I was. I managed to crinkle two photos at the corner before Brooke declared she'd do it.

Since she insisted, I talked to her about the game. Surprisingly, it did help, probably because instead of dissecting everything from a technical point of view, I just laid out why I felt so shitty about it. We'd won, but no thanks to my performance.

"I don't like disappointing the fans or my teammates. Generally, I just don't like letting down the people who put their trust in me."

"Jace," she said softly. "I understand why you feel like this, but everything has ups and downs."

"I know. I just can't help feeling this way."

"What do you think?" she asked once she'd filled the frame.

"I love it."

"I think I'll buy a second one, but smaller."

I kissed her temple. "Sure, babe. Whatever you like. You're doing a great job redecorating this place."

"Redecorating? It's just some frames and plants. Oh, and those comforters last week. And the paintings."

I felt her suck in a breath, and I tilted her head back a notch so I could look her straight in the eyes.

"Brooke, I love that you do all that. You're making this house feel like a home. I don't think I've called a place home since I was a kid."

"Why not?"

"I don't know. Without my parents, the house we lived in just didn't seem right anymore. Then I kept moving, and I think Val's house was the closest that felt like home, until now. So, just buy whatever you like, okay?"

"You should know better than to say those words to a woman."

"I have sisters who love to shop. I know exactly the risks involved."

"Remember that sentence when you come in here one day and don't recognize anything."

"Hey, as long as you don't try to buy me a butt-ugly ottoman like the one at your house, we're good."

Her eyes widened before she playfully shoved me away. "That's it. You just lost your chance at sex for tonight."

"It'll be my pleasure to work my way back in your good graces."

I laughed, pulling her into my arms.

"I love coming home to you, Brooke."

She sighed happily, and I tightened my arms around her. I had no idea how something as simple as having her in my house could make me so happy.

"How do you want to celebrate your victory? And Carl's decision?" she asked.

"We can celebrate however you want. And thank you for making that happen, babe."

"Hey, it's all you. I presented him all facts impartially."

"Yeah, but he wouldn't be interested in the foundation if you hadn't talked to him about it."

"True."

"So, how do you want to celebrate?"

"Maybe we can go out tomorrow."

"Isn't that when you go to happy hour with the girls in your department?"

She pulled out of my arms, wrinkling her nose.

"No. Right now I'm not looking forward to spending time with them outside work to be honest. They're still not over the fact that I'm dating you."

"Why didn't you tell me?"

She shrugged. "It's not that bad."

Everything in her body language contradicted that statement. Brooke was sociable and outgoing, and I knew just how much she valued getting along well with her coworkers.

"Brooke. I want to know when something's bothering you. Even if we can't find a quick fix, we can brainstorm about solutions. I'm your person, remember?"

She smiled, nodding. "I know, but this will pass. I just think I have to grit my teeth through it, you know?"

"That sounds awful. I don't want you to have to grit your teeth through anything. I want to protect you from anything and anyone who tries to hurt you. I'll talk to Graham—"

"No, you won't."

"I'll talk directly to Sheila and Veronica, then."

"Jace, they are my coworkers. I'll deal with it."

This situation was clearly making her uncomfortable, and I didn't want her to feel like she had to make apologies for being with me. I loved her. I'd always been the kind of guy who went with the flow and didn't think much about the future. Now, I not only wanted to think about the future, but I had a clear vision of it. I wanted to give Brooke my last name.

Chapter Twenty-Six
Brooke

The yearly Lords gala event was coming up in a few days, just before the playoffs started. Jace and I decided it would also be a good opportunity to attend it as a couple.

I wasn't sure if it would help turn around the mood at the office, but I loved Jace, and I was determined not to allow anyone to make me feel bad about it, as if I was doing something wrong.

He'd gone solo to the yearly gala event for as long as he'd been attending it. All Lords employees were invited, so I was going anyway, but as a player's plus one, I'd be in the spotlight. That meant I needed a new dress. And since I was splurging on that, why not add some shoes into the mix? Usually I didn't mind shopping alone, because I was the kind of shopper who took forever analyzing every angle, driving everyone else insane, but this time I wanted company. I called Hailey. I liked my style, but Hailey took class and sophistication to a whole new level.

"Rodeo Drive?" Hailey had suggested.

"Ohoho, not ready to empty my bank account yet. Macy's?"

"Done."

Hailey was already in front of the store when I arrived. She was wearing Louboutins, a wrap-around dress, and a light jacket that was appropriate for early November weather. The sun still shone, but once you stepped in the shade, it was chilly.

"How do you walk around with those heels all day?"

"Habit."

"Tell me at least that you take them off while you sit at the desk."

Hailey raised both brows. "That's for cheaters."

"Well, I cheat. All day long. But I wouldn't mind wearing something like that to the gala."

"I know just what you need."

Shopping with Hailey was a whole new level of fun. The girl knew what she was doing.

"I can tell you were a style adviser."

"Val gave me the idea. She'd hired a wardrobe consultant at some point. It was the best student job I've had. Landon and Val were up in arms about it."

"Why?"

"They insisted on paying all my living expenses so I could focus on my studies."

"And let me guess. You disagreed?"

"I didn't want to be a leech. I also hoped that if I showed I could be completely independent they'd stop fussing about me and Jace and, you know, enjoy their own freedom for a bit. Val used to joke that she felt like an empty nester when I went to college. But it was all for nothing. They still fuss over us. I've learned to accept and enjoy it," she finished with a grin.

After choosing a few dresses, I stepped into a changing room.

I'd only just changed into the first dress when Hailey stuck her hand through the curtains, holding a pair of silver strappy sandals that had my mouth watering.

"You're a genius. These go with every single dress we've picked."

"Practice makes perfect. Mr. Louboutin got a lot of my hard-earned money before I learned to buy shoes efficiently."

Somehow I thought that Hailey and I had different ideas about what *efficient* meant. I didn't remember seeing her wear the same pair of shoes twice.

"Girl, this is our winner," Hailey exclaimed when I tried on a dark blue silk dress. It was long, with a generous split up the right leg.

"It is, isn't it? I'm buying it. And these shoes are going to be the new staple in my wardrobe."

"You know, that would also make a great staple in your wardrobe." She pointed to one of the other contenders, a fabulous mix of silk and organza. "Good for cocktails and even evening meetings. It's black so it goes with almost any shoes."

"Oh, Hailey. You're so bad."

"I know, I know. Should have warned you before. I wanted to keep my mouth shut, but that dress is so pretty I just had to make a case for it."

"I've always had a weakness for pretty things."

"Hey, so have I. Don't be so harsh on yourself. Think of it as a present for yourself. That's what I do."

"That sounds like a great strategy. You know how Jace always brags about being the bad influence out of the two of you? He's wrong. The crown belongs to you."

"Finally someone appreciates me at my full value. Can you bring this up at the next Friday dinner? As casually as possible?"

"Yes, ma'am. I'll make your case."

"I wish I could watch my brother's face when he sees you."

***

On the evening of the gala, I was in my bedroom, getting ready, when the front door opened and Jace called my name.

"Still getting ready. You're not allowed to come in my bedroom. I'll tell you when you can come in."

I had yet to finish styling my hair. When I only had a few strands to roll around the hot iron, Jace appeared in the doorway.

"Hey," I admonished. "I told you I'll let you know when I'm ready."

Jace walked in, stopping just behind me and

catching my gaze in the mirror.

"What's wrong with watching you get ready? It's my favorite thing to do, especially when you remove your makeup and I'm the only one who sees you that way."

My stomach did a small somersault at how intimate this felt. How could Jace make me feel so special with such simple words?

I couldn't believe he'd be gone for two weeks after tonight. The Lords had qualified directly into the semifinals for the cup, but they had a few friendly games in between, all outside of LA. I was already missing him.

"I have something for you," he went on, holding a large jewelry box up. I smiled at the Bennett Enterprises logo. I was such a fan.

My heart went pitter-patter as I took it from him. I felt Jace's gaze on me as I opened the lid and stared at the most beautiful set I'd ever seen. Rose quartz earrings, a pendant, and a tennis bracelet.

"Wow. Jace, they're absolutely beautiful. But this is too much."

He placed a palm on my belly, resting his chin on my shoulder.

"You said you liked presents."

"I meant cutesy stuff."

"You're mine, Brooke. Let me buy you things. They make you happy. I like making you happy."

"They're beautiful. Thank you. And they go perfectly with my dress."

At Jace's silence, I became a little suspicious.

"Jace?"

"Hmm?" Stalling. Now I was *a lot* suspicious.

"You knew what color I was wearing?"

"Hailey mentioned something."

"Tell me she didn't send you a picture of the dress."

"No, no. She didn't go that far. She just helped me choose them. Will you wear them tonight?"

"Of course."

"Here, let me put them on."

He made quick work of putting on the earrings, then the necklace and the bracelet.

I held my breath when he placed a small kiss just under the clasp on my wrist. My pulse intensified, and Jace smiled against my skin, feeling it. I shifted my weight from one leg to the other, making my dress ripple. I knew the precise moment when Jace noticed the split, because a low, primal sound escaped him. He slid his hand straight through it, touching the bare skin of my thigh. I whimpered, attempting to ignore the heat radiating from the point of contact.

I lost that battle when Jace lifted my dress and instructed in a low, commanding voice, "Hold this."

***

Everyone dressed to impress at the gala—the Lords' employees as well as the guests. I honestly thought that it wouldn't be a big deal to pose for photographers. I'd been wrong. Despite having Jace at my side, it was an intimidating experience. Flashes came from various directions, and I had no clue where to look.

And then there were the questions. I'd known there would be a few reporters attending, but I'd assumed they'd have zero interest in me. I'd been wrong. Jace's arrival with me on his arm had spurred many questions.

"Who is she?"

"Brooke handles the Lords' sponsorships. And she's my girlfriend," he said proudly before whisking me further into the building, away from the photographers.

"Are you okay?" he whispered.

"My head's spinning. But in a good way. I think." I grinned. "You called me your girlfriend."

"Gotta let everyone know you're mine, babe." He made to lean in, but I took a step back quickly.

"Hey! No PDA, remember? This is a Lords' event. Everyone from the office is here."

A smile played on his lips. "I publicly announced you're my girlfriend, and I don't even deserve a kiss?"

"You got plenty of kisses before we got here. And you'll get plenty more when we leave."

Jace now looked at me with a dangerous glint in his eyes. I was saved by Dad joining us.

"Brooke, you look lovely. Can I steal Jace?"

"He's all yours."

Chapter Twenty-Seven
Brooke

It was endearing to watch Jace introduce me to everyone with pride in his voice. We were not joined at the hip the entire evening, but even when we weren't together, Jace stopped by to bring me a fresh drink, or just to ask me if I was having fun.

"Why did I ever think it was a good idea to come here?" he murmured.

"Because it's the year's biggest event?"

"Yeah, but I'll be gone for two weeks. I'd rather spend this evening alone with you."

I sucked in a breath, speechless.

"I can't wait to get home with you," he went on. He pushed a strand of hair behind my ear, and by the way his hand lingered at the back of my head, his fingertips gentle on my scalp, I knew we were not going to sleep much tonight. But I was all for sexy, night-long goodbyes.

I did a fair amount of networking with the sponsors. It was the first time I'd meet some in person, and I was determined to make a good impression. In my experience, there was no better way to build trust than face-to-face. It was just how human nature worked.

248

As one of the main sponsors, Carl Hill was also attending, and I spent some time chatting with him.

As the event wound down, the reporters left, along with some of the guests, including Dad. It became harder to avoid certain people's eye rolls—such as Veronica's and Sheila's. Tina, on the other hand, had genuine smiles for me, even remarking, "You two look sweet together," which I took as a sign that it hadn't been foolish to walk in on Jace's arm.

When I went to the dessert buffet to replenish my plate, Levi approached me.

"Enjoying the evening?" he asked dryly. I'd caught him glancing at me a few times as if he was preparing himself to pounce, but he hadn't had the chance to speak to me until now.

"It's a nice event."

I needed to be smart about this. I was certain he wanted to pick a fight, and I wanted to avoid a scene at all costs. He hadn't been happy about the fact that more and more sponsors were steering clear of him and that Carl Hill had gone for Jace.

"I saw you schmoozing up to sponsors. Trying to secure some more contracts for your boyfriend?"

"Levi, if you have any complaints and concerns, we can talk about them when you come back from the away games."

"I want to talk now. How about that?"

I looked him straight in the eyes, realizing I

couldn't avoid this. Before I could reply, though, Jace walked up to me.

"Everything all right?" he asked.

"Sure. Levi was just about to tell me—"

"That she shouldn't get comfortable in her position just because she's sleeping with you."

I froze. He'd spoken loud enough for those close to us to hear. Several people had turned to look at us.

"Levi," Jace said calmly, "apologize right now."

"And table this discussion until you return from the games." My voice was firm.

"Yeah? Why? So I can return and find out that a spineless new hire has turned over the best sponsoring opportunities to the player she's fucking?"

I blinked, trying to gather my bearings. Jace reacted faster. His hands were on Levi's collar.

"Don't talk about her like that. You have a problem with me, fine. But you apologize to Brooke. Right now."

"I don't think I'm going to do that. This club thinks the sun rises and sets out of your ass, and I've had enough of being treated like a second-class citizen."

"If you feel like a second-class citizen, it's because your game is becoming worse by the week," Jace said.

Maybe because Jace was known for being the voice of calm and reason on the team, Levi kept pushing at his buttons. "She must be a damn good fuck for you to lose your cool. Maybe I'll give her a try too."

The fight began the next second. I wasn't sure who threw the first punch, but I suspected it was Jace. He doubled over when Levi hit him in the stomach, but straightened up fast, pouncing on Levi again. They smashed into the buffet table, sending several plates crashing to the ground.

I became aware that I was shouting Jace's name. The entire team gathered around us. Two of them grabbed Jace, two Levi, pulling them apart.

Jace was livid. The veins on his neck were bulging and his face was red. To my dismay, I noticed his lip was split. Levi's eye had taken the brunt of Jace's fist.

"What the fuck?" Andrew called out. "Are you two crazy?"

He was looking at Jace as he spoke, which I found unfair, because Levi had instigated this.

"Both of you, go home," Andrew continued. "Whatever this is better be over by tomorrow. I want everyone's head in the game."

Jace took a deep breath. I tugged at his arm, then interlaced my hand with his tense fingers.

He looked down at our hands, squeezing mine twice before asking me in a low voice, "Are you ready to go?"

"Yes. Yes, I am." I was relieved. For a brief moment, I'd thought he'd insist we stay. Levi was holding his tongue. He knew better than to spew the same shit as before with their captain watching.

To my dismay, I realized everyone had gathered around us. I zeroed in on Carl Hill, who was watching the scene glumly. Shit! There were a lot of sponsors attending tonight, and just like it was easier to make a good impression in person, the bad impressions were also more lasting. At least there hadn't been any reporters left.

As we made our way out of the room, out of the corner of my eye, I saw Veronica and Levi talking.

Jace and I were silent as we walked to the car, but once we were both in our seats, I turned to him.

"Are you hurting?"

"I've had worse on the field. Nothing to worry about. I can't believe Levi would have the guts to talk to you like that."

"He's not a fan of me. But I hoped he'd have the decency to sit down with me and tell me his complaints in a civilized manner. I'm sorry this escalated so badly."

"Brooke, you have nothing to apologize for. I love you. Anyone who disrespects you will have a big problem with me. I won't let anyone get away with talking to you like that. Ever."

I smiled, leaning in to give him a quick kiss on his cheek.

"I love you too."

Jace held out his palm. It took me a second to understand what he wanted, and then I put my hand in his. He brought the back of my hand to his mouth, kissing it.

"Focus on the road, Jace."

"I can multitask."

"Uh-huh. Sure you can."

"Are you doubting me?"

"Oh, no. I don't doubt your multitasking skills. They're just very, very specific. They usually involve me being naked."

Jace chuckled, kissing the back of my hand again.

"And as much as I'm thankful for you defending my honor, you shouldn't have hit him. It'll make things difficult for the team."

"The team was the last thing on my mind. I'm your person, Brooke."

"You are," I whispered, barely able to refrain from kissing his cheek again. I wasn't going to be able to stop just at his cheek this time, but I really needed to be patient and wait until we were not on the road to reward him and take care of him.

We'd agreed to spend the night at his house, because he was leaving tomorrow morning. Once we arrived, I went directly to the freezer, taking out some ice. Jace had insisted he didn't need it, but I had a hunch his lips might disagree tomorrow.

He was waiting for me sprawled on the bed, wearing only boxers. Feeling overdressed, I took off my dress, remaining in my underwear.

He scrutinized me for a few seconds before

ambushing me. The man moved so fast, I didn't realize what he was up to at first. He clasped a hand around my wrist, an arm around my waist, and tackled me until I was on the bed, under him. The bag of ice slipped from my hand, landing on the floor with a thump.

He nestled his hips between my thighs. I sucked in a breath when I felt his hard-on press against my pubic bone. Jace smiled cheekily before leaning in for a kiss. He captured my mouth without hesitation.

As we paused for breath, though, I saw him grimace. He tried to school his features, but he wasn't fooling me.

"Lie on your back," I instructed, pointing a finger at him.

He reluctantly rolled onto his back. I picked up the bag of ice from the floor, holding it to the corner of his mouth. I also lowered the cover to his middle, inspecting the general area where I thought Levi's punch had hit.

"Does it hurt?" I asked softly, trailing my fingers between his navel and his stomach.

"No, but you can kiss it anyway." He grinned.

"What?"

"You could play nurse."

I rolled my eyes. "I can't believe I didn't see this coming."

I straddled one of his legs while I held the ice on the corner of his mouth.

"Are *you* okay?" he asked.

"Yes."

Truthfully, I was worrying about the repercussions of tonight's incident. I was sure things wouldn't be easy for me at the club on Monday. I was also certain some of the sponsors were having second thoughts, but I didn't want Jace to worry about that. He had a string of important games to concentrate on.

"You're not going to get much sleep tonight," he informed me.

"Don't you need rest?"

"I'll sleep on the plane. It'll give me an excuse to ignore Levi."

"You think this will affect the game?"

"He's a pro. I'm a pro. My wanting to break his nose won't be good for the team dynamic though. Just what we needed with the semifinal coming up."

My stomach rolled with a bout of anxiety. I wanted to put him at ease, but I didn't know how. Any reassurances would be empty words, since I knew he had a point. Winning wasn't just about technique, it was also about state of mind. I hoped with every fiber of my being that Jace wouldn't resent me for his friction with Levi. I knew he wouldn't do so consciously, but sometimes when things went awry, we couldn't help needing to blame someone, even if it was someone we cared about.

Jace must have sensed my unease, because he rested his hands on my thighs, pulling me a notch closer.

"Babe, everything okay?"

"Sure."

"If something's wrong, I want to know. I can't fix what I don't know."

"Jace, it's just been a crazy night, that's all. Okay, this is melting already. Want me to bring a new batch?"

"Nah, this'll do the trick."

"I think so too. I'll just throw it away," I muttered, on the way to the bathroom. Jace followed me. I stood over the sink after throwing out the bag, smearing hydrating lotion on my hands. Jace kissed the side of my neck, watching me in the mirror.

"Talk to me, Brooke. There's something on your mind."

"Of course, there is. Tonight, didn't go as planned. I'm just processing everything. Like you."

"But something is bothering you. Your muscles lock up when you're stressed."

He feathered his hand on my belly, which was clenched tight.

"I'm just worried about what might happen tomorrow. On the field, at the office."

"Whatever happens, we'll get through it, Brooke. I'm right next to you. Even if I'm away, don't forget that I'm on your team."

I smiled tightly but was unable to meet his eyes. I didn't know how to explain to him that even the thought of him getting mad at me or blaming me for any mishaps on the field caused me heartburn.

He lowered his hand and took a step back. I slipped past him, heading into the bedroom.

To my relief, Jace didn't push more, though I felt him watching me intently all the way to the bed. I was sure he could tell I was more stressed than I was admitting.

Instead of joining me, he went to his dresser.

"What are you doing?" I asked.

"Still have to pack a few things."

The knot in my stomach tightened as I watched him move throughout the room, picking up clothes and socks, stuffing them in his bag. Tension hung between us, and I didn't know how to act or what to say.

When he finally turned off the light and slipped into bed, he wrapped his arm around my waist from behind. I turned around, lacing an arm over his neck and straddling him with one thigh. I wanted to be completely wrapped in him.

"Is your lip okay?" I whispered.

"More than okay."

The room was completely dark, but I felt him inch closer, moving his head from his pillow onto mine. My toes tingled when I felt his hot breath above my upper lip before he sealed his mouth over mine. Jace kissed me, tangling our tongues in a lazy rhythm. One of his hands gripped the thigh that was on top of him, moving it further up. The tip of his cock nudged my clit. I gasped at the unexpected pleasure that shot through me.

He reached toward the nightstand for a condom. After putting it on, he entered me slowly, his thrusts mimicking the rhythm of his tongue.

I felt every inch of him sliding in and out, his hand alternating between nudging my clit and gripping my ass to hold me at the angle he wanted, reaching a place so deep inside me that I cried out against his mouth.

"You're mine, Brooke. No matter what. You're mine, and I love you. Do you hear me?"

"Yes. Yes."

With every thrust, he owned me more, taking everything he wanted, claiming everything I had to give.

Chapter Twenty-Eight
Brooke

Next morning, I woke up late. I scrambled out of bed, showering and dressing at top speed, pulling my hair in a low ponytail that screamed bad hair day, but between being late or looking unfashionable, the latter was preferable. Why had they held the gala on a weekday?

I was about to skid out the door when I noticed a brown paper bag on the table in the living room with a note next to it.

Woke up too early and bought you breakfast. I'll miss you. Have a great day.
I love you.

I grinned as I carefully tucked the note in my bag.

On the drive to the club, at a red light, I checked my emails, and found out that my apartment was going up for sale.

I had one month to move out. I drew in a deep breath, telling myself this wasn't so tragic. Rent elsewhere would be higher, which meant I would be saving less, but it wasn't anything I couldn't deal with.

I arrived at the club in time, ready to tackle whatever else the day had in store for me. My inbox had emails from three of the five sponsors who had attended the event last night, asking me to call them.

A sense of foreboding gripped me. I hoped they were simply looking for reassurance that Jace was not a violent man and last night's incident had been an outlier.

My hopes turned to dust during the first phone call.

"Carl, I suggest you wait a few days before making such a drastic move."

He didn't just want to drop Jace, he wanted to cease collaboration with the Lords.

"Look, unhappy incident or not, I can't associate my brand with any kind of scandal."

"There is no scandal. It was a fight between teammates. All the reporters had left. Only those who attended are aware of it."

"You and I both know these things can repeat or escalate."

My temples were pounding. This could not be happening.

"I understand your concerns. Why don't we discuss this in person?"

"Feel free to schedule a meeting with my assistant. But I'm warning you, I won't change my mind."

He sounded firm, but I wouldn't let this go without a proper fight.

The second call went about the same. By the time I made the third call, I was bracing for another full blowout, but Jeremy, one of the sponsors who had signed Jace on to market their new sportswear line, merely wanted another player for his campaign.

Still, this was a disaster. The Lords could lose two sponsors, Jace three.

I hated it, but I had to let Tina know. Not only did I need her advice, but she had to talk to the head of PR. If news circulated that two of the Lords' sponsors were pulling out, even the sponsors who had not attended the event would start calling us, wondering what was wrong.

Tina took the news better than I expected.

"They are being unreasonable. If this was a case of substance abuse or media scandal, I'd understand, but an altercation between players is not that unusual. Besides, our boys have a great chance of winning the cup. That's what they should care about. You said you set up meetings?"

"Yes."

"I'll go."

I'd lose face with those sponsors if my boss attended a meeting I had set up, but since I was also responsible for this mess, I couldn't argue. And maybe she could do more damage control than I could, even though the last thing I wanted was for her to think I couldn't do my job.

Everyone was on edge, waiting for the game the next day, which we watched together in the viewing room. This game was not part of the playoffs for the Cup. Since the Lords had finished at the top, they went directly to the semifinals. But in the break until then, they had two friendly games with international teams.

We'd prepared a buffet and even bought champagne to celebrate, but we didn't get a chance to pop it open, because the Lords lost. The reporter covering the game spoke to a few players afterwards. Andrew got the brunt of the difficult questions, but when the reporter asked Jace why the team dynamic seemed different tonight, several of my coworkers glared at me. I couldn't meet their eyes.

I called Jace as soon as I left the building, but he didn't answer. I stayed up late, waiting for his phone call. I wanted to soothe him, but he didn't call back.

The first thing I did next morning was to check my phone for any missed calls, but I didn't have any. I had no clue what to do. Call him again? He would be training right about now, since they had another game in three days. I sent him a quick message.

Brooke: I'm sorry you lost the game last night, but I'm sure you'll be back on track for the next round.

I kept checking my phone throughout the day, even more so once I knew my boss had finished the meeting with Carl Hill. She'd had the two other meetings yesterday before the game, but I hadn't had a chance to talk to her about them because she didn't return to the club to view the game with all of us.

I couldn't wait for her to be back. I wanted to clear the air on this topic. She arrived at four o'clock, and I practically bounced off my seat, catching up with her before she reached her office.

"How did it go?"

"I have a conference call I'm late to, but I'll explain everything tomorrow during our four-month review meeting."

"Okay."

A pang of unease made my gut churn. I emailed her to ask if I had a green light to nudge the sponsors via email. My unease flared into panic when she sent me an email later, telling me she'd be taking over the communication with the three sponsors.

I was even more aggravated when Veronica smugly said, "Tina asked my opinion on your performance, and I was more than happy to share details."

I tried to tell myself that it wasn't anything to worry about. Superiors sometimes took matters into their own hands when it came to sponsors, and asking coworkers about performance was not unusual.

I kept telling myself that, but I still tossed and turned the entire night. Jace had called just before bedtime, but I didn't answer. I didn't have it in me to pretend I wasn't worried sick, and I couldn't unload on him now. He had another friendly game tomorrow.

I woke up at the crack of dawn. Unable to go back to sleep, I started with my morning routine, making myself as presentable as possible. I was the first at the club that morning. My four-month review meeting was at eight o'clock, but Tina arrived earlier, and we started right away.

I cut to the chase as soon as we sat down. "How did the meetings with the sponsors go?"

"I managed to talk them off the ledge, in that they'll remain with the Lords, but Carl Hill won't move forward with Jace as the face of the company. Jeremy also wants someone else instead of Jace."

"Oh! But if I try—"

"No!" Her tone was so cutting that I froze in my seat.

"I went back and forth with them for quite a bit, and this was the compromise we reached. I don't agree with their logic, but they've got the upper hand."

"But Jace—"

"Look, I understand you want to fight on Jace's behalf for personal reasons—"

"That's not true. It's just not fair for him to lose out on these opportunities."

Tina was silent for a beat, crossing her hands over the table.

"He did get in a fight, Brooke. It's not like he's completely innocent. It's an unfortunate mix of circumstances, but it is what it is. Now, I would like to move on to your four-month review."

"Okay."

"The club is very pleased with your performance. You're tenacious and hardworking. You surprised us with the renegotiations and the magazine feature for the team. But at the moment, I don't believe that prolonging your contract would be a good idea."

My insides felt glacial. I was stunned, but I gathered my wits enough to ask for clarification. "But you just said how pleased you are with my performance."

"I am. But in the current climate, I think it's best if you don't remain with the Lords."

"Current climate? What are you talking about?"

"Brooke, all three sponsors know why the altercation took place. The sponsors also voiced worries that you might not be impartial given your relationship with Jace."

I felt as if someone was slapping my face continuously.

"Tina, you know that's not how I work."

"I do. But I also know that unfounded as they might be, such doubts and rumors must be cut from the root."

"Even if it means you have to let go of an employee that achieved more than was in her job description?"

"Even so. Veronica also voiced the same concerns as the sponsors."

I struggled to keep my voice polite. "You know she's gunning for my job."

"She has been with the Lords for a few years. I trust her input."

My fingers were numb from gripping the edge of my chair so hard. My mind was racing so fast that I couldn't focus on a single coherent thought.

"My decision is final," she said.

"Does anyone know?"

"Not yet. You're free to take this up with your dad, or Jace, or even Graham."

Apparently, she'd mistaken my question as a threat.

"That's not what I meant," I began, but she interrupted me.

"When you started here, you assured me you didn't want me to give you special consideration just because you had personal connections in the club."

"I meant that."

"Good. I will write you an excellent recommendation letter. You can remain here until the end of the day to wrap up any open issues, and you will also have access to your email for the rest of the week so you can inform all your accounts that Veronica will take them over from you."

I nodded, leaving her office with dignity, even though I was crumbling on the inside.

The day was absolutely excruciating. Because I was not the type to simply say goodbye via a mass email, I stopped by everyone's desk to tell them I was leaving.

I couldn't handle Veronica's smug expression while I explained the intricacies of some accounts to her, but I only snapped at her once. At four o'clock, I left the LA Lords building one last time.

I drove aimlessly around town, not really wanting to go home. I was sure that the calamity of this day would hit me the second I stepped through my door.

Eventually, I got tired of driving around and headed home, stopping by a gas station to buy a few bags of popcorn and chips. I deserved some comfort food tonight. As I'd predicted, I nearly buckled under the weight of today's events when I arrived home.

I was jobless. Tina had said she'd write me a stellar recommendation, but every employer would question why I was being let go if I did so well. This was supposed to be my fresh start, a new chance, and I'd screwed it up. Then I remembered I had one month to move out. Just what I needed. An expensive rent when I had no job.

I felt like I was back to square zero, in the exact same spot I'd been six months ago when I left Cami's magazine. No job and being forced to leave my home.

I was so mad, I could barely think. Mad at the sponsors for jumping to the wrong conclusions, at Veronica for stabbing me in the back, at Tina for not sticking up for me, choosing instead the easier option of letting me go. Most of all, I was mad at myself for getting in this situation.

I wasn't going to lie, I even was mad at Jace,

because if we'd waited just a few more months, maybe things would have panned out differently. If he hadn't gotten into that fight…. If, if, if….

I knew I had to call Jace. I wanted to be the one to tell him about the sponsors. I played with the phone in my hand, dialing and canceling before the connection was made about ten times before deciding it wasn't the best idea to call him before a game. He'd call afterward. In truth, I was postponing the call because I was afraid he'd be disappointed he lost those sponsorships, and ultimately, disappointed with me.

Unfortunately, Noah and Cami had shown me how disappointment could seep into every aspect of a relationship and change it, mar it. I didn't want Jace to think less of me.

When the game began, I moved to the living room, turning on the TV, watching the Lords jog out into the arena. It had been a good call not to tell him about the sponsors before the game. My heart grew a little heavy at the prospect of the post-game call. Maybe I'd leave out the fact that I was fired. I was getting madder about it by the second, and there was a real risk I'd take my anger out on Jace. Besides, he would get up in arms about it, and with the string of games coming up, he needed his mind clear.

Chapter Twenty-Nine
Jace

"Great game, everyone," Andrew exclaimed. We all cheered back. The mood was always filled with an infectious energy after a win, especially one so close to the cup game.

"Meet you in the hotel bar in half an hour?" he said once the bus stopped in front of the hotel.

"Yeah. I'm starving."

A few others agreed with me.

"I'll stop by the bar first and tell them to have snacks ready for us," Andrew continued.

I headed straight to my room with one goal in my mind. I wanted to talk to my girl. Hadn't heard from her in a while, and I missed her. She'd texted me before the game to wish me luck and tell me she'd watch it. I felt ridiculously proud that she took her time to follow the game, because I knew she did it mostly for me.

I sat outside on the balcony as I called Brooke.

"Great game," she greeted.

"Which shot did you like most?" I asked, just to tease her.

"Hey, don't mock me. Now, if you want to know what your sexiest pose is, that I can tell you."

I chuckled. "That's what you paid attention to?"

"Oh, yeah. Gave it my full attention."

"It's good to hear you."

"You too. So, listen, I wanted to talk to you about something."

"Go ahead."

She went on to tell me about some of the sponsors dropping me, which was a bummer. I'd already promised those paychecks to the foundation.

I had plenty of financial backup, so donating was not an issue. But bringing the sponsors in had had a wider scope—they could provide a network for the students there. I should have seen it coming though, after the blowout on the gala evening. Brooke sounded beat about it, and I wanted to put her at ease.

"Brooke, it's no big deal. I'm not worried. With you on my side, I'm sure we'll get new ones in no time."

"You're the MVP. New sponsors will be beating at your door in no time."

Something about her phrasing sounded off. She wasn't including herself in that scenario.

"I can't wait for the championship to be over. We could go on a vacation afterward, just relax for a week or two."

"We'll see."

There was zero enthusiasm in her voice. I

frowned, suddenly feeling off-kilter. Was something wrong with my girl? She didn't sound like herself.

"Fly in for the semifinal on Saturday, Brooke."

"No, I can't."

"Why not? I've looked at flights. There's one on Friday in the evening, or even on Saturday, and another one going back on Sunday in the evening. You wouldn't have to take a day off, and you'd get me all to yourself the entire Sunday."

"Jace... I can't. I'm sorry."

"You already have plans?"

"Nothing is set in stone yet."

That didn't sound convincing, especially since last time we spoke, she'd said she was just planning to have a lazy weekend. I missed her like crazy. Didn't she feel the same?

"Brooke, what's wrong?"

"Nothing, I just can't swing a weekend trip."

"Is this about Levi? Because you won't even see him, I promise."

I'd managed to ignore him, especially after we lost that first game, and I sure as hell planned to keep him away from my girl.

"No, it's not that."

"Then what is it?"

Brooke was usually talkative, yet tonight it felt as if I had to fight for every word, just like on that night before I left. I'd known something was nagging at her but hadn't wanted to push.

Now I thought it would've been better if I

pushed more and got to the bottom of the problem, because it was harder to communicate over the phone.

"Just… a lot of things I need to take care of."

I let out a frustrated sigh, leaning against the railing of the balcony.

"Brooke—"

"Listen, I need to go. Have fun celebrating tonight, okay?'

She wanted to hang up already? I was too taken aback to think about a better way to reach out to her and get at the bottom of this. We exchanged a hurried goodbye. What in the hell was happening?

I was too restless to stay in my room, so I went straight to the hotel bar. Andrew was already there, perched on a stool, eating a sandwich.

"What crawled up your ass?" he asked as I sat next to him. I was surprised he'd picked up on my mood, but then again, I'd been ecstatic just twenty minutes ago. "Problems with your girl?"

"Is it that obvious?"

"Just an educated guess. There's a reason I'm single. Don't want any bullshit in my life."

I respected Andrew as captain, but our views differed wildly where our private lives were concerned. Sure, a few years ago I would have agreed with him. Maybe even a few months ago, but not after meeting Brooke.

What she and I had was powerful. If something was off, I didn't want to ignore it or just assume it'd go away on its own. In my experience, unspoken frustrations and problems only tended to escalate. I needed to find a better way to reach my girl, that was all. I was sure we could work out just about anything.

The next two days blurred into each other. Our schedule was draconian: moving to a new city, working out, watching tapes, working out again just before the last friendly game.

We won, but only by sheer luck. I felt boneless when I returned to my room every night. After the game I was so exhausted that I wanted nothing more than sleep, but I'd promised Milo I'd call as soon as I could, so I dialed Lori's number. The two of them, Evelyn, and Graham were on vacation.

Milo answered. "Uncle Jace, that was *so* cool. Dad said it was your best game."

We went on to discuss every detail. His enthusiasm made me grin. Milo reminded me of myself at his age. He could have probably gone on forever, but I heard Graham's voice in the background after about an hour.

"Milo, please pass me the phone. I'd like to talk to Jace."

"Bye, Uncle Jace. Dad wants to talk to you."

"Great job," Graham said a few seconds later. "Kind of makes me wish I'd been there for a game."

Before Lori and Milo were part of his life, Graham used to travel with the team on important games.

"You can always fly in for the semifinal."

"Nah, and miss out on this? If there's one thing Milo loves more than soccer, it's scuba diving. But we'll make it to the final if the Lords play."

"Way to lay on the pressure," I joked.

"Listen, I wanted to talk to you about the issue with Brooke. I just found out today, because I told Tina not to email me anything except an update report every two weeks."

"What issue?"

"Her contract wasn't extended."

I sat up straight, unable to wrap my mind around that at first.

"Wait... she's been fired?"

"That's what I got from the report."

"Why?"

"Haven't spoken to Tina yet. I opened the report after the game was over."

"I didn't know about it."

Graham said nothing. My heart was pounding. Why the hell didn't Brooke say anything to me?

"Graham, let's talk another time. I need to call Brooke."

"Sure."

The second the call disconnected, I dialed her number. I got up from the bed, heading to the windows. The room at this hotel was on the twentieth floor, and they didn't have balconies up here. I opened one of the windows, but I still felt like I wasn't getting enough air.

Brooke didn't answer, but I called her again, and this time, she picked up.

"Hey, sorry, I didn't hear the phone. Great game—"

"Why didn't you tell me they didn't extend your contract?" I wasn't in the mood for tiptoeing around.

"Oh… how did you find out?"

"Graham received his report."

"Okay."

"Brooke, babe, why didn't you tell me?"

"I just didn't want you to worry about this when you have so many games to focus on."

"Fuck the games, okay? I don't care about that, or the sponsorships. I told you I want to know when something is wrong. Is this why you didn't want to come to the game?"

"I wasn't feeling up to facing the team or for you to have to pick sides. And I'm also regrouping. Sending applications, stuff like that. It's why I don't even want to think about vacations. I also have to find another place to live."

"What, why?"

"The apartment is going up for sale."

"Move in with me."

"Jace, thank you for saying that, but I don't want you to feel pressured into this. I'll find a solution."

What the hell? Pressured? I'd just offered. I rested against the window, trying to cool down. I couldn't understand what was going on and decided to ask about the facts. Maybe then I could piece things together.

"What happened?"

"Two of the sponsors first wanted to drop the Lords completely, but Tina talked them into hanging on to the team. They also voiced the worry that I hadn't been impartial when I suggested you for the solo spot."

"It's my fault for getting in a fight with Levi. Everything else is bullshit."

I realized for the first time why she hadn't come to me with all this: she was mad at me.

"Is it really such a stretch for them to believe that, though?"

"What do you mean?"

"That you kept insisting, and I kept giving in," she snapped.

"Fine, I insisted. But what do you think would have been different if I hadn't?" I snapped back.

"I don't know. I just can't believe I'm not learning from my mistakes."

I felt every muscle in my body go on lockdown. I'd expected her to be angry about my fight with Levi, but this went deeper. For a few seconds, I could only hear her breath mingling with mine. I was afraid of what she'd say next, but she didn't speak at all.

I just had to man up and ask.

"And now you're regretting it?"

"Jace, I want to focus on the things I have to fix. I just don't have the energy for planning vacations or anything else."

She didn't have the energy for *me*.

Fuck, that sounded a whole lot like she did regret it but wanted to spare me from hearing it out loud. And right now, I realized that I didn't want to outright hear it. I honestly couldn't handle Brooke saying she regretted it, or perhaps that it hadn't been worth it.

I was afraid that I was on the verge of losing the woman I loved, but I had no idea how to move forward, what to say to make things better. What if she'd just shut me down?

"And I want to be there for you every step of the way, Brooke. I will be."

"Jace, you have a semifinal coming up. You need your head in the game."

I tried to guess if there was more to her words than she let on, but I wasn't good at interpreting intentions and deciphering deeper meanings.

"Good night, Brooke."

"Good night."

Chapter Thirty
Jace

I went to bed much later than usual. We had an early flight the next day. Even though we had no other game until the semifinal in Miami, our schedule was still packed with interviews and promotional appearances through California. I wanted to drop everything and head back to LA, but it wasn't an option.

When Coach sat next to me, I was fully expecting to get an ass-chewing from him.

"I talked to Brooke this morning," he began. "Just found out Tina let her go."

"I found out last night. It's my fault for getting into that damn fight."

"Jace, you always keep a cool head on the field. In the rare instances I've seen you lose your temper off the field, it was warranted. I might not be close to any of you boys, but if I know one thing about you, it's that you fight for what you want."

"That's true, sir."

He clapped my shoulder. "So you'll fight for my girl?"

"Absolutely."

"Good, because sometimes Livie gets too trapped in her head when things need fixing. After my heart attack, it was impossible to reason with her. But I have full confidence you'll find your way through. It's worth it."

If Dad were here, I was sure he'd give me the exact same advice.

As soon as we landed, I had half a plan. I didn't know how to fix things *with* Brooke yet, but I was determined to fix things *for* her. I planned to make people see just how valuable she was. My girl wasn't going to pay for something that wasn't her fault.

It was still seven o'clock in LA, and I went for my morning run first, planning to wait until eight o'clock to call Tina. But after completing the run in the park surrounding the hotel, I didn't even have the patience to walk back inside and shower. I sat on one of the wooden benches on an alley in the park and called at seven thirty.

"Well, this is a surprise," she said.

"Is it?"

"Not really. I'm surprised you didn't call earlier."

"I didn't know. Found out after you sent the report to Graham. Listen, Tina, this isn't fair to Brooke. I got into that fight with Levi. And the bit about her being impartial is simply not true. She has this scoring system where she weighs everything from game stats to number of existing sponsorships, estimated social reach, and about a million other things."

"Jace, I understand that, but I'm in a tough position. The sponsors were ready to walk away from the Lords. They were skeptical of Brooke's recommendations."

"Was it their request for you to let her go, or was that your decision?" I was tapping my foot against the pavement in a jittery move, struggling to keep my voice calm.

"I was doing my job the best I could. Covering all bases."

No, you were just choosing the easiest way, I wanted to say, but I bit back the words. Lashing out at Tina wouldn't help Brooke.

"I want to talk to the sponsors."

"That's not your job," she said harshly.

"No, but in this case, it's more than warranted."

"Still not your job."

"They changed their decision based on my actions."

She ended up forwarding me their numbers, suggesting I wait until ten to call them. I decided to take her advice. My mind was spinning, and I had so much tension in my body that I wasn't sure even another run would help me release it.

Over the next two days, I spoke to the sponsors in between trainings, wanting to fix this. Needing to fix this.

When we arrived at the hotel in Miami, where

the first semifinal game was taking place the next day, the first thing I did was head out for a run. After, I encountered a surprise in the hotel lobby. Hailey was at the check-in counter.

"What are you doing here?" I asked.

"I wanted to surprise you. Took time off so I can watch the game and see the city. Why are you sweaty?" She took in my jogging attire. "You went for a run in the afternoon? What happened? You only run twice a day when you're in deep shit."

I chuckled for the first time today. No one picked up my moods the way Hailey did.

I made to hug her, but she took a step back.

"Brother, I love you. But not enough to give you a sweaty hug. Go take a shower. Meet me at the restaurant afterward?"

"How about you come to my room and we order something in?"

She blinked, then furrowed her brow in concentration

"Don't turn the lasers on me," I warned.

"You leave me no choice. You give off unhappy vibes. I should have brought Lori and Val with me. You look like you need an intervention. Why didn't you say anything?"

"You just don't have a pause button, do you?"

Hailey grinned. "You already know the answer to that. You're just like me. The good news is, I can get the girls on the phone. We can do an intervention via a conference call."

"Please, don't."

"Fine then, I'll channel my inner Val and Lori. But I need more reinforcement for that than room service. I saw a promising food truck nearby. I'll grab us something and meet you in your room."

"What would I do without you?"

"Probably brood." She patted my cheek, the way she did when I was a kid before pointing me to the elevator. "Shower. Now. You're a bit stinky."

I was in a much better mood as I went to my room. I would've loved to be in LA for the next Friday dinner. Being with my family always helped me see things more clearly. I couldn't explain why, but being surrounded by my siblings always helped me be able to strip the unessential things away and focus on what was important.

Val especially had a way of putting things in perspective, but so did Hailey. Channeling Val... she was definitely good at that. She used to do that all the time when we were kids, thinking she could get to boss me around if she acted more like Val. It didn't work, but it was a lot of fun to watch.

Hailey took her sweet time, knocking at my door half an hour later. She had large paper bags in both hands. I relieved her of them at once, carrying them to the small table.

"I thought you were buying some snacks from the food truck."

"Yeah... I changed my mind and also went to the grocery store. Bought dessert and some wine."

"I don't drink before games."

"It's for me, not for you. Thought I might

need some reinforcement."

"Creative reinforcement for channeling Val?"

"Yep. And for being a voice of reason and dishing sage advice."

"Maybe you won't have to do either."

She parked her hands on her hips. "Sorry to burst your bubble, but you look like you need both. Usually Chardonnay is of great help for inspiration. Didn't find any, but I'll make do with what I have."

"Let's eat before it gets cold."

My sister kicked off her shoes, sitting in one of the chairs with her legs tucked under her.

I sat opposite her, digging into my burrito. I'd pushed myself a little too much during today's second run, and I was starving.

I felt Hailey stare at me.

"You're giving me the laser eye glare again."

"Just trying to guess what the damage is. Will told me you have some problems with the sponsors."

"When did you even find out? That only happened a few days ago."

"You underestimate me. But you don't fret over those usually, so there must be something more."

I shook my head, smiling.

Hailey pointed a finger at me. "That right there is a sad smile. You don't do sad smiles, Jace. What's wrong?"

"Brooke and I aren't in a good place." All the worries I'd managed to subdue during my run crashed into me at once as I spoke.

"Why not? What happened? Tell me you're not getting cold feet because things are getting too serious." The look in her eyes was murderous.

"I'm not."

"Oh, okay."

"It's the opposite."

"Brooke has cold feet?"

I shook my head, doing my best to summarize everything. Apparently, the Connor rumor pipeline wasn't that efficient, because Hailey had had no idea Brooke's contract hadn't been renewed.

"Jace, of course she's probably not too happy with things right now."

"With me. She wasn't happy with me," I stressed. What ate at me was that I didn't know if Brooke was simply mad at me, or if her feelings for me had changed on a deeper, fundamental level. Even if that was the case, I was going to fight my way through all of it. I loved her.

"Jace, a relationship isn't about being happy one hundred percent of the time. That's not possible. Mom used to say that the secret to a happy marriage is working together to get through the moments that don't make us happy. She said that during a Christmas morning when she and Dad were semi-fighting."

"Was I there? I… don't remember that."

"I do believe Will was rolling his eyes, Landon stuck his fingers in his ears, and you were copying him."

"That sounds like me."

"You know, I always thought that after they passed away, you were the most closed off. Even to us. For a while I was afraid you wouldn't open yourself up at all, but then you did—to us, at least. But you haven't really let anyone else in... until Brooke. I see how you look at her, how you're a bit different when you're around her. She makes you happy. Don't let her go, okay?"

"I'm not going to."

I knew what Hailey meant, and I wasn't going to let anything get in my way, much less myself.

Hailey smiled. "So... when were you planning to propose?"

"How did you know?"

"Oh, dear brother, you still have no clue how online advertising works."

"What?"

"When we chose the rose quartz set, you looked up engagement rings on my laptop when I wasn't looking. Guess what kind of ads I'm being bombarded with."

So much for secrecy. "Maybe I just wanted to check how our Bennett cousins' business was going."

She wiggled her finger before taking the dessert out of the bag. "No, no, no. You're not fooling me. Online advertising is way more targeted than you think. If it's showing me engagement rings, it's because you looked at them. And no man looks at engagement rings unless he's serious about buying one. Since I got ads for different ones, I'm not sure if you looked at a lot of them because you were curious or had trouble deciding, but I made a folder of my favorites, just in case you needed a second opinion. I can show them to you anytime. Ready when you are."

Chapter Thirty-One
Brooke

I had never felt more on edge than I had over the past three days. However, I was persistent in my job search. It gave me a sense of purpose. I was also toying with the idea of talking to the sponsors, making an impassioned case for Jace and the education center.

Sitting at my kitchen table, I made the first call to Carl Hill.

"Hi, Mr. Hill. Brooke Derringer here."

"Hello, Brooke."

"Can I take up ten minutes of your time?"

"Of course."

"Just a disclaimer, I am not calling on behalf of the LA Lords."

"I see. You're on a personal quest."

"Something like that. I understand all your misgivings in regard to me, and I respect them. I will be honest, I don't agree with them. I have thoroughly explained the factors I considered when making recommendations, and my decision was based on hard facts. Jace is a stellar player, has built a fan base you can tap into, and is generally very easy to work with. But as I said, I understand you have misgivings. However, I'd love to talk to you about the foundation. They are doing a great job there, and regardless of your involvement with Jace, the foundation is a great PR case for you."

To my surprise, Carl chuckled.

"You know, Jace called me two days ago."

"Oh, so you spoke to him about the foundation already."

"Not exactly. We spoke about you. He was singing your praises, much as you are doing with him now."

Jace had called Hill? Excitement coursed through me, lighting me up.

"As to the foundation, that cooperation is still under consideration. I happen to think it's a great cause."

"It is."

"Sorry to cut the conversation short, but my assistant just informed me about an incoming call from overseas. I need to take it."

"Thank you for your time. Have a great day."

"I will. You too."

Jace and I had texted in the last few days, but it had been mostly short updates, and I feared that I'd driven a wedge between us when I lashed out at him. I was very sorry for that. I hadn't meant to, but I'd been upset and so very stressed about having to deal with everything imploding around me.

The call to Jeremy went in the same fashion— Jace had spoken to him too. I couldn't ignore the hope blooming in my chest any longer.

I was still waiting on Tina's recommendation. When I received the first email from a prospective employer asking me for it, I told myself I'd give her another day before calling. But now I'd just received a second email telling me they wanted to see the recommendation from my most recent job, so I had no other choice but to call her. I was sure she was backlogged. Tina might have many faults, but she wouldn't withhold this on purpose.

She answered after a few rings, and it was clear she was driving and had put me on loudspeaker, because I could hear traffic sounds.

"Brooke, hi! I'm on my way to a meeting now. Can I call you back later?"

"Oh, sure. I just wanted to drop you a quick reminder about the recommendation."

"Crap. I forgot to send you that. It's just... I've talked to Jace, and then I started thinking. Well, procrastinating would be the more appropriate word."

"Jace spoke to you? I didn't ask him to, you know."

"Oh, he made that clear. He's very fond of you."

"He said that to you?"

That seemed very unlike Jace.

"No, he roasted my ass for being unfair to you. I just put two and two together."

I grinned to myself. He'd spoken to Tina and each of the sponsors, defending me. That was... well,

I couldn't describe what I was feeling even to myself.

"I'll send you that recommendation tonight, okay? Really have to go."

"Thanks."

I felt a spike of adrenaline when the line disconnected. I needed to talk to Jace *right now*. He could be training, though, so I sent him a message instead.

Brooke: Spoke to Carl, Jeremy, and Tina. Thank you for talking to them. It means a lot to me.

He called me three seconds later.

"Hey," I said breathlessly into the phone as I leaped to my feet, walking from my kitchen to my living room.

"Hey!"

"Thanks for talking to Tina, and the rest."

"I told you I'm your person."

"How are you? Prepared for tonight?"

"We're all good to go."

He sounded strained. My stomach seemed to constrict into a tiny ball that leapt to my throat. I sat on the steps of the porch, resting my elbows on my thighs.

"Jace, you sound… off. What's going on?"

Silence. He was hesitating. I walked out the back porch, steeling myself.

"Did you mean that? About regretting us?"

I felt struck dumb. "I said that?"

"Don't remember the exact wording."

"Of course, I don't regret us."

"I know I kept pushing, but it was just because I couldn't be without you, Brooke."

"You're—"

I broke off at the sound of various voices in Jace's background. He wasn't alone anymore.

"Coach wants to talk to us."

I thought I heard a familiar female voice among all the male ones.

"Is Hailey there?"

"Yes. She took off a few days to watch the games. Will you watch tonight?"

"You bet I will. I'll be cheering for a certain handsome MVP."

"Hopefully the Lords'."

"Haven't made up my mind yet."

"I miss you, Brooke."

"I miss you too."

I was smiling from ear to ear as I finished the call. My heart was beating so fast that I actually pressed my palm on my collarbone, trying to calm down a little and regulate my breathing.

Returning to my laptop, I intended to continue with the tasks I'd planned for today, then decided to change my plans.

I'd been so busy licking my wounds and fearing that Jace would think less of me and that it would in turn would taint or lessen his love for me that I somehow led him to think I regretted our relationship.

Never.

When I first met Jace, I was not ready for

him. I'd been defensive, still putting myself together, almost convinced I wouldn't be able to dream again. But now I was ready for him and his love.

I opened up an airline website in my browser. I was flying out to Miami. Tickets were relatively inexpensive because there were many flight options.

I could take care of everything else later. The recommendation could be emailed from everywhere. I could answer my phone from Miami as well as I could from here.

I booked a ticket on the first plane, which gave me just enough time to reach LAX. It was morning, and the game was in the evening. With the five-hour flight time and the three-hour time difference, I could make this work, but just barely. There better be no delays.

I'd never packed so fast. A few pairs of jeans and T-shirts. Toiletries. I'd nearly forgotten my nightgown, though I was fairly certain Jace wouldn't have minded. When I texted Franci to cancel our TV date tonight, she cheered for me.

Franci: Yes!!! Go get your man.

Once I landed in Miami, I discovered that several other passengers from my flight were there to watch the game, but I didn't find anyone to share a cab with because they were staying at a different hotel. I checked the time as I hopped into an Uber, barely refraining from urging the driver to go faster.

I knew the team's schedule. They were going to leave from the hotel to the stadium in half an hour, and I wanted to meet Jace before. I wanted him to know I was here.

I tapped my foot on the floor of the car, biting the inside of my cheek. When we reached the hotel, I practically jumped out of the car, slinging my backpack over one shoulder.

Once I was in the lobby, I realized I didn't know the number of Jace's room. Reception wasn't going to simply tell me without calling him first, and that would ruin the surprise.

Then I remembered Hailey was here too, and I called her.

"Great to hear from you," Hailey said.

"Hailey, hi! So… um, I'm in the hotel where you and the team are staying. Could you tell me what room Jace is staying in?"

"You're at the hotel?"

"Yes. In the lobby."

"Ooooh, I'm in the lounge. Wait, I'll come meet you."

"Is Jace with you?" I asked in a panicky voice. "I want to surprise him."

"Just me."

Hailey joined me a few seconds later, pulling me into a hug.

"So you're here to surprise my brother, huh?"

"Yes."

When she let go, I thought Hailey's smile was a little smug—or knowing, perhaps?

"Hailey, is there something you want to tell me?"

"What? No, not at all. I'm just glad you're here. Jace will be very happy," Hailey said, a little too quickly. Something was definitely going on. At any rate, I didn't have much time for guessing games now. I wanted to catch up with Jace before the boys left for the stadium.

"What's his room number?"

"2012."

"Thanks. I'll see you later."

I darted toward the elevator, impatiently pressing the button, even though someone else had already pressed it.

When the elevator doors finally opened, I was the first to dart inside. I was the only one going to the twentieth floor. I tried to keep my composure while walking toward Jace's room, but my heartbeat was so erratic that I had trouble inhaling properly.

By the time I knocked on his door, my entire body was on edge.

"I'll be right out," Jace called. "Just a minute."

I knocked again and heard Jace sigh in frustration, then the sound of footsteps walking toward the door.

When he swung it open, his expression was serious, but then the grim set of his mouth gave way to an enormous smile. He held his arms open, and I walked right into them. He pulled me inside the room, and I dropped my backpack to the floor, lacing my hands at the back of his neck. Jace kissed me hard.

"Why didn't you tell me you were coming?"

"Wanted to surprise you."

He bit my bottom lip lightly, sending a searing hot impulse through me.

"I don't like us fighting," he whispered against my lips. "But if it means I get surprises like this one, I could get used to it...."

He feathered his lips along my jawline, up to my cheek. He skimmed his hands from my hips up to my back, then to my ass, as if he wanted to touch me everywhere at the same time. I was content just to be in his arms again.

"I've missed you, Brooke. There are a million things I want to tell you."

"We'll have plenty of time tonight."

"You're sleeping in my room." His tone was firm, bossy.

"Well, I haven't booked a room for myself, so that works for me."

His phone buzzed, and Jace grimaced.

"That would be Andrew, reminding me I'm late."

I clutched at his shirt, knowing that he had to leave but unwilling to let go. Just a few more seconds. Jace kissed me again, tangling our tongues fiercely, making me shudder.

"Hailey has my VIP tickets," he said afterward.

"I'll talk to her. I already ran into her in the lobby. Now go, before Andrew storms inside here."

"I'm glad you're here, Brooke. It means a lot to me."

"Go get them."

After Jace left, I hopped in the shower. The players had to be there early, but I still had plenty of time left. I texted with Hailey so we could share an Uber to the stadium.

I had come prepared with the jersey I'd bought a while ago. I put it on, ready to cheer for my man. I pulled my hair in a ponytail and smeared on some eye shadow and lipstick, though I was sure I'd chew off the lipstick by the time the game was over. Jace didn't seem as if he ever cared if I was wearing makeup or not, but I wanted to look impeccable, especially after rushing to his room looking less than put together.

I descended to the hotel lobby a little too early, but Hailey was there as well. She looked impeccable, in high heels and a beige dress reaching down to her knees and hugging her figure. Not many people could pull off walking into a stadium looking like that, but Hailey wasn't just wearing a style. She owned it.

"Jace is often late, and you're always early. Is there a correlation?"

"I think he was always late just to spite me." Hailey grinned, taking in my clothes. "Nice. Haven't thought about wearing a jersey."

"Hailey, you look as if you've never worn a jersey in your life."

"I did when I was a kid. Up until Val gave me the fashion bug. Started to 'borrow' her clothes when I was fourteen. She pretended not to notice, but then all her clothes would mysteriously find their way back from my room to hers."

"Well, Val was a great sister. I fought with mine over clothes on a weekly basis." I was too excited to stay put. Apparently, so was Hailey, because she suggested we could leave already.

"Yeah, let's go. Who knows how long it'll take us to get inside."

Since we had VIP tickets, it took no time at all. Even after buying drinks and snacks, we still had thirty minutes until the game began.

The players were already out on the arena, performing their warm-ups. The stadium was smaller than the Lords', and because our tickets were front row, I had no trouble catching Jace's attention when he looked up.

I turned around briefly so he could see the number, and when I faced him again, my heart stuttered at the pure joy on his face. I caught Hailey's expression as I sat down. There was that knowing smile again.

"You make him so happy."

"It's not hard to do that. He's always such a positive person."

"I've known him for far longer than you have. Trust me, there's happy, and then there's this." She pointed toward the field. "I knew it. You're—"

She stopped abruptly, pressing her lips together. Ah-ha. My instincts had been spot on. That knowing smile could only mean one thing. Hailey was keeping secrets.

"I'm what?"

"Great. You're great."

"Hailey, you honestly don't think you're fooling me, right?"

"My lips are sealed. And you can tell Jace I told you nothing."

"Nothing about what?" I bluffed.

"Nice try."

Wow. Hailey was getting better at keeping secrets. I didn't have time to ponder creative methods that would lead to secret spilling, because the game began. I'd never seen a game quite like this one.

Andrew scored at the seventy-five mark, and then Jace at the eighty-first. I had no clue who was cheering harder for Jace: Hailey or me. I was pretty sure I wasn't going to be able to speak the next day. Adrenaline coursed through me for the rest of the game, and even after it was over.

"Shall we go to their locker room?" I shouted over the sounds of the crowd.

"It's best if we head straight to the hotel now," Hailey said. "It'll be madness outside if we stick around until the team leaves."

"You're right."

I was just too excited to jump right back into Jace's arms. On second thought, perhaps it was best to wait until we were at the hotel to jump him, or everyone was going to witness some PDA.

Chapter Thirty-Two
Brooke

Leaving the stadium wasn't as easy as getting inside had been. Everyone was rushing out at once, and finding a cab was a nightmare.

In the end, we only arrived at the hotel about ten minutes before the team. The bar and restaurant area had been closed off. Only the team and their family and friends were allowed inside, which meant the celebration was a private affair.

Even so, quite a few of the other hotel guests were fans who'd attended the game and were now in the lobby, waiting with jerseys and hats ready to be signed.

Hailey and I went straight inside the restricted zone, waiting at the bar along with a few other friends and relatives of the players.

When the team finally came inside the private area, everyone clapped, then Jace made a beeline straight for me. He took one look at my jersey before kissing me. He tasted like Gatorade and mint, and by the way he pressed his hand on my lower back and the lazy strokes of his tongue, I could tell we wouldn't linger at this party for long.

Jace's kiss consumed me. I wasn't aware of anything except him: his mouth exploring me with growing urgency, his hand pressing possessively at the small of my back.

Belatedly, I realized someone was clearing their throat.

"Hello, brother. I'm doing all right. Thanks for asking," Hailey said. We pulled apart, chuckling. Jace kissed his sister's forehead.

"Thanks for coming to the game, brat."

"That's my repayment? I come all the way here so you can call me brat? You were fabulous."

The two of them went on to discuss some of the crucial moments of the game. I joined in, trying my best to hide my smile when Jace rested his hand at the small of my back, slipping the tip of his thumb in the waistband of my jeans.

"Let's get out of here," he whispered once Hailey moved away to speak with a guest.

"Jace! People want to see you at the celebration."

He made a small, guttural sound at the back of his throat. His eyes were hard and determined, and I was ready to bet he'd just take my hand and lead me out of the room, but to my surprise, he didn't insist.

His grip on me just grew a little more possessive. Especially after he left me alone for a few minutes to get some drinks and a guy started chatting me up. Upon his return, Jace glowered at the guy.

"Oh, my bad. Didn't know she was taken," the guy muttered before scurrying away.

"I leave you alone for a few minutes, and someone's already replacing me."

"No one can replace you, Jace. You're one of a kind."

He grinned. "I like what I'm hearing."

"I was trying to find a polite way to work you in the conversation, but your way of bulldozing over him works too."

Guess who didn't appreciate Jace's bulldozing manners? Hailey.

She lifted a brow when Jace cockblocked a guy offering to buy her a drink.

"Jace, I'm a grown-ass woman."

"And that is Andrew's cousin. I know for a fact he's a man-whore."

"Right. So, you would've reacted differently if, say, a guy from the team was hitting on me?"

Jace stared at her. "Hailey, these guys are not exactly saints."

She rolled her eyes before glancing at me. "See what I have to put up with?"

"Yes. But not to worry, I'll find a way to change this. Might take me some time, but I'm persistent."

Jace blinked.

"Little brother, dial back that big brother attitude… or our deal is off."

I looked between them, eager to know more.

"What deal?"

Jace shook his head. Whatever game they were playing, it was certainly one for Hailey and zero for Jace.

***

Jace

I only wanted one thing: to take my girl upstairs and show her just how happy I was that she'd flown here. I was happy about the win, of course, but all that was just background noise.

I'd planned to only stay at the party long enough not to be considered impolite, and according to my calculations, that period of grace expired now. I pulled Brooke closer to me. Her breast pressed into my side. When I began to lazily stroke the base of her spine with my thumb, she straightened up, licking her lips.

"Brooke, I want to be alone with you."

She shuddered deliciously against me, giving me a small nod. I took her hand, leading her out of the restaurant, through the lobby, and into the elevator. I laced an arm around her shoulders once the door closed, pulling her mouth up to me, giving her a taste of what was about to come.

Brooke sighed into my mouth, clutching at my shirt. When the doors opened, I pulled back, smiling down at my girl, who pouted, tugging at my shirt to bring me closer again.

"This is our floor, babe."

"Oh."

We almost jogged to the room, and the second we were inside, I kissed the side of her neck, pulling the elastic band from her ponytail. Her hair spilled down her back, the strawberry scent of her shampoo wafting around me.

"Thanks for flying here. It means a lot to me."

"I'm sorry if I gave you the impression I was regretting anything. I wasn't. I'm not. I just… well, I was afraid you'd begrudge me for what happened with the sponsors, that you'd be upset. I've…well, I know from experience that when things go wrong professionally, that tension takes over the relationship, driving a wedge, so…"

"Brooke. That would never happen. Ever. Do you understand?"

She nodded. "I'm sorry for lashing out at you. I was taking out my frustrations and fears on you, and it wasn't fair."

I whirled her around.

"You were right, though. I kept pushing."

"Well, if you hadn't, who knows where we'd be now. Maybe we'd still hang around as friends, having movie nights."

"Babe, there's no way I would've lasted that long without making a move on you." She attempted to look down, but I cupped her face with both hands. "I'm sure we're going to have ups and downs, but I'll love you through all of that. All I ask is that you love me back."

"I will. I *do* love you."

"You're everything I didn't know I needed."

Her breath caught, and she looked up at me with a dreamy expression.

Before Brooke entered my life, I hadn't

understood my brothers when they claimed that meeting their women had turned their worlds upside down. But now I did. I'd work hard to see that look in her eyes every single day.

I couldn't stand not kissing and not touching her anymore. After taking off her jersey, I kissed her collarbone, starting from the right shoulder, moving my lips slowly, enjoying her reactions to me: her breathing becoming more labored, the goose bumps popping up on her skin, the light flush on her neck. All for me. When I cupped her bra, she rolled her hips, humming my name. I wanted to explore her for days.

I drew my hand slowly down her belly to the fly of her jeans. She sucked in a breath when I opened it, and I slipped my fingers inside her panties, nearly bursting in my pants when I felt how ready she was. I didn't go slow after that. I yanked away her jeans while she worked at ridding me of my clothes too. When we were naked, I kissed her long and deep until I felt her quiver lightly. Then I cupped her ass with both hands, lifting her up. I smiled against her mouth when she wrapped her legs around my middle.

Then she lowered herself just a little, so the tip of my cock was wedged between us, and a deep groan rumbled at the back of my throat.

I laid her on the bed but didn't join her, despite her tugging at my hand.

"I want to look at you, Brooke. Lying here, waiting for me. Wanting me."

I placed one knee on the mattress, dropping a kiss on her right ankle.

"I want to kiss every inch of you."

"Jace," she protested.

"And I will do it."

I kissed up her right leg before focusing on the other one. I could feel her becoming more impatient. She was fisting the bedsheet, or my hair whenever I was in her reach. Needing more access, I straddled her. She gripped my shoulders, bringing me down on her. I skimmed the tip of my nose down her collarbone, tracing the same path up with my lips. She swallowed, rolling her hips, gasping when the tip of my erection nudged her clit.

"Fuuuuck, Brooke."

My muscles locked down as I pulled back to slide on protection before losing my head completely.

Then I entered her slowly, feeling her pulse around me. Her eyes flared wide, and her grip on my shoulders was crushing. She sensed this intense feeling of togetherness too. I moved slowly in and out. I wanted to be entwined with her so deeply that our connection could never be broken.

I kissed her feverishly until I slid both my hands under her ass to lift her up. Pushing my forehead into the pillow for leverage, I pressed my cheek to hers, wanting as much connection as possible.

On a gasp, Brooke clenched her thighs, making it almost impossible for me to move, and then I felt her unravel. I held back my own climax for as long as possible, but when she tipped her head between us, muffling her sounds of pleasure against my chest, I was a goner.

I was constructing a small plan at the back of my mind, but I kept it a secret for now, even though we didn't sleep at all. We talked about everything, simply enjoying being with each other.

Chapter Thirty-Three
Brooke
Three weeks later

A few weeks after the game in Miami, Tina called to ask if I was still interested in working at the Lords. Karma had worked quickly. Veronica had not lasted ten days in my job. She'd quit, claiming it was overwhelming. Tina had concluded that she'd jumped the gun, and she'd like to have me on the team.

I politely turned her down, because I didn't think going back was the best option. Besides, I'd accepted a job I couldn't wait to start back in the fashion industry, as a VP of business development for a European shoe designer who wanted to expand in the US.

Karma had also worked on Levi. At the end of the season, he was ranked last in terms of performance, which led to him being released from the team.

Jace was officially the MVP for this year, which had made Carl and Jeremy change their mind *again*. They were moving forward with Jace, especially once the Lords won the MLS cup.

They also decided to go through with their respective cooperation with the education center.

"I'm so excited about the job," I told Jace.

"You'll do great. I'm happy for you, but I'll see a lot less of you."

"Jace. You only saw me during lunch breaks, at most."

"Don't forget the gym."

"Oh, yeah. That too. I'll be slacking off without a sexy view to motivate me."

"We can set up a home gym. I'm always willing to drop my clothes to motivate you."

"Hmm... now there's an offer I can't refuse. Besides, I have to make sure you keep in shape until the season starts again, Mr. MVP."

The season would begin again in March, which meant Jace had a lot of free time over the next few months. The only thing he had to take care of was not getting out of shape.

We were in his living room, sprawled on the comfy carpet. I was lying on my belly, reading a book. Jace seemed to thoroughly appreciate the view. He was expertly massaging the soles of my feet.

Decidedly, life couldn't be any better. I'd moved in with him right after the semifinal, and the man was forever pampering me, but today was different.

I had no idea why he was being so generous as to dish out foot rubs, but I wasn't about to look a gift horse in the mouth.

Jace moved his hands from my feet to my

calves, unexpectedly leaning in to bite my ass gently. I yelped, nearly elbowing him in the head.

"What are you doing?" I asked between giggles.

"What does it look like?"

"You're shamelessly attacking me. But I think what you're really after is getting me naked." Which really wouldn't involve too much effort since I was only wearing a dress.

"Babe, if I wanted to get you naked, I'd be carrying you into the bedroom over my shoulder by now."

He kissed up my exposed back slowly, alternating between chaste and open-mouthed kisses. I shuddered every time I felt his tongue. No matter what Jace said, he had a terrible track record of jumping me when I was showing so much skin. My track record of resisting him was equally terrible. I waited with bated breath, trying to anticipate his next move, but he simply whispered, "I love you, Brooke."

He rested on one elbow next to me, keeping an arm on my back. I pushed away the book, turning to face Jace, resting on an elbow as well.

"I love you too."

"I have something for you." His voice sounded a little thick.

"A gift?"

He smiled mysteriously, then pulled a little jewelry box from his back pocket. I grinned, sitting up and rubbing my hands in excitement. Maybe it was a set of earrings.

Jace sat up as well, watching me with warm eyes. He was strangely silent. When I opened the little box, I sighed. Jace hadn't gotten me earrings. He'd gotten me an engagement ring. A round diamond with small aquamarines surrounding it. I couldn't breathe for a few seconds, captivated by the beauty of the ring and everything it meant.

"Brooke, I think I fell in love with you long before I realized it. You started out by only wanting to be "friendly" with me, and before we knew it, you were my person, and I was yours. Will you marry me?"

He was close enough that I could feel him holding his breath. I smiled, nearly shouting, "Yes."

Jace gave me a broad, wicked smile, but his hands were a little tense as he retrieved the ring out of the box, taking my right hand.

"Left hand," I said hoarsely. "Engagement rings go on the left hand."

He laughed, switching hands. I loved seeing him this happy, to know I was the reason for it. I sat in his lap, lacing an arm around his neck, keeping my left hand between us, so I could admire the ring properly.

"It's beautiful. I love you."

He kissed my forehead, then my temple, before skimming his lips to my mouth.

"I can't wait to call you my wife."

"First I'll be your fiancée."

He brought his hands to my hips, gripping

them rather possessively. "How attached are you to that title?"

"I'm rather fond of it. I'd like to keep it for a while. Is there something you want to tell me?"

"Just that I'd like to get married as fast as possible. What do you say?"

Just a few months ago, I'd been honestly convinced I wouldn't be able to let anyone in again, but Jace made me fall head over heels. He moved his palms from my hips to my waist. I loved feeling those strong biceps flex under my hands.

"Yes. Yes, all the way."

I grinned. Yes, this was Jace Connor. He went balls to the wall whenever he wanted something, and he wanted *me*.

Epilogue
Brooke

We broke the news to the Connors at the next Friday dinner. We arrived a little late at Val's house, so the gang was already sitting at the table, chatting and eating.

Jace held up my hand for everyone to see.

"Wow, congratulations," Val exclaimed. "I can't believe we didn't get wind of this."

Hailey was flashing that smug smile again. I didn't miss it, and neither did Val.

"You knew," Val accused. When Hailey nodded, Val glared at Jace.

"Hey, I didn't mean to tell her. I just made the mistake of looking up rings on her laptop."

"Ah, this was the secret you mentioned at the hotel party," I said, finally getting it.

Jace nodded gravely.

"I know I don't have the right to, but I feel kind of betrayed that you kept his secret," Val said.

"Me too," Lori added.

Hailey smirked. "I'm aware of my faults, and I've always strived to improve them. This one just… took a while longer."

"We've also set a date," Jace said gleefully, squeezing my hand under the table. I squeezed it right back, feeling an army of winged creatures flutter in my belly.

"We want a summer wedding."

"This upcoming summer?" Lori clarified, looking slightly alarmed. I nodded, which prompted her to take her iPad out.

"Um… Lori, we don't want anything big," I tried while Lori pulled up a calendar.

"Everything still needs to be perfect," she explained.

Graham kissed her cheek. "You're very good at pulling weddings together on short notice. Remember how you organized everything for Amber and Matt in four weeks? You have more than six months now."

"Yes, but this is my brother." She looked up from her iPad, between the two of us. "We need to set up a meeting to discuss everything."

Jace glanced at Landon and Will. "Help. How do I make her dial it down a notch?"

Will held up both palms. "You're on your own, brother."

"I'll give you tips later," Landon said, earning a glare from Lori.

"Wow. Hailey's learned to keep secrets, and Jace is getting married before Will and me," Val exclaimed. "This day is just full of surprises."

Will shook his head, hiding a smile as he handed Hailey a five-dollar bill.

"What was the bet?" Jace asked immediately.

"She insisted you'd set the date first. I bet on Carter and Val. Wait a second! Hailey, did you already know about the ring when we made the bet?"

"Of course not. I'm not a cheater." She pocketed the money with a wicked smile.

After everyone had their bellies full, Lori pulled me and Jace to one side. "Want to look at some wedding stuff online?"

"Sure," I said.

"I'll go set up everything on my laptop."

I winked at Jace, placing a hand on his arm. "No worries. I've got this."

"I think I love you even more right now. I just want you to have my last name, babe. Everything else is up to you."

"You like living dangerously? I might get gung-ho about everything."

"If it makes you happy, go ahead. At any rate, we're good at navigating the unexpected. After all, you just wanted to be *friendly* with me in the beginning."

I laughed. "True. I just didn't know who I was up against back then."

"And now you do?"

"Oh, yeah."

"I love you, hot stuff."

"I love you too. Any day now, I'll come up with an appropriate nickname. Something to do you justice."

Lori and I started by looking at dresses, and once they knew what we were up to, the other women gathered around us, offering their opinions. Our men were sitting further away, but every once in a while, one of them would stop by to bring us snacks or drinks. It was a lot of fun, but I warned everyone that I wasn't deciding on anything tonight. I was snapping pictures of my favorites.

Occasionally Jace would stay long enough to peek at what we were doing, and I made a big show of hiding the screen. Hailey looked between us with a big smile.

"I'm so happy he found you," she whispered after he left. "I'm going to be the only single Connor at your wedding," she added with a wistful tone that was very un-Hailey. "Promise you won't have a singles table."

I shook my head. "Of course not."

"Those went out of style years ago," Lori explained.

"Whew. Dodged a bullet," Hailey said with mock relief.

I exchanged a glance with Paige, Maddie, Val, and Lori, biting back my own smile.

During one of the Friday dinners, we'd predicted that Hailey would be dating someone seriously by the time the next Connor wedding took place. Of course, back then, I'd had no idea that the next wedding would come up so fast, which raised the stakes a bit, but I had full confidence in Hailey.

Other Books by Layla Hagen

The Connor Family Series

Book 1: Anything For You

Hotshot CEO Landon Connor has many talents. He's successful and driven, and maybe a little too career-focused. Some (like his big and boisterous family) would even call him a workaholic. Landon has good reasons for putting his personal life on hold…

But meeting landscape designer Maddie Jennings makes him question his choices. He can't get enough of her sweetness, or her sensual curves. Maddie Jennings is all he sees, and everything he wants.

Maddie hasn't met anyone quite like Landon. He's sexier than anyone has the right to be, and more intense too. He's a little bossy, a lot hot. Despite fanning herself every time he comes near her, she tries to ignore their attraction. Maddie isn't sure that she and Landon are quite right for each other.

When Landon romances her with late night walks and sinful dancing, she can't help giving in to him. His touch is intoxicating, and their passion is scorching hot. His love is beautiful

But can Landon open up his heart for longer than a summer?

AVAILABLE ON ALL RETAILERS.

Book 2: Wild With You

Wedding organizer Lori Connor loves her job. Planning people's happy ever afters have catapulted the single mother to success. When she meets the best man at the latest wedding, sparks fly. Graham Frazier is more than Lori has bargained for.

The charismatic soccer club owner is disillusioned by marriage after his divorce. He's also hot as sin… and kisses like a dream. Graham's touch is sizzling. Soon, he bosses her into accepting gifts and spending the night at his house (his excuse is good: she can't possibly drive after working a wedding, can she?).

Graham pursues her relentlessly, wanting those long legs wrapped around him and her smooth skin under his lips.

Then he meets her son, and that boy charms him even faster than his mother did.

Before Graham know it, Lori's son has him wrapped around his little finger.

But are Lori and Graham ready for their lives to intertwine in ways they haven't even imagined before?

AVAILABLE ON ALL RETAILERS.

Book 3: Meant For You

Will Connor lives his life by simple rules: take care of those he loves, give one hundred percent to his job, and never ignore his instincts. So when he meets Paige, he doesn't plan to ignore their crazy chemistry, or the way her pretty smile strips him of all defenses...

As the development director of a non-profit, Paige Lamonica has met her fair share of people. But Will is something else entirely. The hot detective is a little too confident, and far too easy on the eye. She loves that he goes toe-to-toe with her at every turn.

When Will asks her to attend his sister's wedding with him, she thinks he just wants to throw off his scent some relatives with a penchant for matchmaking.

She couldn't be more wrong. Will wants her.

When she teases him, he teases her right back. When she pushes his buttons, he repays her with scorching hot kisses.

Paige discovers that there's more to Will than she thought. With every layer she peels off, she craves more...

But as the daughter of an army man, Paige has never wanted to get involved with someone on the force. Can Will persuade her to give in to their growing love?

AVAILABLE ON ALL RETAILERS.

The Bennett Family Series

Book 1: Your Irresistible Love

Sebastian Bennett is a determined man. It's the secret behind the business empire he built from scratch. Under his rule, Bennett Enterprises dominates the jewelry industry. Despite being ruthless in his work, family comes first for him, and he'd do anything for his parents and eight siblings— even if they drive him crazy sometimes. . . like when they keep nagging him to get married already.

Sebastian doesn't believe in love, until he brings in external marketing consultant Ava to oversee the next collection launch. She's beautiful, funny, and just as stubborn as he is. Not only is he obsessed with her delicious curves, but he also finds himself willing to do anything to make her smile. He's determined to have Ava, even if she's completely off limits.

Ava Lindt has one job to do at Bennett Enterprises: make the next collection launch unforgettable. Daydreaming about the hot CEO is definitely not on her to-do list. Neither is doing said CEO. The consultancy she works for has a strict policy—no fraternizing with clients. She won't risk her job. Besides, Ava knows better than to trust men with her heart.

But their sizzling chemistry spirals into a deep connection that takes both of them by surprise. Sebastian blows through her defenses one sweet kiss and sinful touch at a time. When Ava's time as a consultant in his company comes to an end, will Sebastian fight for the woman he loves or will he end up losing her?

AVAILABLE ON ALL RETAILERS.

Book 2: Your Captivating Love

Logan Bennett knows his priorities. He is loyal to his family and his company. He has no time for love, and no desire for it. Not after a disastrous engagement left him brokenhearted. When Nadine enters his life, she turns everything upside down.

She's sexy, funny, and utterly captivating. She's also more stubborn than anyone he's met…including himself.

Nadine Hawthorne is finally pursuing her dream: opening her own clothing shop. After working so hard to get here, she needs to concentrate on her new business, and can't afford distractions. Not even if they come in the form of Logan Bennett.

He's handsome, charming, and doesn't take no for an answer. After bitter disappointments, Nadine doesn't believe in love. But being around Logan is addicting. It doesn't help that Logan's family is scheming to bring them together at every turn.

Their attraction is sizzling, their connection undeniable. Slowly, Logan wins her over. What starts out as a fling, soon spirals into much more than they are prepared for.

When a mistake threatens to tear them apart, will they have the strength to hold on to each other?

AVAILABLE ON ALL RETAILERS.

Book 3: Your Forever Love

Eric Callahan is a powerful man, and his sharp business sense has earned him the nickname 'the shark.' Yet under the strict façade is a man who loves his daughter and would do anything for her. When he and his daughter move to San Francisco for three months, he has one thing in mind: expanding his business on the West Coast. As a widower, Eric is not looking for love. He focuses on his company, and his daughter.

Until he meets Pippa Bennett. She captivates him from the moment he sets eyes on her, and what starts as unintentional flirting soon spirals into something neither of them can control.

Pippa Bennett knows she should stay away from Eric Callahan. After going through a rough divorce, she doesn't trust men anymore. But something about Eric just draws her in. He has a body made for sin and a sense of humor that matches hers. Not to mention that seeing how adorable he is with his daughter melts Pippa's walls one by one.

The chemistry between them is undeniable, but the connection that grows deeper every day that has both of them wondering if love might be within their reach.

When it's time for Eric and his daughter to head back home, will he give up on the woman who has captured his heart, or will he do everything in his power to remain by her side?

AVAILABLE ON ALL RETAILERS.

Book 4: Your Inescapable Love

Max Bennett is a successful man. His analytical mind has taken his family's company to the next level. Outside the office, Max transforms from the serious business man into someone who is carefree and fun. Max is happy with his life and doesn't intend to change it, even though his mother keeps asking for more grandchildren. Max loves being an uncle, and plans to spoil his nieces rotten.

But when a chance encounter reunites him with Emilia, his childhood best friend, he starts questioning everything. The girl he last saw years ago has grown into a sensual woman with a smile he can't get out of his mind.

Emilia Campbell has a lot on her plate, taking care of her sick grandmother. Still, she faces everything with a positive attitude. When the childhood friend she hero-worshipped steps into her physical therapy clinic, she is over the moon. Max is every bit the troublemaker she remembers, only now he has a body to drool over and a smile to melt her panties. Not that she intends to do the former, or let the latter happen.

They are both determined not to cross the boundaries of friendship…at first. But as they spend more time together, they form an undeniable bond and their flirty banter spirals out of control.

Max knows Emilia is off-limits, but that only makes her all the more tempting. Besides, Max was never one to back away from a challenge.

When their chemistry becomes too much to resist and they inevitably give in to temptation, will they risk losing their friendship or will Max and Emilia find true love?

AVAILABLE ON ALL RETAILERS.

Book 5: Your Tempting Love

Christopher Bennett is a persuasive man. With his magnetic charm and undeniable wit, he plays a key role in the international success of his family's company.

Christopher adores his family, even if they can be too meddling sometimes... like when attempt to set him up with Victoria, by recommending him to employ her decorating services. Christopher isn't looking to settle down, but meeting Victoria turns his world upside down. Her laughter is contagious, and her beautiful lips and curves are too tempting.

Victoria Hensley is determined not to fall under Christopher's spell, even though the man is hotter than sin, and his flirty banter makes her toes curl. But as her client, Christopher is off limits. After her parents' death, Victoria is focusing on raising her much younger siblings, and she can't afford any mistakes. . .

But Victoria and Christopher's chemistry is not just the sparks-flying kind. . .It's the downright explosive kind. Before she knows it, Christopher is training her brother Lucas for soccer tryouts and reading bedtime stories to her sister Chloe.

Victoria wants to resist him, but Christopher is determined, stubborn, and oh-so-persuasive.

When their attraction and connection both spiral out of control, will they be able to risk it all for a love that is far too tempting?

AVAILABLE ON ALL RETAILERS.

Book 6: Your Alluring Love

Alice Bennett has been holding a torch for her older brother's best friend, Nate, for more than a decade. He's a hotshot TV producer who travels the world, never staying in San Francisco for too long. But now he's in town and just as tempting as ever... with a bossy streak that makes her weak in the knees and a smile that melts her defenses.

As a successful restaurant owner, Alice is happy with her life. She loves her business and her family, yet after watching her siblings find their happy ever after, she can't help feeling lonely sometimes—but that's only for her to know.

Nate has always had a soft spot for Alice. Despite considering the Bennetts his family, he never could look at her as just his friend's little sister. She's a spitfire, and Nate just can't stay away. He loves making her laugh... and blush.

LAYLA HAGEN

Their attraction is irresistible, and between stolen kisses and wicked-hot nights, they form a deep bond that has them both yearning for more.

But when the chance of a lifetime comes knocking at his door, will Nate chase success even if it means losing Alice, or will he choose her?

AVAILABLE ON ALL RETAILERS.

Book 7: Your Fierce Love

The strong and sexy Blake Bennett is downright irresistible. And Clara Abernathy is doing everything she can to resist his charm.

After spending her life in group homes, Clara yearns for the love and warmth of a true family. With the Bennetts treating her like their own, she can't possibly fall for Blake. That would be crossing a line...

But when Clara needs a temporary place to live, and she accepts Blake's offer to move next door to him, things escalate. Suddenly, she's not only supposed to resist the man who's hell-bent on having her, but the TV station she works for is determined to dig up some dirt on the Bennett family.

Blake knows family friends are off-limits, and Clara is more off-limits than anyone. But Clara's sweetness and sass fill a hole in him he wasn't even aware of. Soon, he finds himself gravitating toward her, willing to do anything to make her happy.

Blake enjoys bending the rules—much more than following them, but will bending this one be taking it too far?

AVAILABLE ON ALL RETAILERS.

Book 8: Your One True Love

She's the one who got away. This time, he refuses to let her slip through his fingers.

Daniel Bennett has no regrets, except one: letting go of the woman he loved years ago. He wouldn't admit it out loud, but he's been pining for Caroline ever since. But his meddling family can read him like an open book. So when his sisters kick up their matchmaking shenanigans, Daniel decides to play right along. After all, he built his booming adventure business by making the most out of every opportunity. And he doesn't intend to miss an opportunity to be near Caroline.

Caroline Dunne knows better than to fall for Daniel again. But his seductive charm melts her determination to keep her heart in check. Even with their lives going in separate directions, neither can ignore the magnetic pull between them.

But will they find the second chance they've both wanted all along?

AVAILABLE ON ALL RETAILERS.

Book 9: Your Endless Love

An incurable romantic with a chronic case of bad luck with men…

Museum curator Summer Bennett knows that happily-ever-afters are not make-believe. After all, her siblings all found their soulmates, so she's optimistic her prince charming will come along too…eventually. In the meantime, she focuses on her job and her volunteering—which brings her face to face with one of Hollywood's hottest A-listers.

When Alexander Westbrook flashes America's favorite panty-melting smile, Summer's entire body responds. When she asks him to get involved in the community where she volunteers, Summer is shocked that the Hollywood heartthrob agrees right away. Two weeks working side by side with the world's sexiest guy, and the game is on.

Far from the public eye, Summer discovers she likes the real Alex even more than his on-screen persona. Secret kisses and whispered conversations spark a fire in her that nothing can extinguish. If only his life wasn't splashed all over the tabloids…

Alex can't keep his eyes–or his hands–off of Summer. But she's too sweet, and too damn lovely to be swept up in his Hollywood drama. His career is at risk, and an iron-clad clause in his contract with the studio makes a relationship impossible. But staying away from her is out of the question.

AVAILABLE ON ALL RETAILERS.

The Lost Series

***

Lost in Us: The story of James and Serena

There are three reasons tequila is my new favorite drink.

• One: my ex-boyfriend hates it.

• Two: downing a shot looks way sexier than sipping my usual Sprite.

• Three: it might give me the courage to do something my ex-boyfriend would hate even more than tequila—getting myself a rebound

The night I swap my usual Sprite with tequila, I meet James Cohen. The encounter is breathtaking. Electrifying. And best not repeated.

James is a rich entrepreneur. He likes risks and adrenaline and is used to living the high life. He's everything I'm not.

But opposites attract. Some say opposites destroy each other. Some say opposites are perfect for each other. I don't know what will James and I do to each other, but I can't stay away from him. Even though I should.

AVAILABLE ON ALL RETAILERS.

***
Found in Us: The story of Jessica and Parker

Jessica Haydn wants to leave her past behind. Hurt by one too many heartbreaks, she vows not to fall in love again. Especially not with a man like Parker, whose electrifying pull and smile bruised her ego once before. But his sexy British accent makes her crave his touch, and his blue eyes strip Jessica of all her defenses.

Parker Blakesley has no place for love in his life. He learned the hard way not to trust. He built his business empire by avoiding distractions, and using sheer determination and control. But something about Jessica makes him question everything. Not only has she a body made for sin, but her laughter fills a void inside of him.

The desire igniting between them spirals into an unstoppable passion, and so much more. Soon, neither can fight their growing emotional connection. But can two scarred souls learn to trust again? And when a mistake threatens to tear them apart, will their love be strong enough?
AVAILABLE ON ALL RETAILERS.

***
Caught in Us: The story of Dani and Damon

Damon Cooper has all the markings of a bad boy:
• A tattoo
• A bike
• An attitude to go with point one and two

In the beginning I hated him, but now I'm falling in love with him. My parents forbid us to be together, but Damon's not one to obey rules. And since I met him, neither am I.

AVAILABLE ON ALL RETAILERS.
***

Standalone USA TODAY BESTSELLER
Withering Hope

Aimee's wedding is supposed to turn out perfect. Her dress, her fiancé and the location—the idyllic holiday ranch in Brazil—are perfect.

But all Aimee's plans come crashing down when the private jet that's taking her from the U.S. to the ranch—where her fiancé awaits her—defects mid-flight and the pilot is forced to perform an emergency landing in the heart of the Amazon rainforest.

With no way to reach civilization, being rescued is Aimee and Tristan's—the pilot—only hope. A slim one that slowly withers away, desperation taking its place. Because death wanders in the jungle under many forms: starvation, diseases. Beasts.

As Aimee and Tristan fight to find ways to survive, they grow closer. Together they discover that facing old, inner agonies carved by painful pasts takes just as much courage, if not even more, than facing the rainforest.

Despite her devotion to her fiancé, Aimee can't hide her feelings for Tristan—the man for whom she's slowly becoming everything. You can hide many things in the rainforest. But not lies. Or love.

Withering Hope is the story of a man who desperately needs forgiveness and the woman who brings him hope.

It is a story in which hope births wings and blooms into a love that is as beautiful and intense as it is forbidden.
AVAILABLE ON ALL RETAILERS.

***

ONLY WITH YOU
Copyright © 2018 Layla Hagen
Published by Layla Hagen

FIGHTING FOR YOU

LAYLA HAGEN

Made in the USA
Columbia, SC
18 June 2019